PRAISE FOR

GUARDING TRUTH

ELITE GUARDIANS: SAVANNAH | BOOK THREE

LYNETTE EASON

KELLY UNDERWOOD

sunrise
PUBLISHING

Guarding Truth
Elite Guardians: Savannah, Book 3
Copyright © 2024 Sunrise Media Group LLC
Print ISBN: 978-1-963372-00-7
Ebook ISBN: 978-1-963372-02-1

This book is a work of fiction. Names, characters, places, and incidents are
either products of the author's imagination or used fictitiously. Any similarity to
actual people, organizations, and/or events is purely coincidental.

All Scripture quotations, unless otherwise indicated, are taken from the Holy
Bible, New International Version®, NIV®. Copyright ©1973, 1978, 1984, 2011
by Biblica, Inc.™ Used by permission of Zondervan. All rights reserved
worldwide. The "NIV" and "New International Version" are trademarks
registered in the United States Patent and Trademark Office by Biblica, Inc.™

For more information about the authors, please access their websites at
lynetteeason.com and kellyunderwoodauthor.com.

Published in the United States of America.
Cover Design: Hannah Linder

To my parents who have always believed in my dreams,
even the crazy ones.

ONE

REMOTE VILLAGE IN THE HINDU KUSH
MOUNTAINS OF AFGHANISTAN,
NEAR THE TAJIKISTAN BORDER
THURSDAY, 4:00 A.M.

"Time's up. Hostile vehicles spotted. Approaching in less than five minutes."

Caleb Styles nodded to his fellow Army cyber intelligence analyst, Lazlo Thomas, without taking his eyes from the screen in front of him. "And...done. I just uploaded the last software patch. Time to get out of here." He powered off his laptop, shoved it in his backpack, and followed Laz out of the makeshift tent that served as a command center for the Army outpost.

Not that he could miss the man's dark curly hair with a length that tested the boundaries of Army standards. Caleb preferred his dark-brown hair trimmed with military precision, never knowing when he'd be called into the field on trips such as this.

"Slow down a bit, would you?" Caleb caught up and matched Laz's warp-speed pace. Dirt swirled around his feet, the moonlight illuminating the path through the camp. He matched two steps to every one of Laz's long strides. Despite Caleb's six-foot fit and toned frame, Laz had a good four inches on him.

They walked past four other identical brown temporary structures used to house a contingent of soldiers and supplies. Men hustled, preparing to help defend the nearby villages from the impending Taliban forces.

"Sorry, I'm not slowing down until there's plenty of space between us and the Taliban."

"Yeah, I'd like to get out of here before the fighting erupts." Even though they'd both made it out of basic training alive, Caleb spent most of his days behind a computer screen, keeping cyberterrorists from taking down the Army's system. It meant being in the field on special assignments on occasion to make sure communications hadn't been compromised.

Laz slowed to a normal pace. "I can only imagine the kinds of torture devices the enemy would use on intelligence analysts if we got caught here."

Caleb glanced at his friend through glasses fogged from the sweat dripping from his brow. Despite being shielded by mountain ranges on both sides, in the valley, sweltering temperatures ruled the day and night. Even in October.

"Don't worry," Caleb said. "I'll do everything in my power to get you back to base so you can ship out. I know you've got a girlfriend back home. Ready to propose yet?"

Laz's pearly whites lit up under the moonlight at the mention of his girlfriend. What would it be like to have someone waiting for him back home? The trajectory of Caleb's life didn't include a wife and kids. However, one glance at Laz's face, and for a second Caleb reconsidered.

But he'd never been able to risk his heart for a chance at happiness.

"You know," Laz said in a singsongy cadence, "I heard the

Rangers have made a special trip to pick us up. And do you know who made it out of Ranger School in one piece?"

Oh, he knew all too well.

Juliette Montgomery.

Caleb would have elbowed Laz in the ribs if the man hadn't been moving at the speed of a cheetah. "You just had to go there. Juliette and I will always be friends. There are lots of Rangers in the area. I'm sure she's—"

"Caleb?"

His heartbeat ticked up at the sound of his name from the voice he knew instantly. He slowed and turned.

"Jules." His basic training days came flooding back to him. They'd partnered up on many assignments, partly because most men didn't want to be on duty with a woman. But the other part of him had volunteered because he'd enjoyed spending time with her.

Juliette stood with three other men, dressed in fatigues. Despite her petite five-foot-three stature and shoulder-length dark-blonde hair, she looked every bit the part of a warrior.

Her golden-brown eyes twinkled in the moonlight for a fraction of a second before going into soldier mode. "No time to catch up. We've got to move." She motioned to one of the three vehicles, and just like that, they were a team again, as if no time had passed since they'd last been together.

Caleb and Laz helped hoist supplies, duffel bags, and weapons into the trunks of the vehicles, as four aid workers were also being evacuated because of the expected danger.

Once loaded, Laz, Caleb, and Juliette took the middle of the three-car caravan. Laz took the front passenger seat, leaving Juliette and Caleb in the back seat.

"Buckle up," Juliette said. "Our driver is Sergeant Hank Williams, better known as Hank the Tank. He's got a lead foot. That's why we're in the second car. To slow him down." The bucket car seat looked like a child's dollhouse chair when Tank's muscular frame slid under the steering wheel.

"Better watch it, *Hazard Pay*," the driver said, adjusting his mirror to smirk at Juliette.

"They still call you that?" Caleb tried to stifle a laugh but it came out as a snort. Laz joined in. "At least some things never change."

Juliette folded her arms. "One crazy stunt in basic training and I'm branded for life."

"That one stunt solidified your career as a soldier," Caleb said. "Four armed men had you trapped. It was game over. That would have sent most men packing."

Caleb had cleared the path for her but couldn't get to her in time. He hadn't expected Juliette to rush into enemy lines like a bullet shot from a gun.

Laz laughed. "I watched you take down those guys headfirst. The look on their faces was priceless. No one saw that maneuver coming."

Caleb remembered the day with perfect recall, thanks to his eidetic memory. "To this day, soldiers still refer to that as the Kobayashi Maru. You know, where Juliette changed all the rules to get herself out of a jam."

Juliette groaned. "You and your *Star Wars* references."

"*Star Trek*. When are you going to get that right? Captain Kirk changed the rules of the test—"

Juliette and Laz burst into laughter. "Some things don't change," Juliette said. "You still drone on and on about sciencey techy stuff that most of us can't comprehend."

"We all learned our lesson after that stunt." Laz turned his neck to look in the back seat. "Never underestimate Juliette Montgomery."

Caleb glanced at her. They always fell back into that comfortable rhythm as if no time had passed. "Jules can hold her own, that's for sure."

Tank chuckled and turned to look at Caleb. "Well, that and no one calls her *Jules*."

Heat crept up Caleb's neck. Had he overstepped? She'd worked and fought her way through Ranger School, a feat very few women accomplished. Maybe she had changed.

"I'll allow it, Tank," Juliette said. "We go way back. And Caleb has pulled me out of trouble too many times to count. He's earned the right to call me *Jules*." She caught Tank's eyes in the rearview mirror. "But you two better not try it."

"Never." Laz saluted her and watched out the windshield. Tank put the car in gear and hit the gas to follow the lead car.

Caleb longed to take a deep breath that didn't consist of dirt and diesel, but this was just the start of their journey to the Tajikistan border. While not far, their destination meant crossing through the mountain pass on roads that barely qualified as safe for a bicycle, let alone a three-vehicle caravan filled with people and supplies.

"So, what brings you all the way out here?" Caleb shifted in the cramped back seat so he could talk to Juliette over the grinding of tires against the earth and rocks below. "Since when are Rangers doing extractions?"

She nodded. "We happened to be in the area on another assignment when we got word that the fighting had shifted and were called in to help with the evacuation. But I could ask the same of you. Even though I'm sure you can't tell me about it, given your super secret clearance level."

"Looks like both of us are doing what we love. Congrats on making it through Ranger School."

She smiled. "I had plenty of practice with all those overnight duties we pulled in basic. I mean, we had some good times on patrol. Hanging out and dreaming of our futures while patrolling the camp—it wasn't all work."

His dreams had always included her. Maybe one day he'd have the courage to tell her.

A bump threatened to send him airborne except the seat belt locked him in place. He grabbed the steel handlebar on the side of the Humvee to steady himself. They climbed higher up the mountain.

"How is your niece?" Juliette asked. "Ivy, right?"

"Ivy's a handful—super smart. I went home last month to see my sister. Tessa will need to stay on top of things with that girl. Already skipping grades."

The sunrise backlit the mountains, changing their dark shadows to splashes of light and color. A bright spot in an otherwise dreary brown, never-changing setting.

Kind of like being in the presence of Juliette. She added a hint of adventure and mischief to his usually quiet and introverted life. Most of his time was spent in front of a screen, not jumping out of planes on dangerous missions like Juliette.

"Whoa, hang on folks." Tank's booming voice rose above the rush of wind outside the Humvee. The car in front slammed on the brakes, and Tank skidded their vehicle close to the edge of the road.

Caleb looked out Juliette's window and stared at the murky blackness below them. The space between them and the edge of a cliff shrank to a few feet. Juliette morphed into warrior mode, her hand reaching for the M16 perched in a rack behind them. "Why did we stop, Tank?" Her eyes flickered between the side window and the front seat.

"Looks like something in the road. I don't have a good feeling about this." Tank also reached for his gun, and Caleb rested his hand on the butt of his sidearm.

The whistle of the rocket-propelled grenade hit Caleb's ears before the blinding light of the explosion lit the darkness. The car in front of them burst into a fireball, sending shrapnel flying into their car.

A chunk of Humvee door hit the front of their vehicle with enough force to knock them closer to the ledge. Tank stomped on the brakes, but the car spun. The front of their vehicle teetered on the edge of the cliff and then took a nosedive.

Metal creaked and Juliette screamed. The vehicle skidded down the side of the mountain. The seat belt dug into Caleb's shoulder, but it was the only thing keeping him from hitting his head on the roof.

Boom.

The car collided with...something. What was it? Dust poured into the cabin, so thick Caleb couldn't see inside or out. Someone coughed. He reached out his hand to feel around the back seat and connected with Juliette's hand. She squeezed back.

"Nobody move," Caleb said. "We must have hit a tree or rock that broke our fall." At least they were upright, but his side of the car had taken the brunt of the crash. He tried the door but it wouldn't budge.

He needed to make sure everyone survived. "Everyone okay? Call out."

"I'm alive," Juliette replied.

A grunt sounded from the front seat. "I—I'm alive but hurt." The voice was Laz. "I'm pinned under the dashboard and can't move my leg."

Tank didn't reply. The smell of diesel burned Caleb's nostrils, and the vehicle let out a slow groan. They needed to move. Now.

A seat belt unbuckled. "I'm going to go out the door and get Tank and Laz out. You get ready to jump out when I have them."

"Jules, no. If you move, we might fall. It's not safe." If a rock was blocking their fall, it might not hold them for long. "We're not done falling."

Caleb's gut clenched at the sound of the opening door.

"I have to get them out. I'm the lightest in the car. We have to try."

From Caleb's vantage point, he saw nothing but the sun

rising outside the front windshield. Out the window, he saw the outline of the boulder that had slowed their descent down the mountain. The boulder was the fulcrum and their car the seesaw. "Be careful, Jules. We're still in danger of dropping some more."

Once the dust settled, he could see the front seat. Tank wasn't moving, and a streak of blood trickled from his forehead down his cheek. The door scraped.

"I'm out," Juliette called back. "We crashed into a rock, but it kept us from going over the side of the mountain. It's steep."

More daylight lit the sky, and Caleb watched Juliette hold on to the vehicle for support while she made her way to the front.

She reached through the glassless window of the driver's side door. "I can't find a pulse. I'm heading around to Laz. We've got to get them both out of here—"

Rocks and pebbles tumbled down the side of the mountain, causing the Humvee to shift. Juliette lost her footing and slipped out of his sight with a yelp.

Smoke filled the cabin. Caleb crawled through the back seat and went out Juliette's open door.

"Please, Lord, let this rock hold us," he whispered.

He maneuvered his way to the edge of the rock.

"Jules!"

"I—I'm stuck." He followed the sound of her voice and saw her clinging to a tree branch. Her speech slurred and a gash on her forehead seeped blood.

A pop sounded from behind him, and he turned to see black smoke pouring from the engine. Not a good sign. The car might explode.

He had to save both Laz and Juliette.

"Laz, you have to get out."

"Can't move, bro. Save Juliette. Get her out of here. I'll be all right. I'm sure help is on the way."

His lie cut to Caleb's core.

One of his two friends could die here tonight.

Caleb sent up a prayer and committed to his choice.

He lowered himself off the rock and down toward Juliette's position. The tree branch was her lifeline, and that head wound was still bleeding. He grabbed her arm just as she let go, and strained to lift her. When he got her into his arms, he said, "Wake up, Jules. I'm never going to leave you behind."

———

A bright light blinded Juliette. A lightning bolt of pain sliced through her even as a voice pulled her out of her slumber. She cracked her eyelids open and flinched.

"Juliette, you're awake," an unfamiliar voice said.

"Where—" She cleared her throat. "Where am I?" Her mouth tasted like she'd swallowed a gallon of sand.

"Don't try to talk," the man said. "I'm Doctor Sharipova. You're in the hospital in Tajikistan. You've been in a coma for two days after you hit your head when you slid down that mountain."

A steady beep brought some clarity to her thoughts.

The mountain. Caleb. Laz and Tank.

Why was she always the first to rush into danger? And she'd been the one to need a rescue. If only she'd gotten Laz and Tank out of the car.

Instead, she'd fallen.

"Juliette? How do you feel?"

"Tired" was the only word she managed to push out of her burning throat. A whiff of antiseptic cleaner sent her gag reflex into overdrive. She forced her eyes open and squinted at the man in scrubs standing next to her bed.

"Caleb?" One-word questions would have to suffice for now, until the fog lifted from her mind.

The doctor glanced at the nurse, and she whispered

something Juliette couldn't hear. The graying man with thick eyebrows and a stethoscope around his neck flipped through pages on a clipboard. "It looks like your friend sustained some third-degree burns. After pulling you to safety, he assisted two others from the burning vehicle."

She tried to sit up but didn't get very far. "Are they all okay?" The nurse held a cup of water while Juliette sipped.

Images of Caleb lifting and carrying her up the side of the mountain assaulted her memory. His words echoed through her soul. *I'll never leave you behind.*

The doctor consulted his clipboard again and frowned. "I'm sorry to report that Sergeant Williams didn't make it. He had massive internal bleeding from some shrapnel."

He flipped another page, his somber expression making Juliette's pulse spike. "And Lieutenant Lazlo Thomas died during surgery from extensive bleeding from a severed femoral artery. Doctors did everything they could to stop it, but in the end, his injuries were too severe."

A tear escaped and rolled down her cheek. She and Tank had gone through Ranger School together. And Laz?

No. No. No. She swiped her face. This wasn't happening. Caleb couldn't lose Laz, one of his closest friends.

And this was all her fault.

"Am...am I okay?" All she needed to know was if this would send her home. Because the best way for her to cope with the loss of two friends would be to get back to work.

She heard the creak of the chair as the doctor sat, and she braced herself for more bad news.

"Your injuries were extensive. A concussion, broken arm, and we had to perform surgery to repair some internal bleeding, but there shouldn't be any long-term damage. However, we discovered something else."

His heavy sigh indicated the good news was about to come to a crashing halt. "While you were at the hospital, we performed a biopsy. I'm so sorry to tell you that the tests show you have breast cancer. It's an aggressive tumor at stage three. The recommended course of action is that you return to the United States to begin treatment."

Cancer? She'd rather be a Ranger, dying a hero's death. How could her own body do her in?

Another whirring machine woke her up. The room was dark, and the doctor had left. She used every ounce of energy to swing her legs over the bed and stand. She moved her gauze-wrapped arm and winced. The pain reminded her to take it slowly.

Caleb consumed her thoughts. She wouldn't rest until she saw Caleb for herself. She clung to the IV pole like a crutch and hobbled down the hall, wishing for pants, but with her arm, she'd never be able to get them on. So she'd parade around the hospital in a white-flowered polyester gown. At least it covered everything.

A few nurses shot her quizzical looks, but they didn't stop her, so she moved forward. She stopped in the hallway at the door with the white markerboard that had *Styles* written on it.

She should have been able to get both Laz and Tank out of the car. Instead, she'd slipped and tumbled down the mountain. And Caleb had had to save her over rescuing the others.

And now? She was being sent home to save herself.

Juliette pounded her fist against the wall holding her up and fought the onslaught of tears. Her job was to serve and protect others, and she'd put her team in jeopardy and lost.

Her body ached and her head throbbed, but it was the broken heart that might kill her. In one enemy attack, she'd lost two friends. Was she just supposed to go home and wallow in the abyss of loss? Everything within her wanted to pick up a gun and fight more battles, take vengeance for Laz and Tank.

Instead, her own body was attacking her.

She composed herself for Caleb's sake and cracked the door open. Caleb rested in the hospital bed, his shoulder in a sling.

His pale color matched the stark white sheets. She closed her eyes and remembered his powerful arms scooping her up to safety.

At the expense of Laz and Tank.

Caleb was the hero. And as much as she wanted this man by her side while she faced chemo, oncologists, and enough drugs to run her own pharmacy, Caleb had a future.

And it didn't include her drama. He'd already paid the price when he'd had to rescue her over Laz. He didn't need to take on her problems.

She shook her head. "You deserve a future that doesn't include taking care of me." Her whisper bounced off the beige walls of the square room, sounding louder than it should have.

Cancer was her battle. She refused to be a burden to anyone. Especially Caleb.

Her decision solidified in her mind but not her heart. Because she'd always have a tender spot for Caleb.

She held her head high, left Caleb, and walked back to her room. She'd check out and be on the first flight home.

Alone.

Caleb might never leave her behind, but she had to leave him. For his own good.

TWO

THREE YEARS LATER
MONDAY, 8:15 A.M.

"Nobody move. This is a good ole-fashioned bank robbery."

Juliette Montgomery froze in line for the bank teller. Four masked men had burst through the front doors of First United Bank of Savannah, guns blazing.

Screams echoed through the lobby, and her hand went instinctively to where her gun usually rested, but she'd left her sidearm at home. It was just one quick trip to the bank before breakfast.

And now men dressed like ninjas held innocent people hostage.

Noelle Burton, Juliette's colleague and friend, rolled her eyes. "I never should have agreed to breakfast with you," Noelle said through gritted teeth. "Danger always seems to follow you. Just one errand?"

"Everyone quiet and on the floor. Now."

Juliette complied, moving at a snail's pace so she could survey the lobby. Nine patrons. Three bank employees. Four gunmen. One security guard that a gunman had dragged to the back of the bank.

And two professional bodyguards with the Elite Guardians Agency.

Juliette shimmied six inches to the left so she could hide behind the table with the deposit slips. Noelle dropped and crept to the right. Juliette shot off a text to Matthew Williams, friend and officer with the Savannah Police Department. Then she hit the Record button.

A shot, followed by more screams, bounced off the tile floor and reverberated through the lobby that looked more like an exhibit hall at the Louvre than a bank in downtown Savannah. The paintings on the wall were probably worth more than the historic house that her grandmother had left her. She lived in the basement apartment and had leased the top two floors to the Elite Guardians.

"Toss your cell phones to the center of the lobby."

Drat.

She left the video recorder on and slid her phone toward the pile of others while one twitchy bad guy went from person to person to ensure compliance. Juliette committed to memory the man's cold gray eyes and height. Five foot ten-ish. Lanky.

One of the robbers, the shortest of the men, took a can of spray paint to the fancy artwork. Blood-red paint dripped down the side of one of the paintings as the man etched one word.

Rushmore.

The spray painter joined the other masked man in the back room, presumably to force a bank employee to open the safe. That left Twitchy and one other beefy guy, who looked like he lived in a gym, to guard the lobby. If she was going to make a move, it needed to be now.

Two against one? She'd faced bigger odds than that.

Juliette wasn't a wait-and-see-what-happens kind of woman. She acted first, then thought about the ramifications later. No way would she let innocent people be hurt on her watch. She was a bodyguard, and she mentally took on twelve new clients.

She glanced at Noelle, sending her a silent message of her intent to intervene.

Noelle squinted and shook her head. She mouthed, *Are you crazy?*

Juliette shrugged. No way would she cower on the ground while these men took what they wanted and threatened innocent civilians. Now, what could she use as a weapon? Juliette searched the room and spotted an award proudly displayed on the corner of a desk a few feet behind her. The crystal trophy had "best customer service" engraved across the front, but what caught Juliette's eye was the sharp point at the top of the keepsake. Heavy and sharp—just what she needed for the perfect improvised weapon. She inched her way to the desk and waited until the bulkier of the two men headed toward the back of the bank.

"Do you really think you'll get away with this?" Juliette stood, faced the bad guy. The man swung his gun in her direction.

"Down. Now."

Noelle stood. "Listen, just let the people go. You don't want to hurt anyone." The second the gunman took his eyes off Juliette, she grabbed the award and rushed the man. He was a hair too slow, and Juliette clocked him in the head with the corner of the crystal before he had a chance to get a shot off. Noelle kicked the gun from his hand.

A few bank customers cheered from their positions on the floor. But this wasn't over. One down, three to go.

Sirens wailed in the distance. Juliette went to grab Twitchy's gun. The man clutched the gun but held his sleeve over his forehead to staunch the blood from where the award had clipped him. But a voice stopped her in her tracks.

"They called the cops?" The three men rushed from the back

of the bank, guns blazing. Juliette and Noelle held their hands up.

"Back on the ground," one of the men growled, pointing a gun in Noelle's face. Juliette and Noelle hit the floor and lay on their stomachs, hands over their heads.

The man Juliette assumed to be the ringleader of the group jumped up on a desk. She noted his blue eyes and pale skin peeking through the eyeholes of his mask.

"Listen up!" The man angled himself right in front of a security camera. He sent a shot into the ornate chandelier in the middle of the room, sending shards of crystal scattering. Shrieks tore through the room, and patrons covered themselves the best they could.

"We are Rushmore." The man's deep gravelly voice commanded the room amidst a few muffled sobs. "The CEO who runs this bank is Edward McMillan. He stole money from the people, and we're here to claim what belongs to the hardworking citizens. The courts might not have convicted him, but we will."

It would have been hard to have missed the news of Edward McMillan's acquittal for fraud and other unethical practices. The story had been blasted by all the twenty-four-hour news outlets for days. But that didn't demand this demonstration of vigilante justice.

The bank robber in charge stuck his hand in a backpack, pulled out a wad of cash, and threw it in the air. Hundred-dollar bills scattered everywhere. From her position on the floor, Juliette watched the four men waltz out the front door, strolling like they were on vacation and not fleeing a bank robbery. Money rained down around them like confetti.

Juliette and Noelle were on their feet the second the door banged shut behind the thieves. "What was that?" Noelle looked at Juliette.

Juliette turned to peer through the front window. People began congregating in front of the bank, scooping up the money.

"I have no idea who Rushmore is." Juliette nodded to the back room. "Hopefully the police get here soon, but I'm going to check to make sure no one is injured."

Patrons began to stand and brush glass off themselves. Juliette walked to the vault room and saw the security guard on the floor. He was conscious, and she helped him to an office chair.

"Are you hurt? Do you know what's happening?" Juliette tempered her desire to pepper him with more questions. But she wanted to make sure the man didn't have any injuries that required immediate medical attention.

"I'm Daniel Archer, security guard on the nighttime watch. It all happened so fast. They forced me to open the safe. One man hit me on the head, and the next thing I know, I saw you." He touched the golf-ball-sized lump forming on his head. Tall, mid-thirties, with an athletic build, the man should have been able to put up a vicious fight before going down, but it hadn't looked like any of the gunmen had been injured.

"Do you know what they wanted?" Noelle asked.

"Looks like they wanted the cash," Daniel said. "It's the second branch they've hit this week."

Noelle squinted her eyes, mirroring Juliette's own thoughts. Bank robberies were hard to pull off with all the security measures banks had in place. These men had waltzed through the front door and grabbed a bunch of cash only to throw it away.

And who was Rushmore?

"Police!" More voices filtered in from the lobby, followed by an army of heavy footsteps.

"In the back," Juliette called out.

Detective Matthew Williams with the Savannah Police Department burst through the door with his gun drawn. He scrutinized Juliette, Noelle, and the injured security guard, and put his gun away. "Is everyone okay?"

"This is Daniel," Juliette said. "Looks like the bad guys conked him on the head."

Matthew shook his head at Juliette. "Of course, if there's danger, I'll find you in the center of it. I got your text. Thanks for the heads-up. No one hit the silent alarm."

Paramedics rushed in to attend to Daniel, who appeared to be dizzy but otherwise faring well. Matt, Juliette, and Noelle headed to the lobby. Police and paramedics poured into the building, talking with witnesses and treating wounds. A few people had some cuts from the shattered chandelier, but injuries were minimal.

Ladecia Slaton, Matt's partner, joined them. Juliette was on a first-name basis with both of them, as her bodyguard duties sometimes collided with their cases.

Decia took notes while Juliette recalled her descriptions of the four men. "We took down one robber, but he escaped in the end. He has a nice-sized gash across his forehead and cheek."

"So, you let them get away?" Matt crossed his arms, squinting at Juliette. "Your skills getting a bit rusty there, Montgomery?"

Matt tried to hide a smirk. The man towered over Juliette by about ten inches, which gave him an intimidation factor that was only enhanced by the police uniform. But they'd been friends long enough for him to have had a front-row seat to Juliette's sarcasm. And he dished it right back to her. Matt was thirty—a year younger than Juliette. Too bad he only had eyes for the black-haired gothic beauty, Raven, the Elite Guardians' administrative assistant. Even though he'd never admit it.

She shrugged. "It's not every day you break up a bank robbery while running errands. How many robberies have you foiled today?"

Matt shook his head. "You never should have faced off with

an armed man. Let alone the other three in the back. One of these days, you're going to get hurt."

"I agree," Noelle interjected. "You took a risk today, and it paid off, but you could have put us all in jeopardy if those guys had started shooting. We work as a team, remember?"

How could Juliette forget? Noelle reminded her constantly that the Elite Guardians thrived on teamwork. Juliette had endured the "we're bodyguards not soldiers" lecture a time or two. Juliette smiled at Noelle and changed the subject.

"Who is Rushmore?" she asked.

"Rushmore is a thorn in my side these days," Matt said. "It's a hacker group that believes in vigilante justice. They target financial institutions and corporations. This is the second bank heist in three days, both First United Bank branches. Let's hope we catch a break soon."

"Was it the same situation, where the gunmen dumped all of the cash in the streets?" Noelle asked. "Because they have motives other than money."

Decia ran a hand through her shoulder-length brown hair and snapped her notebook shut. At five-foot-eight and in a police uniform, the woman commanded attention when she spoke. "Rushmore have organized themselves online and targeted different cities. They seem to focus on CEOs and wealthy individuals within corporate America. They've got some sort of Robin Hood complex going on, targeting the one percent they perceive to control the money. But no one has seen them commit a physical crime. It's always been cyberterrorism."

"And thanks to these two"—Matt nodded at Juliette and Noelle—"we now have better descriptions of some of the members."

Decia tapped her pen against the cover of her old-school notebook. "Juliette might have made an enemy of a very dangerous group. You'd better watch your backs."

Juliette observed quietly as the police took over the scene, roping off the lobby with police tape while officers corralled witnesses to interview.

Noelle kept a scowl permanently fixed to her face. Juliette sighed. "If I hadn't intervened, they might have taken hostages."

Hands on hips, Noelle stared Juliette down. "You don't know that. Look, your soldier-warrior mode has to take a back seat. Those guys weren't looking for a fight, and you tried to start one. I'll always have your back, because that's what friends and colleagues do. But you work with a team now, as a bodyguard. You can't keep taking unnecessary risks."

Juliette walked away so Noelle wouldn't see how her words brought up an onslaught of memories.

Civilians would never understand, unable to fathom the depths of duty and loyalty that propelled Juliette into action. Noelle might be a former detective, but had she watched her friends die in battles? Juliette refused to play it safe. If anything, she needed to fight harder to protect the innocent.

Even if it put her in the crosshairs of cyberterrorists. Or her coworkers.

———

MONDAY, 9:00 A.M.

Caleb Styles reached out his hand to smash the snooze button on the buzzing alarm clock. Only he couldn't connect with it.

Another vibration sent a rumble through him. Not the alarm clock, but his phone. He lifted his head off the dining room table. When had he fallen asleep?

He grabbed the cell phone and swiped to answer it.

"Hello, Mr. Styles? This is Principal Rodgers from Ivy Covington's school calling."

Ivy.

He cleared the sleep from his throat. "What trouble has my

niece gotten into this time?" The twelve-year-old couldn't seem to go a day without some sort of incident. He wasn't cut out for parenting a normal preteen, let alone Ivy with her off-the-charts IQ. It had been almost three years since Tessa had died, and he and Ivy still acted like outsiders in Savannah.

"You'll need to come pick her up. A teacher caught her hacking into the school computer to change another child's grade."

He almost asked if she was positive it was Ivy, but this had his niece's signature written all over it. The girl loved to push the boundaries of her intellect.

"Ivy's behavior is escalating," Principal Rodgers said. "These calls are becoming a weekly habit. Last week it was skipping calculus, but hacking is a serious offense. I could expel her for this."

If Ivy got kicked out of the private school that was costing Caleb a small fortune—he didn't have a backup plan for this. He put his elbows on the table and rubbed his eyes. If only he had a second to shave first, but time wasn't on his side today. "I'm on my way." He disconnected the phone and surveyed the mess he'd made on the dining room table. This was what he got for bringing work home.

Computers, papers, and half-drunk cups of coffee littered his table, creating a physical manifestation of his out-of-control stress levels. He thrived on neatness and order, and the mess made his skin crawl.

He tucked his Bluetooth earbuds in and called Blake Abernathy, his long-time friend and co-owner of Cyberskies Security. Blake picked up before the first ring finished. "Are you on your way to the office?"

Caleb searched the table for his keys and found them under a stack of unopened mail, reminding him how much he'd neglected basic life chores the past few weeks.

"Blake, I've been working around the clock since the bank

robbery on Friday. I took home all the laptops scheduled to be sent to the bank to make sure they have the latest security updates. But I've got a situation at Ivy's school I need to attend to first."

Caleb could hear him typing in the background. "You always have an Ivy situation. But we've got a predicament of our own. Turn on the news. First United Bank was robbed. About an hour ago."

"What? Was anyone hurt?" Caleb's head pulsed, but there was no time to grab an aspirin. A second bank robbery? He dashed out the front door of his apartment. "Tell me more."

"It was the same scenario as Friday's robbery. Gunmen walk into the bank, spray-paint *Rushmore* on the bank wall, and walk out while throwing wads of cash in the air."

Rushmore. The thorn in his side. Caleb ran a hand through his hair, which was much shaggier than he liked it. He mentally added *get a haircut* to his running to-do list and hit the stairs, wishing his three-story historic apartment building had an elevator. "Rushmore is a group of hackers. Why are they walking into banks with guns blazing? It doesn't make sense."

"I agree. We received that email threat from them about a cyberattack on the bank, but I didn't expect them to walk into the bank and rob it. I'm taking their threat seriously and have called the FBI. We can't let the hackers win, Caleb. Everything we've worked for will go up in smoke if Rushmore decides to attack the bank systems."

"All it would take is for one bank employee to open an email with malware. Our business would go up in smoke. No one wants to hire a cybersecurity firm that let hackers freeze personal bank accounts and steal money." He'd lose every cent he'd invested in Cyberskies. His livelihood, everything he had, would be worthless with one cyberattack.

Caleb held the glass front door open for his neighbor, Abigail Prewett, who struggled with groceries in her hands. The older lady tried to talk to him, but he pointed to his earpiece that he was on a call and she waved him on.

He stepped out of the building and took a deep breath. October in Savannah gave the town a reprieve from the humidity. If he didn't have multiple crises on his hands, he might consider ditching work.

A sigh filled the other end of the phone and brought him back to reality. "Sorry, Caleb. I didn't mean to dump this on you. You're just as stressed as I am, plus you have Ivy's behavior issues to deal with. What are you going to do about her acting out at school?"

He found his Honda CR-V parked in the lot outside the building. His thoughts shifted between the hacker threat and Ivy. Rushmore could cost him his entire company if the bank's security systems failed.

But what *was* he going to do about Ivy?

He connected the Bluetooth to the car speakers and stashed his earbuds in the center console. "You know I always have a plan before I act. But with Ivy, I'm at a loss. She's brilliant but misguided. After losing Tess and her husband in that car accident, she's all the family I have left, but I'm not qualified to be her parent. I'm an analyst, and the things she does aren't logical."

"Maybe you'll have to find new ways to challenge her."

"I've tried. I've always created ciphers and puzzles for her to work on. I've taught her a lot, but she's got it in her head that she's ready to be a white hacker and help save the world. She's trying to grow up way too fast."

"You're the perfect parent for her, Caleb. She's got that same eidetic memory as you. You understand her in ways most can't." True, he saw the world around him in a series of mathematical equations, something he had in common with Ivy. And he knew both the blessings and curses of their eidetic memories. Caleb remembered everything with perfect recall, even the things he'd like to forget.

But while Ivy's genius level impressed everyone, it came with disadvantages. "She's twelve going on thirty. Maybe I shouldn't have let her skip those grades and start high school. She's not ready. I just want her to have a normal childhood." At thirty-three and single, he'd assumed the fatherhood ship had sailed. And now this.

"You've got this. I know you two will find a rhythm. This parent gig is still new for you both."

"Thanks, Blake. Between the hacker threat and a headstrong preteen, I've hit my max for problems."

"Not to mention you have zero social life since moving to Savannah last year. When's the last time you went on a date or even just had a night out without Ivy?"

Caleb shook his head, even though his friend couldn't see the gesture. The image of one woman popped into his mind, and he shoved it out as fast as it came. Juliette Montgomery was in his past. She'd walked out on him without so much as a forwarding address.

"I probably should take your advice. But right now, I'm pulling into the school. Wish me luck."

"Praying for you, man. Let me know if you need anything."

Caleb disconnected the call and trudged into the school office. The brick exterior and lush landscape made the private school seem like a resort rather than an institution.

The receptionist ushered him into Principal Rodgers' office. He sat in front of the principal's desk with an awkward feeling, like he was the one in trouble. He tapped his foot as he counted ceiling tiles in the office. Sixty-two.

He silenced the buzz in his pocket. A sneak glance at his phone showed the headline of a news article Blake had sent about the bank robbery.

One problem at a time. He'd have to think about work issues later.

Principal Rodgers entered the room and sat at her desk. "This is the third incident in four weeks," she said, looking down at him through her long eyelashes. The gob of mascara in the corner of her eye made it difficult for Caleb to concentrate on her words. "We know Ivy is highly accelerated in math and computer science, but she needs to be reeled in. The school has every right to report this incident to the police. Maybe it's time to consider getting help."

Translation: *Are you sure you can handle being a parent, Caleb?*

Why couldn't people just say what they meant? "Sorry, ma'am. I know she's getting out of hand. But if you can give us just one more chance before suspending her, I'll make sure this doesn't happen again." If Ivy got suspended, he couldn't go to work. Assuming he still had a job if the situation didn't improve with the hacker threats.

The principal stared him down, and he forced himself to not slouch in his chair under her scrutiny. Why did this woman have the intimidation factor of a rabid wolverine? After being in the military for eight years, he should be ready to face anything. But he'd left those days behind to take care of Ivy.

The principal sat back in her chair, which squeaked from her ample girth. Her eyes softened. "I know your situation is difficult. Ivy losing her parents has forced her to deal with grown-up things. But I can't have her circumventing the rules and disrupting other students."

"I agree. I just ask you to please give her one more chance. There isn't another school in the area as prestigious as this one that can challenge her."

The woman's face lit up with the compliment of her school, and Caleb prayed it would buy him some time.

"I know Ivy's been in counseling. Maybe you can increase the number of visits."

Caleb nodded. "I've already texted her counselor after the last school incident for Ivy to have more sessions."

The principal stared at Caleb, her unruly salt-and-pepper curls bouncing as she sized him up. "I think you might be the one that needs help. You're doing this all on your own."

First Blake, now the principal chimed in on the relationship desert in his life. He had Ivy, but forming new friendships, even dating, wasn't on his list of priorities. In his mind, that just made things more complicated.

And the one thing he didn't have room for in his life was more chaos.

Caleb forced a smile. "My neighbor, Abigail, has been helping me watch Ivy in the afternoons. So I have some help."

She sighed. "I know it's been a difficult transition for both you and Ivy, but she can't continue down this path. Take her home today and I'll allow her to return tomorrow with one last chance to prove herself. But she'll need to stay in line."

"Thank you, Principal Rodgers."

He left the school office and found Ivy sitting in the hallway on a bench. "Let's go, kid." Ivy grabbed her bag, and they walked to the car. He didn't have the energy or the words to argue with her now. Hacking the school computer? Even when he was a kid he hadn't been bold enough to attempt that. In the future, her computer skills would either lead her to a high-paying job or a prison cell. At this point, it was a toss-up.

Once they got in the car, he let out a breath. "How much did the kid give you?" He held out his hand, and she passed him a twenty-dollar bill.

"Why would you risk getting in trouble, Ivy? I'm taking away all your electronics. No going online."

Ivy folded her arms and sulked in her seat. "He didn't think I had the skills to do it."

"So it was a dare? You hacked into a school computer to prove your ability?"

He should be mad, but the shallow part of him beamed with pride that she had pulled the stunt off. "You need to learn when it's okay to show off your talents. Just because you can do something doesn't always mean you should. You are so smart, but you're going to be in so much trouble if you keep this up. The school has the right to suspend you. Or worse, involve the police."

"Well, maybe you should teach me a few things about hacking. Then I can get a job and help stop crimes and stuff."

Her auburn hair shimmered in the sunlight, even with the beanie she'd slung over her head. His heart caught—she looked just like her mother. They'd both lost so much after the car accident took Tessa.

"You should concentrate on passing the ninth grade without getting kicked out of school. No one's hiring a high-school dropout, even a smart one."

Had Caleb made a mistake when Ivy's test scores had allowed her to skip from the sixth grade straight to high school? Mentally, the girl could handle it. But emotionally?

"You should know better than to hack a school computer," Caleb said. "What's going to happen when they kick you out, Ivy? What if the school had called the police instead of me? What you did is a criminal offense." He willed his blood pressure to return to a normal level. No sense getting into an argument with a sullen preteen.

Caleb had tried to challenge Ivy, even before he'd become her legal guardian. She had a gift, and he'd wanted her to sharpen her skills in math and science. They'd sent special coded messages to each other when he was stationed overseas. For birthdays and Christmas, he'd sent her ciphers and challenges. But life with a twelve-year-old plus a demanding job sucked up every ounce of energy he had.

He pulled into the parking lot behind the apartment complex and looked at her. What would he do if she got kicked out of school? Would they even want to stay in Savannah?

He sighed. "Look, I know you've got a gift. How about I help you with some coding projects. But only if you stop..." Stop what? Hacking into school computer systems? Showing off how smart she was? Everything within him wanted to protect her childhood. He took a breath. "Stop trying to grow up so fast. Even though you're in ninth grade, I want you to be a kid. I know you want to take on the world, but right now, I need you to take school seriously. Make friends, have sleepovers."

She cocked her head to the side. "You want me to make friends with high school students?"

Right. Maybe he should have thought that sleepover comment through. "I just want you to have some fun times in addition to burying your face in a screen all the time."

"Can I go out with a boy?"

Good thing he'd parked, or he would have wrecked the car. "I'm not ready for that."

"Relax. I just wanted to see your reaction. But I *am* in high school now."

She stared at him, and he watched the battle going on in her mind. Like him, she couldn't hide her emotions well and had no filter. "What's going on with you?"

She huffed. "I miss Mom. I want things to go back to the way they were."

Caleb sighed. "I wish the same thing. But we've got to make do with what God's given us. We have each other. And I have a busy week ahead of me with work, which means I need you to stay out of trouble. Besides, you've got to get ready for the robotics competition this weekend."

Her eyes lit up at the mention of the tournament. Her team had made it to the next round of the competition, and her bedroom looked worse than Caleb's dining room table clutter. Electronics were spread from one wall to the other, with cords sticking out from under her bed like a secret science experiment. If only she had traditional kid problems, like having dirty clothes or makeup scattered about instead of spare robot parts littering the floor.

"I'm having trouble debugging the latest version of my bot. Would you help me later?"

"Of course."

Ivy scampered out of the car and raced off to their apartment. But before she could seal herself off in her bedroom, Caleb confiscated all her electronic devices. He double checked under her mattress and her closet in case he'd missed any. Then he changed the Wi-Fi password. Not that it would stop Ivy if she was determined to get online, but it would at least slow her down. The girl had qualified for Mensa at the age of eight because of her advanced math skills.

If only there was an algorithm he could program to give him answers on being a parent.

He handed her a thick book he'd pulled from the bookcase in the living room.

"What's this?" she asked, flipping pages in the manual.

"It's a book on robotics. It will help you with your program. Because no internet for one week."

A look of horror rippled across her face. "How am I supposed to work on the program errors if I can't have internet?"

"And that will be your biggest challenge yet."

Returning to his pile of work rubble that consumed the dining room table, he grabbed an envelope from the stack of mail.

He didn't need to look at the piece of paper to know word for word what it said. But he pulled out the document and stared at it.

We believe it's in the best interests of Ivy for her to be raised by her grandparents.

The words typed on the lawyer's stationery made his skin crawl. The Covingtons had filed a petition to become Ivy's legal guardians. His brother-in-law's family didn't think he was a fit parent.

And maybe they were right, based on today's fiasco. What would happen if Bob and Betty Covington found out that Ivy was about to get kicked out of school for hacking?

———

MONDAY, 11:45 P.M.

Every minute that ticked by seemed like an eternity for Ivy.

Grounded again. No electronics. No computer, TV, radio, or anything. She rolled over on her bed after having already taken two naps.

The pink walls started to close in on her like a coffin.

She flung a stuffed unicorn across the room. Silly toys for a high school girl. She'd only hacked into the school system to prove to the kids in her class she could do it. If only she belonged somewhere for once. But the kids in her new school were older, more sophisticated. And that one boy had made fun of her, so she'd needed to show him up.

Hacking into the school system was as easy as riding a bike. And it made her classmates pay attention to her.

She rolled over again and looked at the door to her room. An upperclassman had invited her to game tonight. Her first high school invitation, the equivalent of a sleepover. They'd stay up late and chat while completing a quest. She couldn't even get a message to her new friend that she'd miss out tonight.

So not fair. She launched her pillow to join the unicorn on the floor.

Her analog watch indicated that it was 11:45 p.m. Ugh. Fifteen minutes until the quest. Time to find a way online. The sound of the shower hissed in the background, and Ivy slipped out of the room. The password to the Wi-Fi wouldn't be an issue. He'd created a challenging system to change the password each time, but give her fifteen minutes and she'd get in. Nothing was hard for her to figure out with her eidetic memory.

The box of laptops on the dining room table called to her like candy on Halloween night. She got out of bed and padded across the apartment, calculating the odds of Uncle Caleb noticing that one laptop was missing. If he came back to work tonight, he'd notice it immediately. But if he quit for the evening, she'd have all night to return the stolen computer. She accepted the odds and slid the laptop from the middle of the stack, careful not to topple the rest of them.

She tucked her uncle's phone into her jeans pocket and bolted for her bedroom.

With a sweep of her arm, she cleared the textbooks off her desk to make room for herself to work.

"Well, this is weird." Instead of a normal operating system, this laptop booted up with only one program showing. She double-clicked one icon, and multiple windows popped up.

"What in the world..." Ivy stared at the screen. Numbers and letters scrolled across the windows. Her heartbeat double-timed. She checked the connection, and the laptop wasn't online, but the program held a massive database of information.

"Yes!" She clamped a hand over her mouth to contain her excitement. This had to be a cipher from her uncle. Just like he used to send her when her parents were alive. He'd probably created a code and left it for her to finish.

Forget gaming. This was much more interesting.

Her mind whirred faster than the program spat out numbers and letters across the screen. The information seared itself into her permanent memory banks, whether she wanted it there or not.

This was some kind of program. And not a good program,

either. Hmm. Maybe Uncle Caleb wanted her to figure out ways to stop this kind of program, like his company did.

"Finally, a challenge worthy of my skills!"

Numbers and letters imprinted on her brain as she read through lines and lines of code. But the code was missing a piece. If she launched it, it wouldn't work.

It would be just like her uncle to plant this for her to find. But what was she supposed to do with this information? Fill in the missing code?

She poked around the rest of the computer, the game long forgotten.

A different file popped up. A text file.

This contained a coded note, and with a little bit of thought, she uncovered an email address and password.

The sound of the shower stopped. Ivy used her uncle's phone to log in to the free email account with the information she'd discovered.

The email account was empty. No new emails or any signs that it was an active account. She clicked on the only folder that showed signs of activity: the drafts folder.

Several unsent emails popped up. She opened one to find more letters, numbers, and symbols. A burst of energy pulsed in her veins. Had she just discovered a cipher? It was another one of Uncle Caleb's puzzles for her to figure out.

She grabbed the pen and notepad, not that she needed it. What she needed to work out was the key to decode the messages.

Ivy scrolled through the string of numbers and letters in the body of the email. It was an email exchange by a few different people, like they were leaving messages to each other. Her hand ached from writing. While information stuck in her brain like glue, writing helped keep her thoughts organized. And she needed a clue to discover the key to the cipher.

Her scattered notes started to make sense as her mind

translated the information to letter and number patterns. Words coalesced into phrases.

The heat is on. He's getting too suspicious.

We need to send a message.

After tonight, we have a new target.

Ivy shivered, and not from the cold air coming from the AC vent. Who were these people? She looked away from the screen, blinking to regain some moisture in her eyes. What were they targeting? After the phrase *new target* was a string of numbers, letters, and degrees.

She opened the search app on her uncle's phone and typed the information into the search engine. Could it be that easy? The results popped up in a fraction of a second.

Ivy clicked on the link, and a map of Savannah pulled up. Bingo. GPS coordinates.

Wait. Was this the supposed target? What kind of game was her uncle playing with her? Was she supposed to go to this location? She zoomed in, and every muscle in her body tightened.

The map had pulled up her uncle's office building. Strange. Maybe he had something hidden for her at work. But this made no sense.

A creak disrupted her concentration. Hadn't her uncle gone to bed?

Another floorboard groaned. The apartment had been built a hundred years ago, so it wasn't a surprise the place rattled. But if it wasn't Uncle Caleb…

She cracked the door open two centimeters and peered out into the living room. Her uncle's room was on the other side of the apartment, and his door was closed. She listened.

A shadow crossed in front of her, and Ivy covered her mouth with her hand. Someone was in the apartment, and she didn't have a way to call or text Uncle Caleb. She had his phone.

So she used the only thing at her disposal and let out a blood-curdling scream.

THREE

The scream launched Caleb into full soldier mode. Before his eyes had opened, he had his gun in his hand and had reached for the bedroom doorknob.

Every nerve ending in his body pulsed with energy while his mind focused on one solitary mission.

Rescue Ivy.

He cracked the door a fraction and didn't see anything in the living room. Waiting a heartbeat, he proceeded across the apartment to Ivy's room. All of his senses operated in red-alert mode.

The hairs on his arm stood up and Caleb froze.

Someone was in the apartment.

A crash rang out from the kitchen, and a blur of black rushed him. He pointed his gun, but something slammed into his head. Dazed, he stumbled backwards.

"Uncle Caleb! Watch out!"

He grabbed the back of the couch for support with one hand, gun still pointing in the direction of the dining room. A man clad in all black grabbed a laptop from the table and flung it at Caleb, and he ducked. The device flew over his head and hit the wall. Before he could regroup and re-aim his gun, the front door was flung open and heavy footsteps pounded down the hall.

Ivy was by his side before he could blink, her arms wrapping around his waist. Her tears wet his shirt. Caleb touched his forehead and saw blood trickle between his fingers.

"I'll get you a towel to press against your head." Ivy sniffed and headed to the kitchen. He followed, not wanting her out of his sight for a second. She grabbed some paper towels from the counter and handed him a wad. He pressed them to his forehead, and the bleeding slowed.

"I called 911," Ivy said. She handed him his phone from her pocket. He'd have to talk to her later about why she had it.

"Your scream scared the intruder away. Good thinking." Caleb sat at the dining room table, careful not to touch anything. Maybe the police could dust for prints. Except he recalled the intruder had been wearing gloves, so prints wouldn't be likely.

A knock at the half-open door stopped his heart. "Caleb? It's Officer Matt Williams from downstairs."

A man stood in the doorframe, since the door hadn't fully closed after the intruder had bolted. "My boss texted me about the break-in when he recognized the address as my building." His neighbor strode in, weapon in hand, but no uniform. The man wore jeans and a Savannah Banana's T-shirt. "I raced upstairs as soon as I heard about an intruder. Are you two okay?"

Caleb had only met Matt once, but gratitude at the man's timely arrival plus the stress of the situation choked his words. "We're fine. Just stunned."

"The paramedics are on their way." Matt surveyed the damage. "Are you able to talk and tell me what happened?"

Caleb stayed seated, making sure he wasn't dizzy from the

bump on his head. He cleared his throat, hoping his voice didn't quaver. He needed to be strong for Ivy. "We had an intruder. Ivy screamed, and I walked into the living room to find a man rummaging through our belongings."

Two paramedics rushed in single file, and they made a beeline for Caleb. His first reaction was to wave them off, but Ivy shook her head, preempting any chance of him not getting checked out. She knew him so well.

An officer peppered Ivy with questions and asked for a description of the intruder. "I don't have an exact description because the man wore all black and a ski mask, but he was around five foot ten. I'd guess he weighed one seventy-five, because he was on the skinny side. He wore black Nike sneakers, probably a size ten if I had to estimate. White guy, based on the skin color that peeked through the edges of the mask. His eyes were blue, and I don't think he was very old. Maybe not a teenager, so I'd guess he's in his twenties. He moved pretty fast, so I don't think he was much older than that. And he was married."

The older officer taking her statement chuckled and sized Ivy up. The guy's pasty skin with dark circles under his eyes conveyed the man's bad luck of pulling numerous late-night shifts.

"Now, little girl, how do you know all this?" The officer's Savannah drawl gave the question way more syllables than necessary.

This *little girl* could run circles around the guy when it came to recalling elements of a crime scene. Ivy stared at the man like the answer should be obvious. Her eidetic memory came in handy for police reports, and Caleb knew exactly how she'd figured the perpetrator was married.

"The bump on his gloved hand suggested the presence of a ring on his left hand."

"Do you want a job, Ivy?" The officer shook his balding head.

"Because we've never had that kind of description before. You'd make a fine officer."

"No, thank you. I'm going to work for the FBI cybercrimes division."

The man made a tsk-tsk sound. "Too bad. I'd hate to lose someone so talented to the Fibbies. I hope you reconsider someday."

"Look, Uncle Caleb. My first job offer." Ivy smiled, and it made Caleb's adrenaline return to a normal level. He hated she'd had to go through the scare of a home invasion. His thoughts flickered back to his job. Did the break-in have anything to do with the hacker threat? The timing of the two events could be a coincidence, but Caleb's gut told him otherwise.

Caleb pulled Matt to the side while Ivy chatted more about her FBI aspirations. "I need to let you know about threats we've received at work. From a hacker group called Rushmore."

Matt inhaled sharply. "I'm familiar with their work in the area."

"I'll forward you the email they sent Blake, my partner, but I'm concerned this break-in is related."

Matt nodded. "I'll look into it. Is there anything else missing from your house? Did the thief take anything?"

Caleb looked around. "I didn't see him take anything, but I counted the laptops and one is missing. He hit me with one, threw another, but there's still one unaccounted for."

Matt made a note with his phone. "I'll add that to the official report. Just keep me in the loop if you hear from these hackers again."

Matt left the apartment along with the other officer and paramedics. Caleb sat on the couch after securing the front door. He'd change the locks in the morning. Ivy snuggled close to him. The strawberry scent of her shampoo restored some semblance of the peace Caleb had lost with the home invasion.

He needed to keep Ivy safe—from robbers, hackers, or whatever terrors life threw her way.

"Uncle Caleb, I'm so glad you were in the Army and knew what to do when that man broke in."

His heart wrenched. "I'll always be there for you. Nothing's going to happen to you on my watch."

She looked up at him. "But who's looking out for you?"

Caleb's heart squeezed. This perpetrator had rocked her sense of security. "I'll take extra precautions, but I don't think that man will be back. I know how to defend myself."

"But in the Army, you had a team of people that helped you." She got up, moved to the bookcase, and picked up a picture of Caleb's graduating basic training class. "You all worked together for protection. You shouldn't be alone."

"Oh, Ivy. I can't guarantee safety, but I believe that God is ultimately in control, even when things don't make sense. I'm choosing trust over fear." He let the words settle in his soul, because his mind continued to sink its teeth into the *what ifs,* and he refused to waste brain space focusing on the worst-case scenarios.

She stared at the picture and then placed it back on the shelf. "Maybe we could play hooky tomorrow. Just spend the day together. I don't think you should go to the office in the morning."

Caleb looked at the pile of laptops. He still needed to check them for any security flaws. "I've got a lot of work to catch up on, and you've got to go to school. After today's incident, you can't play hooky. I can't face Principal Rodgers twice in one week."

Ivy didn't laugh—not that he was known for his humor. He just wanted to see her smile.

"I worry about you, Uncle Caleb. You don't have anyone watching your back."

"Hey, kiddo, come here." He held his arms open and she

filled them. "You don't have anything to worry about. You let me worry about our protection."

Caleb's mind spun with plans for security. Because he'd protect Ivy at all costs. School might be the safest option for her tomorrow while he figured out the next steps. He'd let the school resource officer know the situation. He wasn't taking any chances.

These hackers had messed with the wrong family, and next time, he wouldn't be caught unprepared. Despite reassuring Ivy, in his heart, Caleb wondered when these men would strike again.

———

TUESDAY, 8:30 A.M.

"Can you please try to stay on Noelle's good side today?" Raven Vega greeted Juliette the second she walked through the front door to the Elite Guardians' office.

Great. So Noelle wasn't over her irritation from yesterday's bank robbery. Not the way she wanted to start her day. Juliette and Noelle had forged a friendship, but Noelle ran the office. They didn't always see eye to eye on how to handle certain situations. But someone had had to intervene in that bank robbery before an innocent person got hurt.

She pasted on a smile. "Good morning to you too, Raven." She placed the box of donuts on the edge of the reception desk. If Juliette needed to stay on anyone's good side, it was Raven's. The eccentric administrative assistant's gothic attire only added to her allure. By day, Raven kept all the bodyguards in line and organized. By night, the woman moonlighted as a tour guide for one of Savannah's historical tours, enchanting tourists with tales of the city's mysteries. When Juliette needed to find anything in Savannah, Raven was the first stop.

"Noelle is looking for you. But you have an early morning visitor right now." Raven nodded to the waiting area at her right. Juliette stuck her head through the doorway to the waiting room that used to be her grandmother's formal living room back in the day. A young girl sat in a chair, her backpack crammed under her feet.

She ducked out of the doorway and turned to Raven. "Shouldn't she be in school? Who is she?" Juliette dropped her voice to a whisper. The girl couldn't be more than ten or twelve, and where were her parents? Noelle would have to wait. Juliette's trouble radar dialed into the girl in front of her.

"I don't know. She asked for you by name and said she needed a bodyguard." Raven shrugged.

Okay then. Juliette crossed into the waiting area and stood in front of the girl. "Hi, I'm Juliette. What's your name?"

The girl sized Juliette up with striking emerald green eyes. Before the kid could respond, Juliette's protective instincts overrode all other senses, and she peppered her with questions. "Where are your parents? Do they know you're here?"

Ivy took a deep breath. "I—"

"Actually, how old are you? Shouldn't you be in school? How did you *get* here? I should let you talk..."

"Ease up there, Sherlock." Raven's mouth turned up with the hint of a mocking smile. "Give her a chance to answer."

Juliette shook her head and squatted in front of the girl. "Tell me why you're here."

After a several second pause, the girl spoke with a pace that matched Juliette's rapid-fire style. "I'm Ivy Covington. My parents died in a car accident approximately three years ago. No one knows I'm here. I'm twelve. Yes, I should be in school. I walked from the campus; it's not too far from here. I'm here because I need your help. Well, technically my uncle is the one in trouble."

Ivy Covington. Juliette ran the name through her mind's

database. It sounded familiar, but she couldn't place it. She sank onto the couch next to Ivy's chair. "Why me?"

Ivy pulled out a picture frame from inside her backpack, handing it to Juliette. "Is this you? In the picture from basic training?"

Juliette stifled a gasp. Nostalgia slammed into her like an ocean wave as her past resurfaced. The group photo from graduation day had creases in it, and the colors had faded, but the memories were sharp and clear. Staring back at her from the frame were Caleb and Laz, two of her best friends from that class.

She never let herself think about Laz.

"I haven't seen this picture in years. Basic training was ten years ago. Where did you get this?"

"So, it's you in the picture, right?"

Juliette handed the frame back. "That's me." She resisted bothering Ivy with more questions. The girl needed space to open up.

Ivy flipped the picture for Juliette to see and pointed to one of the men in the photo. "My uncle."

A knot clenched in her stomach. She nodded, now remembering where she'd heard Ivy's name. Caleb used to talk about her all the time. "Your uncle and I were good friends. We met in basic training and both went into separate branches of the Army. I became a Ranger, and he wound up working as a computer analyst. We eventually lost touch though." Recollections swirled around her like fog in the morning.

Caleb Styles. The name sent her mind reeling. The last thing she wanted to do was revisit her Army days. After all this time, what would she say if she came face-to-face with the man she'd left lying in a hospital bed after he'd risked his life to save hers?

She shook her head as if she could dislodge the scene from her thoughts. "Why are you here, Ivy?"

Ivy reached into her bag and pulled out an actual ceramic

pink piggy bank along with an envelope. She dumped out the contents of each onto the end table. Bills and change littered the glass top. Juliette stared at the preteen girl with the piggy bank.

"I have $127.60. I've been saving for robotics parts. I'm in a competition. It's a big deal. I'm building a sumo robot that has—"

Juliette waved a hand. Ivy was so much like Caleb, who added a million details in every story he told, whether Juliette understood or not.

"Right," Ivy said. "I'll get to the point. Your website didn't have any prices for hiring a bodyguard. But this is all I have right now."

"Are you in trouble?"

The girl shifted in her seat. "No. I want to hire you to protect my uncle. He's all I have. I can't let anything happen to him."

Juliette's heart melted. She'd had no idea that Caleb had moved to Savannah. What were the odds they'd wind up in the same city? She'd heard that he'd been sent stateside but had lost track of him after her discharge from the Army. She stood. "Let's go into the conference room, where we can talk in private. I'll take some notes, and we'll figure out what to do."

"You're a bodyguard. You have to help him. I'm hiring you. He won't say no to you." The girl stood, hands on hips, with a fierceness Juliette appreciated.

"Let's talk about it and see if there's a case. We may need to loop your uncle into the conversation at some point."

"He's not going to like that I skipped school and came here on my own. He won't listen. I need you to convince him not to go to work."

"But if he's in danger like you claim, he needs to know. And I assure you, he's quite capable of taking care of himself. But the fact of the matter is, I can't be a bodyguard for someone without telling the person. It doesn't work that way."

Ivy shot her a sullen look that said she disapproved of the

plan to tell Caleb, but she grabbed her backpack and followed Juliette across the lobby, up the stairs, and into a conference room. Juliette grabbed a pen and paper and observed Caleb's niece. She seemed young but sounded like an adult when she talked. The girl reminded her *so* much of Caleb. Smart and analytical. Juliette could almost see her mind whirring with calculations.

They sat at the oval conference room table. The two square picture windows overlooked Lafayette Square, where water misted from the iconic green fountain. A peaceful scene compared to the fierce concern of the twelve-year-old girl.

"Let's start at the beginning, Ivy, so I can best see how to protect your uncle."

"Last night, someone broke into our house. The person was wearing all black like a ninja. My uncle could have been killed, except he pulled out his gun and chased the person away. The police came and everything. I have a bad feeling that something is going to happen at his job. I need you to stop him from going to work." Words tumbled out with the force of a tornado, and Juliette struggled to keep up with the rambling pace.

Could Ivy be any more cryptic and yet so specific at the same time? "How do you know something will happen?"

The girl shrugged. "Whoever broke in might return."

Juliette sat back in the chair, the plush leather squeaking. A break-in would be enough to traumatize an adult, let alone a child. "Have you told your uncle your concerns? Maybe if he knew you were worried about the break-in, he might take some precautions. You know your uncle has military training; he can defend himself. I've seen him in action."

Ivy's head shake had the potential to give her whiplash. "He won't believe me. I'm just hoping you can convince him. He told me you two were good friends. He needs his Army friends. Isn't that your motto?"

A sense of loyalty rattled through Juliette, and her fierce

desire to protect others pumped that familiar feeling through her veins. If the trouble was real, she wouldn't hesitate to intervene. "It's the soldier's creed. *I will never leave a fallen comrade.*"

She cleared her throat, shoving her emotions back into the lock box she'd created in her heart years ago. "We need to bring this situation to your uncle. He needs to be aware of the danger."

Ivy might be the kind of kid that had an active imagination, and it was sweet that she wanted to protect her uncle from an intruder. Then again, peering into Ivy's tear-filled eyes, Juliette sensed something much deeper was going on. But she couldn't take a case based on a gut reaction. Let alone drain all the money from a little girl's piggy bank.

But face Caleb? What would she say? *Sorry I left you lying in the hospital to deal with the grief of losing your friend. You may have saved my life, but I wanted you to have a future that didn't include taking care of me?*

Duty called, and Juliette at least needed to get Ivy someplace safe, if not assess the danger. She led Ivy downstairs to the reception area. "I'll text Noelle," Juliette said to Raven. "I'm going to make sure Ivy makes her way to school or home." Raven nodded without taking her eyes off her computer screen.

Juliette turned to Ivy. "What time does your uncle go to work?"

The girl shrugged. "He said he might work from home this morning and then go to the office later."

Juliette led Ivy down the hallway and through the back door. The house had a courtyard that offered a few parking spaces for the Elite Guardians' staff and any visitors.

Caleb's mini-me jumped into Juliette's car. "Do you like robots?" she asked as she buckled the seat belt.

"What? I have no particular feelings about robots."

"I'm in a robotics competition at school. We're building a

robot that can…" The girl prattled on about the technical specifications of the robot, but Juliette's mind drifted. Just one look at the girl, and Juliette's nostalgia took center stage. The resemblance between Ivy and her uncle made Juliette's heart ache. How would Caleb handle seeing her after all these years? She had been the one to walk away. She'd done it with his future in mind, but would he see it that way? The knot in her stomach tightened.

When Ivy stopped to take a breath, Juliette jumped back into the conversation. "So your uncle doesn't know I'm coming?"

Ivy cringed. "I didn't tell him. I knew he wouldn't want help. But he needs it. He's alone."

Those two words burrowed into Juliette's heart. Caleb deserved to be with someone special. Women always seemed to fall for the nerd, but Caleb had never seemed to notice the command he had over the opposite sex. He was attractive, kind, and super smart. Why was the man still on the market?

They arrived at the address Ivy had provided.

"This apartment complex was an old hospital that was gutted and renovated into apartments." Ivy's lecture style reminded Juliette of a college professor. "The outside still holds its pre-Civil War historic charm, but the lobby and each unit received a complete twenty-first-century upgrade. Modern lighting, new fixtures, but sadly, no elevator."

Juliette hiked up the stairs with Ivy, her heart rate ticking up with each step. How had she not run into Caleb when they'd been living in the same city? She'd been in Savannah for a year.

They rounded the corner of the hallway, and Juliette collided with someone. Strong arms grabbed her to keep from tumbling over.

Not someone.

Caleb Styles.

"Oh, I'm so sorry," she said, willing the rising heat in her neck to stay down.

Her eyes locked with his, and for a second, it seemed like no time had passed between them. It was as if they were still in basic training, hanging out together and laughing while they were both saddled with the late shift for guard duty.

She took two steps back, out of his reach, and the connection was severed. Now she was the woman who had left him three years ago without a word. No explanation. Nothing.

"Juliette?" His arms flopped to his sides, and his mouth gaped open. "I—I don't know what to say. Why—why are you here?"

His eyes shifted to Ivy. "What did you do? I was just rushing out the door because the school called and said you never arrived for first period. And I dropped you off." The car keys jangled in his hand.

Something tugged at the hem of her shirt, and Juliette saw Ivy peeking out from behind her.

"Uncle Caleb, we need help. You need help. And you told me your Army buddies would always have your back. So I googled Juliette, and it turns out that she's a professional bodyguard. So I hired her."

"Surprise," Juliette said, throwing up her hands in mock surrender. "I found her in my office this morning. Thought I'd make sure she got home in one piece."

"Don't worry," Ivy said. "It was only two blocks from school. Not a long walk."

Caleb ran a hand through his hair. When had he let his hair grow out? It wasn't long, but she'd always seen him with his short military style. Not to mention the goatee he sported. But his signature black-rimmed glasses remained the same. The man still looked good, from his nerdy T-shirt to his plaid Converse. He was the same old Caleb she remembered, just a little older with a few gray hairs peeking out of his brown, wavy hair and a couple of fine lines on his forehead.

"Ivy, head inside. I'd like to talk to Juliette for a moment."

Ivy complied and bounded down the hall and through their apartment door. Once the door closed, Caleb leaned against the wall and said, "Jules. I didn't know you were in Savannah of all places. In fact, I had no idea where you've been the last few years." His tone wasn't one of scolding, but of concern.

She shrugged and leaned against the wall, facing him. "I moved to Savannah about a year ago. I had no idea you were in the area." She folded her arms, trying to appear casual, but the rising tide of emotions swelled. "I am so sorry to hear about your sister. When did you take custody of Ivy?"

His shoulders sank and he stared at the ground. "It was just after you left. When I got back to the base after the attack, I found out about the car accident. I finished out my contract and came stateside to be with Ivy."

Right after she'd walked out on him, leaving him in the hospital after he'd rescued her.

Three years ago, the decision had seemed to be in everyone's best interests. But now?

She longed for that spark between them to ignite again. The camaraderie they'd shared. If only she could pick up where they'd left off, before things had derailed like the world's largest freight train.

Did she and Caleb have a shot at being friends again?

Or would she always be the one that left him behind?

FOUR

Caleb blinked, making sure the image standing in front of him in the hallway of his apartment building was real and not some mirage.

Juliette. The woman who'd walked out of his life without even a backwards glance had now entered his world as suddenly as she'd left it.

His mind tried to form words. Say something. Anything. "I just can't get over the fact that you're here, standing in front of me."

"Well, imagine my surprise seeing a twelve-year-old version of you waiting for me this morning with a piggy bank and a story about a break-in."

He suppressed a groan. "I'm so sorry. I guess the events of last night shook her more than I thought. I should have gotten her in to see the school counselor."

She smiled and his pulse hammered in his ears. She'd always had that effect on him.

His whole world was defined by logic and reason. Except when it came to Juliette. His brain short-circuited around her.

"It's crazy to see you as a parent," she said. "It suits you though. Ivy is just like you."

The compliment sent warmth rushing across his face. "Thanks. But what brought you to Savannah of all places?"

"My grandmother passed away about a year ago. I wanted to honor her memory by keeping the house she left me." Her voice had that hint of a Southern accent, and living in Savannah must have brought it out.

Juliette was still as beautiful as he remembered. Her dark-blonde hair was short and stylish, not long like she used to wear it. But her warm golden-brown eyes brought back the flood of fond memories. How many nights had they stayed up late, talking outside the barracks? It had been a long time since he'd had that kind of connection with anyone.

A door opened and Caleb's neighbor, Abigail Prewett stepped out. "Oh, I thought I heard voices."

"Hi, Abby. We were just going inside."

"What happened? Oh dear. Why isn't Ivy in school? Is this because of the break-in?"

Caleb appreciated the older woman for helping pick Ivy up from school when he had to work late, but sometimes her nosiness grated every nerve he had. Abby cared for her grandson, who happened to go to the same school as Ivy. Caleb tried to extend her some grace, because she was a recent widow, having just lost her husband to a rare cancer. Abby understood Ivy more than most people, having been a professor at a technical college before resigning to take care of her husband. The woman geeked out over robots with Ivy and often helped his niece with her programming homework.

But she was still annoying.

Abby sized up Juliette, and a grin spread across her face. The woman was probably in her late fifties and had that Southern grandmotherly charm.

"And who is your beautiful friend, Caleb? You didn't tell me you had a girl—"

"Thanks for checking on us, Abby, but we were just heading in." He had to get Juliette away from his prying neighbor, because he didn't have a logical explanation for Juliette's presence, let alone Abby thinking Juliette was his girlfriend. Before Abby could say another word, he ushered Juliette into the apartment.

"I'm so sorry for the mess in here. Work has been a bit stressful." The table of laptops and papers created a visual representation of the state of his affairs. Messy. Chaotic.

Desperate.

He'd never let anything in his life get this out of control. Juliette would probably question whether he was fit to be Ivy's guardian. Just like Ivy's grandparents.

He cleared some space at the table and offered her a seat. Ivy attempted to sneak off to her room, but he snapped his fingers. With a pout, she took a seat next to Juliette. He sat down and sandwiched Ivy between them.

"What's going on? Someone want to fill me in?" He faced Ivy. "Last I remember, I dropped you off at school. I watched you go in. Why would you go to Juliette for help behind my back? We could have talked about calling her."

A flicker of fierceness flashed across the girl's face. "I'm sorry, Uncle Caleb. But I needed help you wouldn't refuse. And you wouldn't listen to me about not going to work. I saw the picture and thought about your Army friends. They always have your back. You told me that much. Juliette can help. She's a professional bodyguard. I think she even guarded the president once."

He glanced at Juliette. She shook her head and mouthed *no*.

Ivy pouted. "Well, she probably could. She's that good at protecting people."

A professional bodyguard suited Juliette. The woman had dedicated her life to protecting others. She was as fierce a protector as a momma bear with her cubs. It was what made her an amazing Ranger. She risked her life as easily as breathing if it meant saving someone else.

But he didn't need a bodyguard. His mind scrambled to put the pieces of Ivy's puzzled emotions together.

"Why, Ivy?"

His niece shifted in her chair. "What if the person comes back? Or shows up at your job? I know you can defend yourself, but—" Tears spilled down her cheeks, and she turned away.

Caleb shook his head and glanced at Juliette. "Let's start over. We had a break-in last night, but that doesn't mean the person will return. The police said they've had a few burglaries in the area. And I've changed the locks and security code." He threw his hands up, as if to apologize for this bizarre encounter.

Juliette shrugged. "Ivy seems to think something bigger is going on. She walked from the school to my office. I just want to make sure you are both safe."

"Ivy walking the streets of Savannah by herself isn't safe." He turned to his niece, lowering the volume of his voice. "You should have come to me with your concerns." He loved that Ivy wanted to protect him, but she'd gone overboard.

Ivy trembled. "But what if the person shows up at your work? Maybe this isn't about robbing us. Maybe the person is after you. I don't want anything to happen to you."

Caleb's resolve melted at the sight of tears rimming Ivy's jade-green eyes. How could he be mad at her when he had the same fear of losing those he loved?

"I get it, Ivy. More than you know. But I don't think hiring a bodyguard is necessary."

More tears wet the collar of her school uniform shirt. *Oh, Ivy.*

His heart pulsed with love for his niece, but a bodyguard? Who happened to be Juliette Montgomery?

Not going to happen.

He shot Juliette a pleading look, not sure what she could do in this situation. One more reason on his list of why he made a terrible parent. How could he console Ivy after this break-in had destroyed her sense of security?

Juliette tilted her head. "Caleb, what if you agree not to go to the office today? Maybe take a day off."

He put his hand on Ivy's shoulder. "Would that help you realize that I'm safe? I was going to go into the office this afternoon, but maybe I can work from home the rest of the day."

Ivy wiped her eyes with the back of her hand. "Yes. Today and tomorrow. Please don't go to the office. Just stay here."

"But you have to go to school. After yesterday's trouble, you can't miss any more classes. Are you willing to go to classes for the rest of the day? I'll give you back your cell phone so you'll be able to get in touch with me anytime you need me."

"Yes, if you promise not to go to work."

Caleb nodded. "It's a deal. Why don't you get your books and get ready for school."

As Ivy headed to her bedroom, Juliette leaned closer to him. "Do you want to tell me what's really going on?"

He blew out an exasperated breath. "I don't like the recent chain of events. You know I don't believe in coincidences. My company is a cybersecurity firm. The bank that was just robbed is one of my clients."

Juliette's eyes lit with recognition. "I'm all too familiar with the robbery at First United Bank. I was there."

"What? You were there when men stormed the bank with guns?"

She nodded. "I had to make a deposit. Just a simple errand that veered way off course."

"Well, Rushmore has been sending threats to my company,

trying to attack our software. We've been fending them off, but then someone breaks in and steals one of my laptops? It all ties together."

Juliette sat back in the dining room chair. "So maybe you do need someone to watch your back. It might not hurt to have me hang out for a day or two. Just in case you're a target."

"But it's more about my software than me personally."

She squinted. "How much more personal does it get than a home invasion?"

"Well, when you put it that way, it does seem like I'm on the radar for these hackers. But I don't need a babysitter."

"Coffee. You need coffee. Let's drop Ivy off, and then we can discuss this over coffee. And maybe some bear claws."

Juliette and her snacks. He bit back a smile at the memory. The woman had always been eating some kind of sugary snack.

Plus, how could he say no to her pleading eyes?

He relented. "Fine, maybe we can meet for coffee after I drop off Ivy. I haven't had enough caffeine yet today. It would be nice to catch up, and maybe we can figure out how to alleviate Ivy's concerns. We can talk about it."

His breath hitched at the thought of spending time with Juliette. Flashbacks scrolled through his mind of the last time he'd seen her, when he'd lifted her off the mountainside to safety. One of the worst days of his life. And now, three years later, she sat at his dining room table after his niece had hired her to be his bodyguard.

"Let's meet at Bitty and Beau's for coffee in thirty minutes," Juliette suggested.

"Sounds good." Caleb's phone vibrated in his pocket. "Let me take this. It's my partner, Blake." Juliette nodded and headed to the front door to wait.

"Blake, I'm on my way out the door. Can I call you back shortly?"

"It can't wait. We received another threat from Rushmore.

They posted it on their website this morning. They've just declared a cyberwar with Cyberskies. And they named us both personally as their enemies."

———

TUESDAY, 11:30 A.M.

What had she been thinking? Juliette tapped her foot under the café table while waiting for Caleb.

Why had she suggested they meet up? The man could defend himself. But, like Caleb had said, too many coincidences might spell trouble. And she wanted to make sure there wasn't real danger for Caleb or Ivy.

But now the past stared her in the face. Should she bring up that day she'd left, try to explain?

She'd ordered two coffees and two bear claws. Caleb wouldn't eat the pastries, but she'd use it as an excuse to eat two. Sweet snacks were her downfall. The caffeine and sugar rush did little to calm her nerves, but seeing Caleb again had erased the canyons of time and distance between them. Maybe they could forge a friendship again. Because her reaction to his presence made her head swim and her heart beat a little faster.

"Jules." Caleb waved and headed in her direction. Her stomach fluttered. Why was she nervous?

"You still love sweets, I see." The wooden chair scraped against the floor when he pulled it out and sat down. His memory never let anything slide.

"Who, me?" she said, taking a big bite of the warm pastry that might as well have doubled as a dessert. "I never understood how you stayed in shape with your vast amount of sugar intake."

"It's why I get up early and run five miles every other day. Duh."

Juliette had always thought he was handsome, but the small patch of gray at the edge of his dark-brown hair made him even more adorable.

"I see some things don't change," Juliette said, waving her hand across his T-shirt. This one read *Come to the Math Side. We have Pi.* Cringeworthy—maybe—but Caleb owned his quirks.

Caleb smiled and pushed his glasses higher up the bridge of his nose. "What can I say? I'll choose comfort over style any day." Awkward and humble. And he was oblivious to what others thought of him. The man could still command the attention of any woman in the room, even if he didn't notice.

His demeanor shifted to somber. "I am so sorry about Ivy. The break-in must have really gotten to her. She's had a lot of trauma in her life for such a young age. I hate having her out of my sight, but that private school is locked up tighter than Fort Knox. I think she's safer there. Assuming she stays."

Caleb took a sip of the coffee Juliette had purchased for him. She mentally checked herself. This was business. Nothing else.

But an emptiness stirred in her soul. She hadn't realized how much she'd missed his friendship until he was sitting across from her.

She cleared her throat, refusing to let her emotions get the best of her. "She seemed convinced that the person will return. Do you think the robbery was an isolated case?"

"I'm not sure. I didn't see the guy take anything, but one of my work laptops is missing. Ivy startled the guy. It could have ended way worse."

"She's smart. Maybe she picked up on something and that's why she's nervous."

Caleb sighed and the wooden chair creaked as he leaned back. "She's too smart. Ivy qualified for Mensa at the age of eight. I can't keep her out of trouble on the internet. Yesterday, she got busted for changing another student's grade by hacking into the school's system. She's twelve and in high school. I picked one of the most prestigious private schools to keep her challenged, but the astronomical tuition is pointless if she gets kicked out."

The man had his hands full. He'd always been smart and the top of his classes, even graduating from West Point before enlisting. Seemed like Ivy took after him. "I'm so sorry to hear about your sister. Will you tell me a little more about the accident?"

Caleb frowned and swirled the liquid remnants in his coffee cup. "It was about a month after the incident on the mountain. I'd returned to my station when I got the call about Tessa and the car accident. A drunk driver crossed the center line on a highway and killed Tessa and Zach. Ivy had been at home with her grandparents. I took emergency leave. I came back to the Army only to complete my assignment, and once that was up, I left for good to raise Ivy."

Words formed on the tip of her tongue. She wanted to explain, apologize, and even rehash the past. But what if he didn't want to go there?

Would that day on the mountain always be between them?

Time to change the subject. "What are you doing in Savannah?" she asked, taking another sip of her coffee.

"Do you remember me telling you about my friend from West Point, Blake Abernathy?"

She nodded.

"Blake asked me to join him and start a cybersecurity company. His offer came at the right time and we moved about a year ago. Ivy and I both needed a change of pace, so it seemed like a good idea."

An employee arrived at their table and offered to take their used cups. She might need another one to go.

"So, how have you been, Jules?"

At the sound of her nickname, she froze. Leave it to Caleb to cut to the heart of the matter with one word. He was the only person she'd ever let call her Jules. His familiarity unnerved her. He knew her in ways no one else did.

"I've been back in Savannah for about a year. Since my grandmother left me her house, I decided, like you, it was time for a change. Before that, I was in Columbia, South Carolina."

He watched her with those deep brown eyes that probed her soul. With Caleb, surface-level conversation didn't exist.

"Why?"

Another one-word sentence that shattered Juliette's confidence. She took a deep breath. The man deserved an explanation.

She looked him in the eye. "When I was in the hospital— after the mountain—they told me I had breast cancer. It wasn't the injuries from the attack that sent me home. It was my own body."

"Oh, Jules. I'm so sorry. I would have been there for you if I'd known."

His eyes probed hers for her to continue. "That was my concern. You had your whole life ahead of you, and I'd washed out of the Army. Losing Tank and Laz—the grief hit me hard. And then realizing I'd have to give up the Rangers, the loss was more than I could bear. You deserved to have a future without my baggage. You needed to heal too."

Caleb cleared his throat. "It took me a long time to get adjusted to life with Ivy," he said, "and when I was in a place that I could track you down, I tried. I called your parents, and they said that you'd moved but wouldn't tell me where. I tried, Jules, but I had no idea where you wound up once you were stateside."

She wrapped her hands around her cup to steady them. "You tried to find me?"

He nodded. "I didn't like the way we abruptly ended a great friendship."

The formation of tears took her by surprise, and she turned

away to gain her composure. After all these years, she'd thought their friendship had been severed permanently. Yet he'd tried to find her.

She rallied, looked at Caleb and smiled. "After the Army discharged me, I moved back home while I underwent treatment for breast cancer. But the second I was cleared, I moved to Columbia."

"I'm just glad you're well now."

"It was a long and hard battle, but after about a year, I went into remission. But my time with the Rangers was over, and I thought it best to find a fresh start. So I joined the Elite Guardians and became a bodyguard."

"That's great news about your remission—you've always been a warrior. I'm glad you chose a different battlefield to tackle head-on."

His words soothed the hurt places she wouldn't admit existed. He understood. The surgery, doctor visits, chemotherapy, and radiation had bullied her into the fight for her life. And she'd refused to let cancer win. But in the end, it had destroyed one of the biggest things she'd loved.

Being a Ranger.

He broke through her thoughts. "How did you become a bodyguard? It's a perfect job for you, Jules."

Had he read her mind? "My friend, Olivia Savage, owned the Elite Guardians Agency and offered me a job. My first assignment was working with *the* Preston Whittaker." She fanned herself in mock gushing of Preston's celebrity status. Laila Rabbinowitz had become one of her closest friends. Make that Laila Whittaker now.

"Right. Like you'd ever fall for someone's celebrity status."

"True, but one thing led to another, and when my grandmother left me her three-story house in the historical district, I convinced Olivia to open a branch in Savannah. The Elite Guardians lease the top two floors for office space, and I live in the basement apartment." She sighed. "But let's get to the real reason we're here."

Caleb's face fell. "Yes. Let's. Ivy. I can't believe she tracked you down. Obviously, we can't hire you to babysit me without a known threat. I don't know what's going on, but so far it's nothing I can't handle. Ivy's emotions are a whole different story though." He shook his head, concern for his niece etched into the fine crinkles around his eyes.

"It must be hard becoming an instant parent," Juliette said. "But she cares about you, meaning you're doing something right."

Caleb shrugged. "I'd do anything for her. Zach's parents are still in Ivy's life, and we get together at holidays."

She noticed the wince at the reference to Ivy's grandparents. Her heart fractured into a thousand pieces. She understood all too well the loneliness that shredded a person's soul when a loved one died.

"I remember when my brother, Joe, died in combat. I was twelve. He was my hero, and I still miss him every day. And I remember your parents are both gone too."

"We've both had our share of loss. Ivy's the only family I have left."

This man was a professional griever. But Caleb's faith had always carried him through the difficult times. Despite his analytical mind, he'd always found a peace that defied logic. He'd always encouraged her to reach out to God because, according to Caleb, relying on her own instincts would only get her so far. But trusting in someone besides herself was the one risk she'd never been willing to take.

She shoved her emotions aside.

"The last thing I want to do is insert myself into your and Ivy's lives. I just want to make sure you're safe. I'm not sure what to do. I agree that you don't need a bodyguard. But you need to watch your back, because it really could be connected."

Caleb nodded. "I'll work from home today and then see how it goes. I've emailed my assistant to gather some files so I can pick them up on the way home." She didn't miss the stress that created an edge to a normally stoic Caleb. She'd noted the disarray at his house and his slightly wrinkled T-shirt. And not having shaved? That wasn't like the Caleb she remembered.

"Is there something else going on?"

"No, just work stuff. Co-owning a tech start-up is a lot harder than I thought it would be. And raising Ivy always has its challenges." He took a deep breath, indicating the subject was closed. "I'm glad we ran into each other, although I wish Ivy hadn't tried to hire you. I've missed you and have always prayed that we'd reconnect one day."

Juliette tried to hide her shock at his brutal honesty. The one thing she'd admired most about Caleb was that he was a straight shooter. He said what he meant. She swallowed. "Imagine my surprise this morning, seeing her waiting for me."

Would this be the last she'd see of Caleb Styles? She opened her mouth to ask the question, but a café employee came and collected the remainder of their cups and plates. Thankful for the interruption, Juliette stood. As predicted, Caleb hadn't touched the sweet treat, so she grabbed a to-go bag as they made their way out of the café.

Tourist season had ended, but the streets still beckoned to a few out-of-towners ready to unravel the mysteries of Savannah. Somehow, they fell into a comfortable rhythm of walking side by side toward the corner parking garage, not saying anything. They didn't need words to fill the space between them, something Juliette relished from the past.

If only they could rekindle that kind of relationship.

A chill crept down Juliette's spine, spiking her bodyguard instincts into high alert. She scanned the area around them, unsure of what she was looking for. While she didn't want to dismiss Ivy's concerns, there wasn't any proof that Caleb was a target.

They stood at the corner of the street to cross to the garage. A family of four stopped at the curb, ready to head toward the waterfront district for a day of sightseeing. Several other people approached the crosswalk and waited. Juliette caught movement from the corner of her eye and tracked a man in a black hoodie, cutting his way through the pedestrians toward them.

She could only make out the man's profile under the hood, but was that a gash on his cheek? The man turned and made a beeline for Caleb.

"Caleb, watch out!" she yelled.

The stranger bumped Caleb hard, causing him to stumble off the curb and into the street.

Right in front of an approaching trolley car.

FIVE

Caleb's hands scraped across the asphalt, but he righted himself and sprang to his feet. A hand grasped his arm and yanked him back to the curb seconds before a blur of green-and-orange metal from the trolley flashed by.

The gasps of a few bystanders mixed with the rush of wind from the passing cable car. He wobbled and Juliette tightened her grip.

Cell phones hung in the air, consuming every detail of Caleb's tumble.

Only, he hadn't tripped. Someone dressed in all black had rammed into him. He scanned the street. "Did you see who knocked into me?"

Juliette loosened her fingers from around his bicep and shook her head. "I lost him when I saw you stumble into the street. He's gone. But are you injured?"

Caleb did a mental self-assessment and brushed the grit from his hands onto his jeans. "Aside from my pride being a bit wounded, I'm not hurt." He put a finger through a hole in his favorite T-shirt and cringed. And his glasses were missing. He'd have to wear his contacts when he got home.

Juliette rolled her eyes. "I can buy you a new T-shirt, Caleb. Maybe we can find you an even nerdier one."

Her eyes grew serious. "I'm taking Ivy's case," she said. "I'm your new bodyguard. That man intentionally pushed you in front of that trolley."

"I don't believe in coincidences, and if you hadn't pulled me back..."

Sirens wailed in the distance. "Let's not think about what might have happened. You're safe and we need to get you off the street." Juliette grabbed his arm again, and they walked toward the awning of a hardware store to get out of the way of onlookers. As they walked, Caleb scanned the faces of every person in the crowd, committing each one to memory in order to help the police. But he knew the perpetrator had taken off right after the shove.

Juliette waved her hands like Moses parting the Red Sea to forge a path through the gawkers. She led him toward the building, about a hundred feet away from the crowd. "The situation has changed, Caleb. It doesn't take a mathematician to add up these events. The bank robbery. Your home invasion. The man shoving you into the road. This hacker group is coming for you."

Caleb swallowed. "Blake called me before we left. Apparently Rushmore has declared war against Cyberskies." He couldn't form words or wrap his mind around how close he'd come to his own mortality. His skin pricked as his mind recalled every vivid impression of the trolley rushing by him. But one thought shut down all of the others.

Ivy.

"This puts Ivy right into their crosshairs," Juliette said, as if reading his mind. "If these guys are gunning for you, they could go after her."

"If anyone is targeting me, Ivy could become collateral damage." He bit his bottom lip. "Should I take her out of school? Do you think she's in danger?"

He shot Ivy a text to make sure she was okay. He'd relented and given her back her phone so he could keep tabs on her, especially after the break-in. Her instant response of "Fine" slowed his heartbeat to within a normal range.

He flipped the phone so Juliette could see Ivy's text. His phone had survived his tumble into the street by some miracle.

"I'm on it," Juliette said. "I'm calling in for reinforcements. Let me check with Noelle in my office and see if we can get additional bodyguards in place."

Officers Matt Williams and Ladecia Slaton headed toward them while her fingers flew across the screen of her iPhone.

His neighbor placed his hands on his hips. "Did you two decide to team up to find trouble? Because I've seen both of you at crime scenes in the past twenty-four hours."

Juliette put her hands on her hips, ready to volley the sarcasm back into Matt's court. Caleb tried to hide his smile and let Juliette handle the retorts. "We just want to make sure you're earning a paycheck. But we're concerned that these crime scenes are related."

Matt's face grew somber. "How so?"

Juliette turned to Caleb. "Did you notice anything identifiable about the man?"

Of course he remembered every detail, but the hood had covered most of the man's facial features. He closed his eyes and let his memory draw him a picture of every detail. "Tall and lanky man. Pointed jawline. I didn't see his eyes. But he had an angry red cut across his right cheek."

She nodded. "Kind of like someone hit him in the head with a trophy. I thought I saw some sort of scar or wound. I think he's the man from the bank."

"So you can describe him?" A jolt of energy sparked through

Caleb. This could be their first lead. And it all tied back to Rushmore.

"No. He was wearing a mask, but I clobbered him in the face, which explains the wound."

A chill shuddered through Caleb, and he listened to Juliette explain her theory that she'd faced off with their perpetrator during the bank robbery on Monday.

Hazard Pay Montgomery. Jules was still living up to that stupid nickname. Caleb had always hated it. Because it meant that Juliette put herself in danger.

Matt pulled up info on his phone. "If this is the same guy from the bank robbery, we might have our first crack in this case. But it also means Caleb needs someone to watch his back." The officer eyed Juliette, who hadn't stopped scanning their surroundings.

Matthew and Officer Slaton excused themselves to interview other eyewitnesses and see if they could get various cell phone videos with different vantage points of the incident.

"Your new job as a bodyguard suits you," Caleb said.

A hint of red swept across her cheeks. She shrugged. "I enjoy it and still get to use some of my Ranger training. But I think we need to get off the street like you suggested, in case the man in black is still watching. Would you consider heading back to my office so we can discuss your need for further protection?"

"So you're going to take Ivy's piggy bank money after all?"

She put her hands on her hips. "Caleb, are you making a joke? I didn't know you had it in you." He'd never been known for a sense of humor, and most sarcasm was lost on him.

But he wasn't kidding. The last thing he wanted was for Juliette to be officially in charge of his protection.

He shook his head. "I'm not joking. Are you seriously going to let Ivy hire you to protect me? Because if anything, Ivy is the one that needs a bodyguard. Should I take her out of school?

She should be with me. Do you think she's in danger? Maybe I should text her—"

Juliette placed a hand over Caleb's, silencing his jumbled thoughts.

"I think you both need protection—you've had two serious incidents in two days."

His pride took an arrow to the chest. He moved his hand away from hers and tightened his grip around his phone. Did she think he couldn't defend himself? Sure, he'd been an analyst in the Army, but he'd made it through basic training just like she had. "As long as we focus on keeping Ivy safe, then."

He crossed his arms. With Ivy on Juliette's side, it might be two against one. And Juliette's golden-brown eyes were just *pleading* with him to reconsider. He dropped his arms. "Let's go back to my apartment. We'll discuss an action plan. I'd like to get off the street and be home when Ivy gets back from school. My neighbor is picking her up."

Since he wasn't going to the office, he sent a text to his assistant, Michelle Corbin, to see if she would bring the rest of the laptops from the office to his apartment so he could continue to inspect the software. Despite the craziness around him, he had to be diligent about keeping the bank's systems safe.

They walked toward the car. At the light, they crossed the street, Juliette's hand resting lightly on his bicep. While he didn't want her protecting him, he let it go this time. She had pulled him to safety, after all.

There wasn't a space left in the parking garage. They found his car, and Juliette inspected it, even checking underneath with a telescopic mirror.

"It's clear." She stood up and put the mirror into her bag. "I'll follow you back to the apartment."

Juliette stood by the trunk of his car and watched him get in and lock the doors. He thought for a second that she wouldn't leave his side, but she relented long enough to get her car so she could follow him back to his place. It took all his strength to not drive to the school and whisk Ivy out of class. But Juliette was right. They needed to assess the danger level and come up with a plan.

The ride to his apartment seemed long, despite the short distance. He pulled into a space in the parking lot behind his building. The U-shaped apartment complex used to be a hospital but had been converted into twenty-two apartments. All his senses were on high alert as they got out of the car, and Caleb surveyed the area to make sure they weren't being watched. He was on the hackers' radar, which signaled a potential threat to all his neighbors. He caught Juliette doing her own reconnaissance of the area. They were both on duty now.

Back in his apartment, Juliette swept the place for any listening devices.

"I really don't think this is necessary. The thief didn't have time to plant any bugs." But his tone of voice probably didn't fool Juliette. The recent events added up to plenty of reasons for concern. And they couldn't be too careful.

When her search came up empty, she sat down at the table filled with laptops. Caleb moved to the kitchen and grabbed two bottles of water. He placed one in front of Juliette and settled across from her, the mountain of laptops providing a nice buffer space. Despite their past friendship, Juliette's presence jangled his nerves. An odd reaction, like something familiar mixing with the thrill of the unknown. Which, when combined, might be explosive.

Juliette wrapped her hands around the dewy water bottle. "Do you get the feeling that Ivy isn't telling us everything? Why is she so insistent that you not go to work? It's like she knows Cyberskies is a target."

Her words gave credence to his own thoughts. "I've had the

feeling she's been hacking again. And I keep thinking about these hackers. If I were them, and I wanted to make a statement and take down a bank, I'd attack their security software. Which they are doing. But if they're coming after me, Ivy might be on their radar. Maybe she discovered something about Rushmore."

Would these hackers be so bold as to contact his niece in order to get to him? His heart seized at the thought. Ivy was his responsibility, and if his job brought dangerous men to their doorstep, he'd never forgive himself. It would give Ivy's grandparents more ammunition in their quest for custody.

Juliette stood and moved to his side of the table, sitting next to him, erasing the barrier. And he didn't mind. Her presence seemed to calm the tornado of chaos.

"You are a good parent to Ivy," Juliette said. The smattering of freckles on her nose seemed more pronounced than he recalled.

He let out a long sigh. "I've lost everyone else I care about. My mom. Dad. Sister." *You.*

The unbidden thought sucker punched him so hard he nearly flinched. He had lost Juliette. Now she sat in front of him, and the past three years melted away.

But would the past always keep them apart?

A knock at the door interrupted their conversation, and he sighed, not wanting to disrupt this moment of closeness with Juliette. "That's Michelle with the supplies I requested from the office." He opened the door to Michelle Corbin and Blake.

Michelle was the best hire he'd made. She kept him organized, and he honestly had no idea what he'd do without her. She strode in and laid a box of files and some additional laptops on the already cluttered table.

"I had to come over after Michelle told me about the break-in," Blake said. "I wanted to make sure you're okay."

Caleb ran a hand through his hair. "I've been better."

"I see you've been working. Are these all the laptops that were on their way to the bank?"

Caleb nodded. No sense in prolonging the inevitable. "I took all of the laptops we were delivering to our client to make sure the software was properly installed after the first bank robbery."

He offered Blake and Michelle a seat at the table. "I'm concerned that Rushmore is trying to infiltrate our system. I think that's why they broke into my apartment last night."

Blake's face paled. "That's not good. But sadly, my news is worse." His partner eyed Juliette.

"You can talk in front of Juliette," Caleb said. "She's, um, an old friend and a bodyguard."

"You hired a bodyguard?" Michelle's jaw dropped.

"No—I mean, Ivy sort of did...long story—but she's helping me sort through this mess."

"Well, sort through this," Blake said as he dropped his phone onto the table with a clank. "I just received this on the way over." The video opened with bold white letters on a black screen, and Caleb and Juliette leaned in for a better view.

This is Rushmore. You have something we want. And we have something you want.

The video rolled and showed a man gagged and tied to a chair. Caleb gasped. "That's Theo Payne. He's our operations director."

"Now do you see the need for a bodyguard?" Juliette whispered.

Caleb's pulse raced. His job had invited danger right to his doorstep. He refused to let Ivy be the next to become the target.

———

TUESDAY, 2:00 P.M.

English class was such a bore. Who cared where the comma went?

Today they were talking about Shakespeare's *Twelfth Night*. It was just some old dumb play. Why did they have to learn about this stuff when she needed to be perfecting her computer and math skills? Reading and writing just got in the way.

At least she had her phone back. She stuck it between the pages of her English textbook and made eye contact with the teacher to appear engaged. While looking up, she managed to scroll to her chat app at the same time. She'd told her new friend all about the break-in at the apartment after she'd bailed on gaming.

Well, CyberLane was a friend, even though they'd never met in real life. At least they went to the same school. And CyberLane understood Ivy in ways most people couldn't.

CYBERLANE121

> I've got a project for us. A real hacker project.
> My brother is going to pay us to try and crack
> his program. He works for the government. Are
> you in?

Ivy blinked at the whiteboard as the teacher wrote a bunch of words. If it wasn't numbers, Ivy was out. Besides, all she had to do was take a quick scan of the board and commit everything to memory, and she'd ace every test. She'd raise her eyes up now and again to make sure she'd captured a mental image of whatever was written.

A real-life hacker job? Her first? This was what she wanted Uncle Caleb to teach her. She could become the world's best white hacker, testing systems to prevent the real hackers from succeeding.

Her stomach churned as she thought about last night. She needed to come clean about stealing Uncle Caleb's laptop. He might be mad about her hacking, but he needed to know about the program. Last night, she'd made the decision to stay quiet about the laptop so that she could work on the code. Just for one more day. Tonight, she planned to come clean and give her uncle the laptop. Then he'd take the threat seriously.

The program was the most intriguing thing she'd ever come across. It would do serious damage if it were released. If it worked.

But maybe CyberLane could help her make contact with actual hackers so they might figure out who was behind the break-in. Then the police would have information necessary to arrest them. She knew without a doubt they were searching for the laptop she'd taken. And if she tracked them down, Uncle Caleb would be safe. The hackers had stopped communicating in the email account, so she didn't have much else to go on.

She vowed to come clean when she got home today. It was the right thing to do. But she'd help any way she could. Her uncle might see her as a little girl, but she'd put her skills to good use and prove she was capable of more than just math homework. Especially if it kept her uncle safe.

Ivy kept her eyes on the board and tried to type with the page of her book covering her phone.

IREMEMBER4LIFE

I'm in. Send me the deets

CYBERLANE121

Maybe we should meet in person. Can you skip second period tomorrow?

IREMEMBER4LIFE

Duh. Gladly. Meet by the bleachers at the soccer field?

CYBERLANE121

C U there

"Ms. Covington? Why don't you answer the question for us?"

Busted. All eyes turned to Ivy. She scrolled through her memory database for mental snapshots of whatever was on the board. Not even knowing the question, she threw out the first thing that might make sense.

"I think this quote from Shakespeare sums it up best. *'Be not afraid of greatness. Some are born great, some achieve greatness, and some have greatness thrust upon them.'*"

She held her breath. Mrs. Taylor nodded and smiled. "Nice answer." The teacher called on a different student, who had obviously not been paying attention. The kid squirmed.

That was a close call. She should probably do a little better at paying attention. But her mind drifted back to CyberLane's message.

What if greatness was about to be thrust upon her? While she relished the thought of a real hacker job, she had ulterior motives. She wanted more information on the people that had targeted her uncle. The one that had their sights set on her family.

And who better to ask than an actual hacker?

SIX

TUESDAY, 3:30 P.M.

How had Juliette's week gotten so complicated?

It was only Tuesday, and so far, she'd already dealt with a bank robbery, an almost hit-and-run, hackers, and now an abduction—all connected. What would Wednesday bring?

She immediately called the police after watching Blake's video. The image of the man strapped to the chair made her shiver. His bruised face seared a permanent image in her memory bank. Why were hackers breaking into banks and apartments and adding abduction to their list of growing crimes?

Another knock at the door announced the arrival of Matt and Decia. Caleb ushered them into the apartment, and behind them trailed a man who introduced himself as Tim McGregor, FBI Special Agent in charge of cybercrimes.

Things had just escalated to off-the-charts dangerous if the FBI was taking interest in their case.

She studied Caleb. He wore the stress of the past few days like a mask. Dark circles rimmed his eyes, and his jaw muscles flexed from clenching his teeth. His personal safety had been violated, not to mention that it had to be killing him to have so many strangers traipsing through his home. The man had always valued privacy as much as security.

Juliette stepped in to manage the full apartment. "Let's take seats in the living room, and we can start from the top so everyone's up to speed."

"That's my cue to leave," Michelle said.

Blake headed to the door to follow Michelle out until Matt stopped him. "Don't go anywhere. We need a statement about Rushmore and that video." Blake's face blanched but he took a seat. He ran a hand through dark hair that had a few strands of silver peeking through. His foot tapped out a rhythm on the carpet, underlining his tension. Was it the stress of the events or something else? Juliette made a mental note to grill Caleb about his partner.

Caleb took the couch, and Juliette tucked herself next to him. Agent McGregor hefted his bulky frame into Caleb's recliner. The man had a few inches on Caleb, who was six foot. But unlike Caleb, the older man had an intimidation factor that couldn't be beat. She hoped to never be on the receiving end of an interrogation from this man.

Agent McGregor scrutinized both Caleb and Blake. The man never blinked, his stare making even Juliette want to squirm.

"We've had our eyes on Rushmore for a few years," McGregor said. "We've found wannabe members of their hacker group popping up in a few cities around the country. Their whole manifesto is based on getting even with the rich and powerful. In other places, they've hacked into some small, regional banks and siphoned money from several high-end wealthy clients which they 'redistributed'"—he used air quotes—"into other bank accounts. Hundreds of people woke up to find thousands of dollars deposited into their accounts."

Juliette stifled a gasp. "I remember hearing about that."

"Why break into the bank?" Blake asked. "It doesn't make sense. They're hackers."

McGregor shrugged. "They seem to be some sort of vigilante group, robbing from the rich to make amends with the poor. But I've never seen them this bold, to take a hostage or walk into a bank and rob it. It seems like it's one big publicity stunt. They sent out videos on socials showing them waltzing into these banks, throwing cash around. But based on the video message of Theo, you two have something they want." The man sized up Blake and Caleb again, almost as if to silently communicate *I suspect the both of you.*

Caleb shook his head. "I'm assuming they want access to the security software. I suspect they stole a laptop to try and maybe reverse engineer it."

The agent sat back in the chair. "We'd like to have our top analysts on this, but after looking at your credentials, Caleb, I'd like to ask for your help."

Well, maybe she'd read McGregor's suspicions wrong.

Caleb swiped the screen of his phone and jotted down a name and number on a piece of paper he had on the end table. "This is Theo's wife, Georgia. She works odd shifts as a nurse, but she's probably taking time off. I can't imagine what she and her son are going through. You may need to give her a call in case she has info on how he was..." Caleb swallowed. "How he was abducted. She might not even know he's missing yet."

Agent McGregor nodded. "I've got my people working on this. We won't rest until we find Theo."

Juliette's phone buzzed, and she stepped into the hallway outside the apartment to answer it. "Noelle, thanks for calling me. I know you got my text, but things just got more interesting. I just needed to fill you in on my new case."

"Don't you mean *our* case? Because if the danger is as prevalent as you've indicated, Alana and I are free and ready to step in and help. Please let us help you." While the comment might have been a jab about Juliette's lack of teamwork, it didn't matter. This time, Juliette wanted everyone working on Caleb's behalf. She knew Alana and Noelle had her back no matter what. And she needed them.

"Caleb is an old Army friend, and the threats are escalating." She filled Noelle in on Caleb's case. Or make that Ivy's case.

"Wait. Stop. My head is spinning. A twelve-year-old asked you to be a bodyguard for her uncle?"

Juliette sighed. "Technically, yes."

"A kid hired you?" Juliette could envision Noelle's smirk.

"Technically, yes, but I may do this one pro bono. My conscience won't let me pilfer a little girl's piggy bank money. I have some time off coming up anyway."

"No worries," Noelle said. "We'll make it happen. It sounds like Caleb needs someone to watch his back."

"Whether he thinks he does or not." But based on this last conversation with the FBI, Caleb knew the dangers were real, and he probably wouldn't fight her if the Elite Guardians were also watching Ivy.

Juliette disconnected the phone when she spotted Ivy bounding up the stairs. The girl raced toward her and flung herself into Juliette's arms. "I'm so glad you stayed," Ivy whispered, her voice choked with emotion.

Juliette looked up and discovered a familiar face standing next to Ivy. "Abby, it's nice to see you again," Juliette said.

Abby smiled. Her salt-and-pepper hair gave off grandmother vibes even though the woman probably wasn't even sixty yet. "I try to help out when I can. I was already at the school picking up my grandson. What's going on here?" Abby motioned toward Caleb's apartment as a myriad of voices carried into the hallway.

"Where's Uncle Caleb?" Ivy pushed the door open and ran inside. Abby tried to peer around the doorway, but Juliette moved into the doorframe and blocked her view.

Juliette wasn't sure how to answer without upsetting Abby.

"The police had some more questions about the break-in." Which was true in a roundabout way.

Abby nodded. "I heard the commotion last night and opened my door a crack. Saw a man dressed in all black run by. But I gave my testimony to the police already." She continued to try and stick her head through the entryway.

"I'm glad you were safe last night. I'll let the police know you stopped by, and they can contact you if they have any more questions."

Abby nodded and Juliette eased the door shut just in time to hear Ivy's outburst. "Something else bad happened. I just know it. Don't lie to me. Why are the police here?"

Juliette walked into the living room and found Caleb sitting on the couch with Ivy glued to his side. "Someone sent a threatening note to work," he said.

Matt and Decia wrapped up their questioning, and Juliette ushered them out of the apartment. Agent McGregor said he'd be in touch and left, trailing the officers while barking orders to someone on his phone.

Soon it was just the three of them. Juliette sat in a chair across from the couch, and Ivy turned to Juliette with tears in her eyes. "You can't leave. You have to protect Uncle Caleb. What if the bad guys come back?" She faced her uncle. "Promise me you won't go to work tomorrow."

Caleb stared at Ivy. "Why, Ivy? What is the reason for so much fear?"

Ivy crossed her arms. "I can't go to school if you go to work. I'll worry too much."

"Ivy, why are you so sure something will happen if your uncle returns to the office?" Juliette asked. The girl's insistence seemed to point to something specific.

Ivy shrugged. "I just have a bad feeling about his office. Like the bad guys might be there and try to hurt Uncle Caleb."

Caleb shook his head. "Not buying it. Just tell me what you

found out when you were poking around on the internet in places you aren't supposed to be."

Her eyes widened, but Juliette caught a hint of relief. "You're right. I was going to tell you tonight." She got up and trudged to her room, returning with the missing laptop. She handed it to Caleb.

She sat on the couch and stared at her sneakers. "I stole it from the pile on the table. I saw a strange program on it and thought maybe it was one of the puzzles you used to create for me. But as I dug deeper, I knew it was bad. And there was an email account with some people talking about targeting your office. And then someone broke in, so I knew it was for real and not something you set up to challenge me."

Juliette could see the internal stress cracking through Caleb's exterior defenses. He opened the laptop and typed a few things. "This is why someone broke in," he said. "They installed malware on this computer. It's not online, so no one could trace them. But if someone received this laptop and connected it to the internet, the criminals would have access to the bank's system."

Ivy shook her head, her auburn curls bouncing across her forehead. "Promise me you'll stay away from your office. It's not a safe place."

He poked around in the laptop and uncovered another file. "I assume you figured out the key to this?"

She nodded. "It's a personal email account." She pulled a piece of paper out of her pocket and read the cipher. He pulled up the website, but the entire inbox was empty.

"What did it say, Ivy?"

She blew out a breath. "A conversation in the draft folder. About a new target. And then GPS coordinates of your office."

Caleb's chair creaked when he sat back. "Why didn't you come to me? We could have gone to the police, and maybe these bad guys would have been caught."

Ivy's eyes pooled with tears. "I knew you wouldn't like me hacking, and I thought I'd uncover more information to give better leads to the police. I should have said something right away. I'd never do anything that might hurt you. I'm so sorry."

"Your uncle and I will talk about a security plan to keep him safe," Juliette said. "You hired me, remember? You don't need to be in charge of your uncle's security by tracking down leads."

Ivy pleaded with Juliette. "You can't leave his side. Are you staying here tonight? You can sleep in my room. I've got a trundle bed and everything." Ivy bounded off to her bedroom as if it was a done deal that Juliette would have a sleepover.

Caleb's face flushed and he wrung his hands together. His anger was almost tangible. "Rushmore has now messed with my family. If they find out that Ivy saw their program and most likely memorized it..."

Juliette moved next to him on the couch. Not too close though. She wanted to touch him, reach out and take his hand, but she knew he wasn't keen on people invading his personal space.

"I think you are both in danger. And I'm here for you. And before you say it, I don't think you need a bodyguard. You are more than capable of taking care of yourself, but you need sleep so you're sharp tomorrow. Let me take the couch. This way you both can rest well."

Absolutely, the man was more than capable of defending himself. But Caleb needed someone to watch his back. A fierce sense of loyalty welled up inside of her, something she hadn't experienced in quite some time.

She risked it and dared to put a hand on Caleb's arm, and he stilled. "Didn't you once tell me that sometimes you need to let someone else protect you? Let's take it day by day."

He nodded, and she realized her hand was still on his arm. A sizzle of excitement came from her touch. Maybe she should have thought this through a bit more before she'd agreed to spend the night, even if it was on his couch.

But then again, that's what made her Hazard Pay Montgomery. Always rushing in for the rescue, even without a solid plan.

And he was Caleb. The solid, dependable rock that she'd come to rely on once.

"You know I'm not going to just back down from this, Jules. These hackers think they're coming for me. I'll turn the tables on them. Hunt them down, expose their hiding spots in the most remote corners of the internet. They won't get away with this. They've kidnapped Theo, and Ivy's not safe if they uncover what she knows. I'm going on the offensive."

"I expect nothing less. Just remember, we're partners. You know any of the others from our basic training class would do the same thing for you. I just happened to have been close by when the call for duty rang out."

His tight facial expression relaxed a fraction. "Yeah, I guess you're right." Caleb checked his watch. "Maybe I can order us some Chinese food for delivery." Her favorite.

"I'd love that."

"I'll need to call Agent McGregor to let him know what Ivy has uncovered."

"Yes, good idea."

A text to Noelle confirmed her decision to stay, and Noelle responded with an offer to bring Juliette a change of clothes.

Caleb headed to the kitchen, probably to avoid more awkward small talk. Would things between them ever be comfortable again?

He turned back toward her. "Something doesn't sit right about this. Jules, what if one of my employees is a member of Rushmore? Because how else did they get their program on the laptop?"

WEDNESDAY, 6:30 A.M.

Juliette was at least right about one thing. Caleb had gotten a good night's sleep. But from the second he'd opened his eyes, his heart had been racing. She was sleeping on his couch.

He stretched and turned off his beeping phone alarm. Last night after Ivy had gone to bed, he and Juliette had made a plan. They'd called Agent McGregor, who'd come and retrieved the laptop. But not before Caleb had checked out the program.

Based on the email communication from the hackers, he assumed the hackers were targeting the office to search for the missing laptop and destroy any incriminating evidence. Agent McGregor had assigned agents to the office, and the security in the building would double down their efforts in screening anyone who entered.

Caleb planned to attend his staff meeting and then work remotely. But as a leader in the company, he also wanted to make his presence known to alleviate their fears. He refused to hide. Employees would still be grieving Theo's disappearance and probably be nervous about their own safety—his blood boiled every time he thought of Rushmore kidnapping his employee to get to him. He checked his phone, but he hadn't received any updates from Agent McGregor in finding Theo.

His suspicions from last night returned and made his stomach sour. Someone in his company was in league with the hackers. And Caleb would do everything in his power to flush out the mole in his organization.

Laughter filtered through the cracked bedroom door, and he threw on some clothes. He walked down the hall to see Ivy and Juliette sitting at the dining room table.

Juliette pointed to the bar that separated the dining room from the kitchen. "Made you some coffee."

He nodded his thanks and poured himself a cup. Ivy pounced. "Are you going to the office today? Oh, please, let's all play hooky. The three of us can spend the day together. Please, please, please?"

The three of us?

Ivy's voice got whinier with each please. Her intelligence made her seem all grown up, but she was still a little girl, loving silly things and believing that everything was right in the world. He prayed she didn't have to grow up so fast.

"Ivy, I just need to run in for this meeting. It will be half an hour, and then I'm out of there. I have to meet with the executive committee and then address the staff. It won't take long."

When Ivy realized she'd get nowhere with Caleb, she turned to Juliette. "Talk him out of going into the office today. Or at least don't let him out of your sight."

Juliette smiled. "Well, you are footing the bill for my services, so you're the boss. I will stick to him like numbers on a spreadsheet."

Ivy chuckled. Caleb sipped his coffee. He could get used to laid-back mornings like this. When was the last time Ivy had laughed like that? As if she didn't have a care in the world.

"Let's go, math genius," Caleb said. "Get ready and I'll take you to school. You can buy breakfast before first period."

He turned to Juliette after Ivy had scampered off to find her backpack. "You really don't have to follow me around all day. I'll just drop Ivy off, stop in at the office for an hour tops, and head back here. Security has been tightened around the building."

Juliette shrugged. "Like I told Ivy, she's my boss for today. You're stuck with me. Why can't you play hooky for one day?"

He sighed. "I'm not going to get rid of you, am I?" Not that he wanted to. The thought of spending the day with a beautiful, strong, and intelligent woman sent his pulse into overdrive. Especially this one.

She shook her head vigorously. "Nope. I have Agent McGregor's number, and he's keeping me updated. I've got no place to be." She flipped her phone so he could see the text chain.

The reality of their situation hit him like a sucker punch to the gut. "Theo was supposed to be in this meeting too. Which means that it's even more important that I go, offer my condolences and make sure I put their minds at ease that the business is running smoothly. Everyone will want to see the company leaders working hard despite the tragic situation."

"Then we'll make sure that happens."

Ivy emerged from her room with her overstuffed backpack. At the front door, the girl made one more plea for Caleb to stay away from the office, but he shook his head. "I'm just going in for a few minutes. Juliette will be with me. It will be fine." Ivy stomped out into the hallway in protest, and they headed to his car. Their first stop was to drop Ivy off at school. Hopefully she stayed there today. But if not, Juliette had asked Noelle to shadow Ivy. They were just waiting for clearance from the school.

After Caleb and Juliette watched Ivy walk into the school for visual confirmation that she wasn't going to ditch, Caleb pulled out of the school's parking lot and headed toward the office. Juliette remained unusually quiet. Unlike him, she was a talker.

"Are you mad that I'm going in? That I'm not taking Ivy's concerns seriously? Because I understand that the threat is real. But I have people who need me. I can't run and hide." Why was she giving him the silent treatment?

"I'm not mad. I just don't understand why you won't take a day off. Especially in light of Theo's situation. I'm sure people would understand. I mean, I was always the workaholic. It's just strange to see you obsessed with work and stressed to the max."

He ran a hand through his hair, mad that she could read him so well. "Co-owning a company and starting it from scratch with Blake was stressful, and I have a lot on my shoulders. Besides, I need to protect my clients that have placed their trust in my business. Just like you serve your clients."

Juliette glanced at him from her passenger's seat. "I get it. But we also didn't eat breakfast. And I didn't have enough coffee or sugar to keep my mind razor sharp. Can we please stop at the café near your office. Pleeease?"

Her pouty lips and Ivy-like antics worked. "Fine. I can't believe I have to contend with the two of you now. I have some time before the meeting, so let's get you your sugar fix."

She pumped her fist in the air. He parked on the ground floor of the garage across from his office building. The café was on the corner, with a great view of the street. When they arrived, the hostess seated them by the window. He could see his office on the top floor of an eight-story high-rise dotting the Savannah downtown business district.

Juliette ordered bacon and eggs plus a whole pot of coffee, and Caleb ordered the same. Then Juliette amended her order to include a chocolate-covered bear claw.

"Stop judging me," she said in a singsongy voice.

He shook his head. "I didn't say anything."

"You were thinking it—rather loudly, I might add."

"I wouldn't dream of judging you. You put as much sugar into your body as you want."

Why did this feel like a date? They'd started to make inroads to the comfortable companionship they used to have, and it was a breath of fresh air in his smog-filled life.

"Do you miss the Army?" Juliette asked as she attacked her bear claw.

He thought for a moment. "I was never die-hard Army like you, Jules. I was meant to be an analyst, and while I liked my time serving, I'm much more suited to owning my own company. I provide jobs for people, and I get to build my own software. It also lets me afford Ivy's expensive tuition, so it's worth it."

The waitress brought their breakfasts. "Can I say a blessing for the food?" Caleb asked.

Juliette hesitated but nodded. He said a quick blessing and dove into his eggs. "Your faith has sustained you all these years," Juliette said. "In a world that changes on a daily basis, I'm glad you remain constant."

"Actually, God is the only thing that remains constant amidst the chaos. The one I can rely on to never let me down. Even the most complicated mathematical equation would fail if not executed precisely. When the world seems bleak, I still see God in everything around me."

Ah, there it was. One of the main challenges in their friendship. Juliette only trusted herself to protect others. She failed to see how God had rescued her.

Juliette took a big bite of eggs. "You're really good with Ivy," she said. "It's nice to see you in a fatherly role. She's lucky to have you." Maybe he wouldn't say anything about her subject change.

He put down his fork and took a sip of coffee. "Well, she might not think that all the time. I try and challenge her to grow her computer skills, but she gets out of hand with her hacking. I want her to enjoy her childhood, but she's in such a hurry to grow up and do adult things. I just wish I could provide a normal childhood for her."

"But she's extraordinary. Just like you."

Heat climbed into his cheeks at the comment. "I do the best I can. I even found her a counselor through our church, and it seems to be helping. I think."

"Maybe I'll go with you sometime." She took a few more bites of the bear claw.

Had he heard her right? "To church?"

Two things raced through Caleb's mind. First, Juliette had changed her position about God.

And second, she wanted to see him again.

She met his gaze, and he forced himself to not look away. "Yes. Church, as much as I'm uncomfortable with it. You're the most logical person I know. With all of your intellect, if you believe in something, I can't write it off completely. Plus, things changed when I went through cancer treatment. Suddenly I was faced with a situation I couldn't control. It makes a person think, that's all. Sometimes on my sickest days, I just had to believe there was more to life than living and dying. There must be some kind of hope in the middle."

"God's there, Jules. In the midst of our darkest times. You just need to rely on him and not on your own strength and understanding."

The waitress interrupted them and dropped off the check. Juliette poured herself another cup of coffee, and Caleb paid the bill.

"I'm sure Ivy would love it if you joined us for church," Caleb said. And so would he. Which was why he needed to be careful, or he'd be in the same situation he'd been in three years ago. Wanting something he couldn't have. She'd left him. Just like everyone else he'd ever loved. His mom had abandoned him. His dad had died. His sister had been taken from him in that senseless accident.

He wasn't willing to risk his heart only to be disappointed again.

The two walked out of the restaurant. At the corner, they waited for the light to change.

"I'll only be an hour," he said. "I can set you up in a spare office if you have some work to do—"

A tremor moved the ground under his feet. Earthquake? A lamp post in front of them swayed. He blinked, and he was in Afghanistan, watching Juliette fall off a cliff.

He yanked Juliette to the ground behind the smoking Humvee, shielding her from the impending blast. But it wasn't a military vehicle, rather a mailbox. And the screams weren't his teammates trapped in a burning car but people pouring out of his office building.

He forced his mind into the present and watched black smoke and flames engulf the side of his office building.

———

WEDNESDAY, 9:20 A.M.

Ivy checked her phone. She'd ditched second period and headed to the soccer field. A PE class ran laps on the track, but under the bleachers made a perfect hiding spot.

What if CyberLane didn't show?

She paced in the confined area under the rows of concrete seats. Why was she so nervous? It's not like she was worried about cutting class. She and CyberLane had been chatting for a few weeks now. And while Ivy wanted to find out more about the hacker group, what she really wanted was a friend. And CyberLane had connected with Ivy in a way most people couldn't.

"I wasn't sure you'd be brave enough to skip Mrs. Hillard's class," a female voice said from behind her. Ivy turned and found a girl, probably around sixteen years old, with long, dark hair and a neatly pressed uniform that matched Ivy's own.

"CyberLane?"

"Call me Layna."

"Ok. I'm Ivy."

The girl gave Ivy a quirky smile. "I know who you are, Ivy. We've been chatting for a while, and I've been watching you. You've got some mad hacking skills. I hear you have a photographic memory as well."

Ivy shrugged. She had an eidetic memory but didn't want to correct her friend.

"Look," Layna said. "My brother wants to give you a chance to use your hacker skills for good. Can I trust you to keep our secret? Just until he gets the approval to hire us, and then you can tell everyone that you have a government job as a white hacker."

Wasn't that what she'd told Uncle Caleb she wanted? This seemed too good to be true, but why would Layna go out of her way to lie to her?

"Yeah. I won't say anything."

Her friend nodded. "My brother has a big job for us. One that will help the feds stop bad hackers. And he only recruits the best of the best. It's my first assignment. Are you sure you're up for the task?"

Ivy nodded. Layna handed her an iPhone. "I figured your uncle took your phone after that stunt you pulled hacking into the school system. Nicely done, by the way. You passed the first test." So, Layna had sent the boy with the twenty-dollar hack job to erase his grade.

Ivy relished the compliment. This girl was an upper classman, and quite possibly her first friend at this school.

"Keep this phone on you at all times," Layna said. "It's a burner phone so that we can get in touch with you. Don't let anyone find it. Things are about to go down in the next couple of days, and I have to be able to reach you."

Ivy took the phone and shoved it into her pocket.

"What's the project we'll be working on?" Ivy asked.

Layna squinted. "I'm not sure I want to tell you everything. How do I know you won't run and tell your uncle?"

"There's a lot he doesn't know about what I do."

"Like what?" Layna smiled, putting Ivy at ease. "If I can tell my brother something awesome you've done, he'll give you a job, and we'll get to hang out. It will be so much fun. I've always wanted a sister."

Ivy's mind conjured up images of herself and Layna hanging out after school, working online, and using their skills to help people. And she liked the scenes. If only the dreams were real.

But what could she tell Layna that might be impressive? Before she could decide, she blurted out, "I'm helping the police track down Rushmore. I know about their malware program."

Ivy's mouth went dry. Why had she said that? She didn't know this girl, and she'd gone too far by implying she was in on the investigation. And now Layna knew Ivy had seen the program.

But if it helped her find out more information about Rushmore, maybe it was okay.

"Well, that's a juicy secret," Layna said. "Don't worry. I'll keep it to myself and my brother. He'll definitely want to hire you now. Especially if you can help bring down that notorious hacker group. No one knows who they are."

The knot in Ivy's stomach untangled a bit. She was helping the good guys. Her uncle wouldn't stay mad at her if she found information on Rushmore. And then he'd let her work with Layna and her brother. Her mind spun with the possibilities. She'd be just like her uncle. Stopping cybercriminals and fighting for justice. Uncle Caleb couldn't deny her the opportunity if it gave them information on Rushmore. They'd take down the hacker group. He'd have to let her accept the job.

She rubbed her forehead to rein in her thoughts. One thing at a time.

Layna moved closer to Ivy and lowered her voice to a whisper. "No one can know about this. My brother's job is classified. Can I trust you?"

Friends. Ivy nodded. "You can trust me."

"Us hacker girls have to stick together. There aren't that

many of us out there. I need to know you have my back no matter what."

"Of course I do. We're friends." Ivy loved how the word *friends* rolled so easily off her tongue. Most of her other classmates teased her because she knew all the answers. But Layna was different.

"Here," Layna said, taking off one of her many clunky bracelets. "Have this. It's a friendship bracelet. It means we're officially sisters. I've got your back, and you have mine."

Ivy took the bracelet and slid it on. Layna turned like she was going to leave. Over her shoulder, she met Ivy's eyes. "Just keep the phone handy. I'm sure my brother will be calling with good news."

SEVEN

The ground rumbled. A heavy weight pinned Juliette to the concrete sidewalk.

"Caleb? Are you hurt?" She gave him a shove, and he sprang to his feet, ready for action.

He offered her a hand and pulled her to her feet. She wiped the gravel bits from her hands and cheek.

Another rumble elicited more screams. Flames shot from the side of the office.

She had to get the people out of the burning building, but Caleb was one step ahead of her, running toward the lobby entrance, directing people to the parking lot across the street to get them out of the debris fallout area.

"I need to go in," Juliette yelled over the cacophony of shouts and sirens. "People might be trapped."

Caleb had one arm supporting a coughing woman to keep her upright, and he halted Juliette with the other arm.

"The building might not be safe. You're not a firefighter. The sirens mean they're close. Wait for backup."

He ushered the woman to a bus stop bench. Her once white outfit now had black stains. Juliette could smell the smoke from her hair, but she didn't appear to be injured.

No way would Juliette stand by if people needed to get out of the building. "I'm not going to wait around for the fire to spread, trapping more people. I'm going in."

Caleb looped his arm around hers. "Wait. For. Backup."

Traumatized soot-covered people clustered a safe distance from the office. Black smoke clung to the air, billowing from the crater that was once the site of Caleb's office.

She wriggled out of his grip. "What happened to your Army training, Caleb? We need to get the people out."

He spun her around to face him, placing both hands on her shoulders. "You don't think I care? That's my office. My employees." His voice was barely a whisper with the words *my employees.* "But you're not a firefighter or a Ranger, you're a bodyguard."

His words hit their intended mark, snapping Juliette's head back to reality. Caleb was in danger. If he'd been in that office when it exploded...

"You're right. I can't leave you unprotected. Because you need someone to watch your back. This attack was personal. I'm calling Agent McGregor to get you and Ivy into protective custody."

Her heart stopped.

Ivy!

One look into Caleb's eyes and she knew he'd realized the same thing. If these terrorists had stalked Caleb to his office, they wouldn't hesitate to go after Ivy to use as leverage.

All of Caleb's facial features tightened at once. "Ivy. We need to pull her from school, make sure she's safe." He dropped his trembling hands to his side while he fumbled in his pocket for his phone.

"They may go after her, Jules. I can't take that risk. What if they find her at school? We have to do something."

"I'm on it." With her phone in hand, she fired off a text to Noelle. "Noelle is at the school. I asked her to tail Ivy, and last time I checked, she was waiting on the school's security officer to clear her to be on campus."

"We need to go. I have to make sure she's not in danger."

Caleb swiveled his head, and Juliette did the same. She checked for anything out of place. Could the perpetrators be in the crowd, watching their handiwork? She scouted rooftops of other buildings in the area for snipers. Because someone had declared all-out war against Caleb, and his protection was her top priority.

"Let's get out of the open." She led Caleb to the side of a building across the street, away from the paramedics. She caught sight of Agent McGregor and Decia Slaton making a beeline for them.

Before Agent McGregor uttered a word, Juliette pounced. "Can you get Caleb and Ivy into protective custody? They aren't safe."

"Slow down, Ms. Montgomery. I'll see about protective custody if there's a reason for it. But we all need to sit down and have a conversation about this. We still don't know what the hackers want or why they've escalated to this kind of violence."

Juliette huffed. "They've already kidnapped one of Caleb's employees." She waved her arm in the direction of the smoldering building. "That's Caleb's office. I'd say these are pretty good reasons we need to get Caleb off this street to somewhere safe. You even said that Caleb might be instrumental in your investigation. If the FBI knows this, so do the hackers."

They both gave their version of events to Agent McGregor and Decia.

"Excuse me, but I see Michelle from my office." Caleb raced across the road before Juliette could stop him.

She glared at Agent McGregor and gritted her teeth. "Help me protect him. Find us a safe house."

Juliette dashed after her client and found him with his arm around Michelle, whose tears ran streaks through the soot covering her face. "It was so awful," Michelle sobbed. "There was a big rumbling sound, and black smoke filled the whole floor. If anyone had been in your office..."

Caleb nodded to Juliette. "My office was empty. They'd moved the meeting to a conference room on the other side of the floor to use the bigger screens and to accommodate more of the staff. The casualties might be minimal if no one was in the direct blast area." Caleb morphed into a soldier right in front of her. His clinical descriptions harkened back to their Army days. All business. Assess the situation. Check for survivors.

"That's a relief." Juliette didn't see any wounds on Michelle, but she could have inhaled a significant amount of smoke. "Will you get checked out by a paramedic before you leave? Also, you'll need to give a statement to the police."

"I've got this," Decia said, joining them. "I'm Officer Slaton." Michelle nodded and began relaying her version of events to the officer.

Juliette stepped a few feet away and texted Noelle for a status on Ivy. She'd feel better once she knew Noelle had eyes on the girl.

"Caleb!" Juliette's head swiveled toward the man racing across the grass entryway for the office complex.

She stepped in front of Caleb until he said, "It's Blake," and she moved to the side.

Blake approached with another woman, and he tackled Caleb with a bear hug. "I'm so glad you're not hurt. I'd decided to move to the bigger meeting room to fit more people. I was setting up the large conference room when it happened."

Caleb's eyes watered, but he held it all together. He turned to the woman. "Juliette, this is Georgia Payne. Theo's wife."

The petite woman might have been twenty-five but could have passed for much younger. Juliette bet the past few days would add a few stress lines to her flawless porcelain skin. Dark circles rimmed her green eyes, which contrasted with shoulder-length jet-black hair, giving her a gothic vibe similar to Raven's style. This woman had been put through the wringer.

"I'm so sorry about Theo," Juliette said.

Georgia sniffed. "I just hope the police can find him before... they kill him. But he would have been caught in an explosion if he'd been here. Why are they doing this?"

Caleb put his arm around Georgia's shoulder. "We'll get him back."

Blake flanked Georgia on the other side. They were like two pit bulls protecting their owner. "Why are these hackers targeting Cyberskies?" Blake asked. "What do we have that they want?"

No one had answers.

Juliette sized up Blake. The man was probably in his early thirties, tall, athletic, and dressed like he had some serious money in the bank. At this point, everyone was a suspect. She couldn't move past the fact that the perpetrator had known Caleb's meeting schedule. She mentally moved Blake's name to the top of her suspect list.

A smudge of soot was streaked across Blake's forehead. "Someone needs to pay for this," he muttered.

Agent McGregor waved for Caleb to join him, and Juliette tempered herself from intervening. He didn't need her monopolizing every conversation and smothering him. As he had reminded her often over the last couple of days, he could take care of himself.

While he wasn't known for being an extrovert, Caleb still poured out concern for his employees.

Juliette's phone buzzed.

Noelle: It took me a while to clear my presence with school security. But Ivy didn't show up for second period. No one has seen her. School is now in lockdown.

She must not have hidden her reaction well, because Caleb was suddenly inches from her face and grabbed the phone.

"Ivy's missing? We've got to find her. Now."

———

WEDNESDAY, 10:05 A.M.

"This is like a scene from a horror movie." Caleb couldn't shake the images that buzzed through his mind like a high-speed train.

The smoking crater in the wall of his office building.

Ivy, tied up and bruised like Theo.

The masked man standing in his kitchen.

What if Rushmore had kidnapped Ivy? Was she hurt? Or would they kill her to get to him? He shook his head and took two deep breaths to settle the roller coaster of what-ifs building in his mind before they took him on a wild ride.

"We need to get out of here, Jules. Maybe she just ditched class again, but I need to be at the school searching for her. Now."

"I agree. I'll text Agent McGregor to let him know the situation, then head to the school."

They managed to finagle Caleb's car out of the parking garage, which had turned into a triage area for people needing minor medical treatment for burns or smoke inhalation. Juliette jumped in the driver's seat after inspecting the car for any tampering. "You'll speed."

He huffed but relented and tossed her the keys. "As long as

we're moving toward the school, I'm not going to argue at this point."

A police officer waved them through the parking garage gate, and they hit the road.

"I can't lose her, Jules." His voice cracked. "She's all I have."

Juliette glanced at him. "I know. She's so lucky to have you as a dad. We'll find her. Like you said, maybe she's playing hooky. The school has high security, so it's likely she's still on campus. We don't know the facts yet."

Facts were his life. Numbers dictated logic and reason. But this? His niece was missing, and it was all his fault. He might as well sign custody over to Ivy's grandparents.

"I never should have sent her to school today. I should have listened to her." His foot tapped out a steady rhythm on the floorboard of the passenger seat. Could Juliette drive any slower? Oh good, a red light. He was about to tell her to blow through it when his phone buzzed with an incoming text.

It's Ivy. My phone died. I'm using Noelle's phone. Are you ok? She said there was an explosion. Are you safe?

His heart restarted at the sight of Ivy's message. "Thank God. Ivy found Noelle and texted." His fingers trembled as he replied to her text.

I'm not hurt. But Noelle couldn't find you and I was worried.

Three little dots and what seemed like a thousand minutes later, Ivy responded.

I cut English class. I'm sorry.

He relaxed his clenched jaw muscles. Let future Caleb worry about Ivy ditching classes. Right now, all he cared about was her safety.

Juliette's phone vibrated, and she put it on speaker. "Noelle, what happened?"

"I've found Ivy. There's no evidence of danger here. She cut class to meet a friend by the soccer field. A school security officer found her walking from the field to third period like she didn't have a care in the world. I'm with the principal and the school resource officer now."

Juliette pressed mute. "What do you want to do? I can have Noelle meet us with Ivy at the apartment."

Caleb nodded and Juliette unmuted. "Noelle, can you please bring Ivy back to the apartment? I'll text Matt to see if he can send an officer to escort you."

"Sounds like a plan." Noelle hung up.

Juliette turned the car toward Caleb's apartment.

"I'm not going to be at ease until I see Ivy," Caleb said. "This was a false alarm, but what if these terrorists come after her, Jules?"

She pulled into a parking space next to his apartment building. "I think it's possible. They may see her as a link to you. Let's hope Agent McGregor can find us a safe house."

Us? Just like that they were a team again, falling in step next to each other as they headed toward his apartment. Once inside, Juliette rummaged through his kitchen to make them some sandwiches. Waves of nostalgia rolled over him, which only complicated his current situation, because no matter what, he couldn't fall for Juliette.

Not again. The last time that had happened, she'd walked out on him.

He sat at the dining room table and cleared a space for them to eat. She sank down next to him with two sandwiches and bottled waters.

He blessed the food—which she didn't object to—and stared at his plate. His stomach refused to settle until Ivy bounded through the front door.

"What do these guys want with you?" Juliette picked up her sandwich. "Why make it so personal?"

He shrugged. "I took a cursory look at their program. They seem to be intent on releasing an all-out cyberattack against the bank. Are they afraid that I'll stop them? I mean, I will stop them. But why take Theo? My heart aches for his wife and son."

She took a sip from her water bottle. "I keep checking to see if the police have any leads on Theo's whereabouts, but so far, nothing. I think we need to revise our action plan. We need to get you and Ivy out of town for a while."

Caleb nodded. "I hate to run. But if it keeps Ivy safe and in my sights, I'll do it. As long as I can have a computer to keep working, I'll be fine."

Juliette scrunched her face, her tell that Caleb knew all too well. "What's wrong? You obviously have bad news. Spill it."

"I've been texting with Agent McGregor. He's working on getting you into a safe house. But he mentioned it being an internet-free zone. He thinks the best thing for you and Ivy is to get off the grid."

"It might make it easier to keep Ivy in line, but I'm not sure either of us will survive." He offered a sad smile.

"The place won't be ready until tomorrow, so you have time. For now, I think you and Ivy should stay at my place tonight. The police will patrol the area, and I'm sure I can coax some of my coworkers into sharing the night watch. We can't stay here in case someone is watching your place."

Caleb wanted to hit something. So many people now had to put their lives on the line for his and Ivy's protection. "I don't want to put anyone in harm's way. I can stay up and take a shift. It would be just like our Army days. Besides, people are being attacked because of me. Look what happened to Theo. Apparently, I'm standing in the way of these maniacs getting what they want. And they've proved that they'll use people to get to me."

He heard the doorknob rattle and bolted for the door. Ivy flung the door open and fell into his arms, her tears wetting his T-shirt. The smell of her strawberry shampoo tickled his nose.

He squeezed her tight, and she buried her head deeper into his chest.

"Oh dear, is everything all right?" The voice grated on Caleb's already frazzled nerves. Nosy Abby from next door.

Another voice echoed in the doorway. Noelle introduced herself. "Abby, let's talk about what you saw the other night of the burglary." The woman he'd yet to meet was a lifesaver by distracting Abby. His neighbor meant well, but Caleb couldn't handle the intrusion.

"But are y'all going to stay here tonight? I mean the break-in and now this—"

Noelle cut her off. "We're not sure what security measures we will be taking, but we'll make sure to keep Caleb and Ivy safe. Let's get you back to your apartment. Maybe you have information that can help the police catch these guys." Noelle put her arm around the older woman and ushered her down the hall.

Juliette shut the door. Ivy refused to let go and twisted her hands into Caleb's T-shirt. "I'm so glad you weren't in the office today."

Caleb finally let Ivy go, but the girl was glued to his side.

He made Ivy a peanut butter sandwich, and they sat in the living room. Noelle slipped back into the apartment after having tea with Abby and doing a perimeter sweep of the building.

His curiosity got the best of him when it came to finding out how much Ivy knew about the hackers' program. He'd always been able to communicate with her on an adult level. If only she'd had the opportunity to just be a regular kid.

"Tell me about this program, Ivy."

Juliette and Noelle parked themselves at the dining room table, within earshot of the conversation. Juliette caught his eye, and he nodded, appreciating the backup when it came to Ivy.

His niece took a big bite of the sandwich and talked with her mouth full, but he didn't care. "It's a nasty program, Uncle

Caleb. Definitely ransomware. They're just waiting for someone to connect to the internet so the hackers can have complete control of the bank's system. Then I assume they'd send a ransom in exchange for access to the server again."

He took a sip of water. "Could you recreate it from memory, Ivy?"

"Oh, of course I can. I spent time studying the program. I figured you'd take it away from me once you knew that I'd taken the laptop."

At least she was being honest. But it confirmed his worst fear. "What did you find out about the program when you studied it?"

"That it won't work."

His heart stopped. "What?"

She shrugged. "Just what I said. They left out a piece of code. The program won't launch. They made a mistake."

Every muscle in his body tightened. His concern had been that the bad guys would realize that Ivy had memorized their program and would target her to keep her silent. But in his wildest imagination, he'd never thought that Ivy would be able to fix a flaw in the code.

He prayed the hackers never realized what Ivy had seen when she'd stolen the laptop. "Ivy, have you told anyone what you saw on the laptop?"

Her face blanched. "Just one person. My friend at school. Layna."

Oh no. His throat constricted as if all the oxygen in the room had been sucked out. "What did you tell Layna?" And who was Layna?

Ivy fixed her eyes on the carpet. "I wanted to wait until I had more information. But Layna's brother works for the government. He's going to get me a job as a white hacker. Then I can ask him for information on Rushmore."

Oh, Ivy.

Her naivety would be her downfall. Why'd he let her skip all those grades? She was a guppy swimming in shark-infested waters, and he hadn't even offered her a life vest.

Some kind of parent he'd turned out to be. This had Rushmore's handiwork written all over it.

He clenched his hands into fists. His pulse hammered a steady thump in his ears. Rushmore had messed with his family.

This had to end. Now.

"Ivy, why don't you head into the bedroom and pack a bag for tonight? With everything going on, we'll probably check into a hotel for a little while."

She nodded and raced off to her room, apparently not the least bit concerned that she might be in trouble. Caleb headed into his bedroom and opened his safe. He pulled out a stack of cash and counted out five hundred dollars.

He marched into the dining room, where Juliette was talking with Noelle at the table. He dropped the bills in front of her with a thud. "I'm officially hiring Elite Guardians to protect Ivy. Here's a downpayment. If it comes down to her or me, you both take care of Ivy. She's the number one priority."

Juliette stared at the money, then at him. "I'm all-in."

Noelle extended her hand. "It's nice to officially meet you, Caleb. But what Juliette means is, *we're* all in. Alana and I are available to help with security. Is there anything else we need to be aware of?"

Caleb sank into the chair next to Juliette. "Ivy's grandparents, my brother-in-law's family, are suing me for custody of Ivy. If they find out that she's in danger, they could take her from me."

EIGHT

One look at Caleb's red face and fierce eyes and Juliette wanted to hunt down all of Caleb's enemies, including Ivy's grandparents. How couldn't they see what a great father he was to Ivy?

"How can they do this to you?"

Caleb shrugged, the crinkles around his eyes more pronounced from fatigue. "My attorney doesn't think they have a case. Tessa had a will that named me Ivy's guardian. But I don't need terrorists kidnapping her to give them ammunition to take her from me."

Juliette put her hand over Caleb's. He didn't flinch. And she knew his rules about people invading his personal space. Touchy-feely was never an adjective used to describe Caleb.

But he let her hold his hand. Until Noelle cleared her throat. Juliette had almost forgotten she was there. "We need to talk about the danger. Now that the hackers have contacted Ivy, what does this mean?"

Caleb withdrew his hand, and Juliette missed his touch. He

sat back and sighed. "She not only memorized their program but realized that the code isn't right. She can fix their ransomware."

"So," Noelle said, "she can recreate the program, and she can fix it so it works."

"Not to mention that she is now an eyewitness to their crimes," Juliette said. "Ivy knows their entire plan."

Things had gone from dangerous to downright deadly. Juliette's mind whirred with contingency plans for both Caleb's and Ivy's safety. She turned to Noelle. "If the hackers realize their error and know that a twelve-year-old girl could fix the program, Ivy becomes an asset. Caleb is a target to take out of their way, but they might find taking Ivy is more valuable to their operation. They both need protection."

Noelle stood and nodded to Caleb. "Save your cash. You might need it, and considering your history with Juliette, we'll figure out the cost later." Noelle might as well have winked and nudged Juliette with the word *history*.

"Thank you," Caleb said. "Right now, I need to text Agent McGregor. We have a new lead, and I need to let him know the hackers tried to recruit Ivy. Maybe they can check out this supposed Layna. She probably isn't even a student at the school." He tucked the cash into the pocket of his jeans and withdrew a cell phone from the other pocket.

"I think we need to move now," Juliette said. "It's simply not safe to stay here any longer. We can crash at my house overnight and head to the safe house tomorrow morning. At least we'll have the Elite Guardians taking turns watching the place."

"I already told Ivy to pack a bag. We can stay at a hotel, but maybe your place is more secure."

At the mention of her name, Ivy bounded into the room with several heavy bags in tow.

"What? I'm not leaving without my books."

"Don't worry, Ivy," Juliette said. "We'll make room for your books at our slumber party. We'll stay up, watch movies, and eat junk food."

Ivy squinted her eyes, as if pondering Juliette's offer. "Can I pick the movie?"

"If you're like your uncle, I'll be stuck watching *Star Wars*." She made a face, and Ivy laughed.

"Don't be ridiculous. This is a *Star Trek* household. I mean, the original *Star Wars* trilogy is okay, but the new ones…"

Juliette tuned out Ivy's highly opinionated movie review and took in Caleb's rigid shoulders and the hard-as-steel determination in his eyes. These hackers had awoken the warrior in him, and he was gearing up for a fight. She'd seen Caleb go toe to toe with a man twice his size in a basic training exercise. Caleb had a fierce side to him that rarely saw the light of day.

Until someone messed with his family.

He caught her glancing at him as Ivy prattled on about Jar Jar Binks, whoever or whatever that was. Heat fanned across her. She turned her attention back to Ivy and nodded as if this was the most interesting conversation on the planet.

It was not.

A knock at the door sent Juliette's pulse thumping, and Caleb checked it out. He let Agent McGregor into the apartment, followed by Noelle, back from her security sweep.

Caleb tilted his head toward the bedroom at Ivy and she understood. She complied, though her frown followed by an exaggerated sigh suggested that she wanted to be part of the adult conversation. He ushered the agent into the living room.

"Can you make sure Ivy is entertained while we talk?" Juliette asked Noelle.

"On it." Noelle ducked into the bedroom and closed the door behind her.

Agent McGregor took a seat in the chair and cleared his throat. "The safe house won't be ready until tomorrow."

"They'll stay with me tonight, with round-the-clock protection." Juliette sat down next to Caleb on the couch.

McGregor nodded and let out a long breath. He steepled his hands in front of his lips. "I know you won't want to hear this, Caleb, but in light of the new evidence, we'd like for you to consider allowing Ivy to meet with the hacker group."

"No," came Caleb's swift reply.

The man leaned forward in the chair. "We researched the name Layna in the school records. Just like you suspected, there's no student by that name. We think Rushmore tried to contact her, but we'd like to turn the tables on them. This may be the only way for us to take them down. They must have left Ivy a way to contact them."

Caleb glared at Agent McGregor. "I will not let Ivy be used as bait for hackers. We still don't even know where Theo is. She's twelve. And once they find out that she can recreate their program, they'll target her for sure."

"We understand your concern. For now, we're waiting for Rushmore to make contact about Theo."

Juliette interjected. "But what are they going to do once they realize the laptop is in FBI custody?"

No one responded. She knew the answer, and based on Caleb's clenched jaw, so did he.

Theo's life was on the line. So was Ivy's.

Agent McGregor took out his phone. "Consider allowing her to draw the hackers out into the open. Because they already know what she can do."

He handed the phone to Caleb. "This is another conversation we uncovered between the hackers. Our agent was able to decode it based on Ivy's notes. She's on their radar."

Caleb's hand trembled as he took the phone. Juliette pressed in close to him to see the screen. The message jumped off the screen, and her vision blurred at the email chat between the hackers.

General: The girl knows too much. We need to take her out.

Liberator: No. She can help us. You said you could recruit her.

Rough Rider: Agreed. She's an asset. We use her to send a message to her uncle. He needs to pay just like those corporate pigs. He helps them hide our hard-earned money.

"How can we let her face off against these men? She's just a girl." Juliette stood, hands on hips, glaring at the FBI agent.

Caleb sucked in a breath and rubbed his hand across his face, his five-o'clock shadow coming on strong. "I can't let her do this. These are more than just hackers. They're kidnappers and highly skilled thieves. She needs to be protected, not paraded around town so she can be a target."

A pulsing headache threatened to destroy Juliette's ability to keep her cool. She needed to get her new clients settled without the stress of Mr. FBI Agent hanging around. "It's been a rough few days. Caleb and Ivy are going to be protected tonight. We can regroup at the safe house tomorrow. But for now, let's let Caleb rest and think things over."

Agent McGregor shook his head. "We need to interview Ivy regarding all she knows about the laptop, the program, and the hacker group. At least ask if they've told her how they'll be in touch."

So much for resting. Caleb slumped back onto the couch. "You can interview Ivy, but no mention of her meeting with these hackers. Let me decide this, not her."

The agent nodded in agreement, and Juliette retrieved Ivy. The girl plopped down on the couch next to Caleb.

"Did Layna give you a way to contact her?" Caleb asked.

Ivy's eyes widened. "Layna gave me a phone. I'll get it." She dashed into her bedroom and emerged with an iPhone.

"I wasn't supposed to tell anyone about this."

Juliette's heart broke at Ivy's naivety. She sat down next to Ivy, sandwiching her between herself and Caleb. "Ivy, Agent

McGregor informed us that Layna isn't a student at your school. We think she might be part of Rushmore. She's not to be trusted."

"Maybe I can talk to her, then. Convince her to help us. I'm sure—"

"Ivy." Caleb's voice held a mix of censure and compassion. "You need to stay away from Layna. She's not your friend. She's trying to hurt you."

Tears brimmed Ivy's eyes, but she nodded.

For the next two hours, Ivy answered all of the FBI agent's questions about her discoveries on the laptop. By the end, Juliette was drained of every ounce of energy she possessed. She could only imagine how Caleb and Ivy felt.

The crowd of people in the apartment finally lessened as agents packed up the cell phone and laptops and left. Agent McGregor made his departure, and Noelle headed back to the Elite Guardians' office to make preparations for security for the night.

Ivy headed to her bedroom to finish packing, and Juliette moved closer to Caleb on the couch. "It will be okay. Noelle and I will make sure you're both protected."

His eyes darkened. "We'll all make sure someone is with her twenty-four seven. I'm just concerned that someone might figure out that Ivy can remember everything. These bad guys kidnapped Theo, which isn't playing by hacker rules. They're out for blood. My blood. And Ivy's."

She didn't need to be reminded of how dire the circumstances were. "I'm calling in all the reinforcements I know. We'll all do our best to make sure you are both safe."

Something flashed across Caleb's face—a mask Juliette hadn't seen since their basic training days: a look of fierce protection. No one messed with Ivy and got away with it.

"Promise me," he said, his voice barely a whisper. "Ivy is your client. Take care of her."

Juliette grasped Caleb's hand, and again he didn't shrink back. "Caleb, you're one of my best friends, and I've got your back no matter what. I'd lay down my life to protect Ivy. And you. You know I don't back down from a fight, and I protect my people. I'm not going to let anything happen to either of you while I'm on duty."

His grip tightened around hers. "What happened to us, Jules? I miss us. We used to be close, and then you left."

"I know." Her fingers tingled from his touch. "I'm so sorry, Caleb. I made a rash decision, and it was the wrong one. But maybe we can start over? Pick up where we left off?"

Would things ever be the same between them? Because unless Juliette could rein in her emotions, she wanted far more than a friendship with this man.

But did he feel the same gravitational pull, drawing them closer than a friendship?

———

THURSDAY, 12:45 A.M.

A thump shattered the silence, and Caleb jumped off Juliette's couch, his gun in his hand, ready to face off with the source of the sound.

"It's just me," came a whisper from down the hall. Juliette turned on a lamp. "Sorry if I woke you. I thought I'd get some water and bumped into the end table. I didn't want to turn on a light in case you were sleeping."

He sank back on Juliette's couch and stashed the gun in the drawer of the end table. Of course he'd been awake. His mind refused to quit.

"I was up. Just replaying everything on an endless loop."

Juliette handed Caleb a glass of water and sat next to him, curling her feet up under herself.

"I love what you've done with this place, Jules. It suits you."
The soft light filtered through the living room complete with
historical elements that Juliette used as accent pieces. His
favorites were the Civil War–era banker's desk and the antique
typewriter that graced it.

Juliette snuggled into the plush sofa cushions. "I know. It's a
bit eclectic. I wanted to keep the historic charm of the house,
but I needed some lighter colors and a modern flair. I kept a lot
of my grandmother's antique lamps and fixtures and made them
into art pieces. Some of these things have been in my family for
generations. I just couldn't part with them. Even though I grew
up in Atlanta, we visited Savannah every summer, and this place
feels like home."

Caleb sighed. "Do you think I'm overreacting to having Ivy
involved in this investigation?"

"No, I think you're playing it safe. And when it comes to Ivy,
her security is all that matters."

"I can't let anything happen to her." He looked at Juliette.
Seeing her brought back a slew of memories he wasn't prepared
to deal with. But one thought screamed for his attention: he
should have been there for Juliette, holding her hand during
chemo. Why hadn't she trusted him with this burden?

He needed an answer. "Hey, Jules? I'm so sorry you had to go
through cancer treatment alone and I wasn't there for you.
But…why did you shut me out?"

She shook her head. "There wasn't anything you could do.
You needed time to grieve the loss of Laz. Plus, you had your
own drama to deal with. I couldn't let you take on my issues. It
didn't seem fair."

"When you left, I didn't fight for you. I should have done
more to find you."

"I didn't want to be found," she whispered.

He swallowed. Was this just something he'd have to try to
let go of? "I know you'll make a good bodyguard for Ivy. Hazard

Pay Montgomery will show up just when I need her to. Unlike me, who plays it safe every single time." Ivy would be safe with Juliette, but at what cost? He prayed nothing would happen to either of them.

"I'll watch out for her," Juliette said. "And you too."

He swallowed a lump forming in his throat. "Back at you. We're in this fight together."

Sure, they were battling threats from these hackers-turned-terrorists. But the bigger battle, the one his soul raged against every day, still lingered. He still couldn't risk his heart. Because it hurt him to the core to think about the what-ifs. "We always did make a formidable team."

She smiled. "Well, I shoved you out of your comfort zone from time to time."

"We taught each other a lot during some dark days," he said.

"Right. I've missed you being my nerd translator."

"I've missed that too. I never even started your Marvel education."

Her laughter cut him off. "Some things never change. Ivy definitely takes after you." Her words mixed with a giggle and sent his pulse skyrocketing. He fought every impulse to grab her hand, which defied logic. He never let people invade his space. But Juliette? He leaned in closer, erasing the space between them as if the move was as natural as breathing. Her eyes connected with his, making him want to dive into the depths of their past and discuss the things that had remained unsaid for years. The hurt and loss. The pain that connected them.

Whether it was fatigue or Juliette's magnetic presence scrambling his brain, he struggled to form coherent sentences.

"I'm sure losing your sister was hard on both you and Ivy. I can't imagine. Especially after losing Laz." Whoa. Apparently Juliette wasn't having the same brain scramble.

"Hard? Try apocalyptic devastation. Finding out Tessa had died in a car crash just brought me right back to that day on the mountainside, watching Laz die and being helpless to rescue him. I got to the Humvee too late. I've lost everyone—my parents, Laz, Tessa..." He didn't finish the list. "The grief piles up to where it's easier to shut down than risk my heart. I can't lose Ivy."

And I can't lose you again.

The unbidden thought short-circuited his brain. Where had that come from?

"What happened with your mom?" Juliette leaned closer—close enough that he caught a whiff of her coconut shampoo. "You don't talk about it. Ever."

He sighed. He didn't want to share, but the way she put her hand on his arm coaxed the story out of him. "My mom walked out of my life. I was six, and she just said goodbye like she was heading to the office. And never came back. Tessa and I grew up taking care of each other. Because after that, my dad found companionship in the form of whiskey. Alcohol took him from us early."

Her hand covered his, sending an electric current racing through his body. "I can't imagine being so young and having my family destroyed like that," she said.

"According to my dad, she'd never wanted to be a mother."

"Well, I'm not leaving you or Ivy." He blinked in surprise, and she added, "While I'm on duty as bodyguard, anyway."

The words squeezed his heart. Wasn't there any way he could get her to stick around once the bad guys were behind bars and life got back to normal again?

Normal. That's all he wanted for Ivy. He wanted her to have a childhood free from the adult stresses like he'd faced. But look how much grief she'd already encountered in her twelve years. "Ivy's lost so much. I'm so angry that these hackers are trying to destroy the last ounce of innocence she has in this world."

His eyelids grew heavy, and Juliette stood. "It's late. We both need some sleep." She said goodnight and headed to her room.

It didn't take Caleb more than a few minutes to pass out.

A thump sounded in the dark, and Caleb was up off the couch with a gun in hand before his eyes fully opened. A motor roared in the distance. He shook off the vivid nightmare of Ivy being chased by a man in black.

He checked his watch. Five a.m.

"What was that?" Juliette whispered, her gun in hand.

"Ivy?" he mouthed.

Juliette moved close and kept her voice low. "I just checked. She's asleep."

They crept across the living room to the front door, each ancient floorboard creating a symphony of squeaks and groans.

Juliette peered out the window next to the door. "I heard some kind of crash. Alana is on duty, and I texted her to check it out." They checked other windows and didn't see anything suspicious.

"Well, I'm up now." Caleb stretched, reassured by the knowledge that someone was checking on the source of the noise. But his gun wasn't going to leave his side just yet.

Juliette headed to the kitchen and filled the empty coffee pot with water. "I guess we're both up for the day," she said. "We should probably sit and talk about a strategy before Ivy wakes up."

Caleb sat and propped his elbows on the kitchen table, resting his head in his hands. "I hate to have Ivy out of my sight, but I want to see my office. Find out how bad the explosion was. They should be able to let me in if it's structurally sound. Maybe Noelle or Alana can take Ivy to the safe house, and we can stop at the office. I get the feeling that at least one of the hackers could be someone that works for me. If so, I'd like to find some evidence before they destroy it completely."

"Once it's business hours, I can ask if the building has been cleared and if we can have access. I'm sure Matt can get us special permission."

A knock sounded. Caleb jumped to his feet, and Juliette rushed to the door to check out the peephole. "It's Alana. And she's with someone." She swung the door open, and in strode a black-haired woman with incredibly intense eyes. Between those and her all-black outfit, she was definitely a believable bodyguard—fierce. A man appeared in the doorframe, leaning on Alana for support. He looked rough, like he'd gone down in round one with Mike Tyson. His face sported multicolor bruises with a nice-sized gash across his forehead.

Caleb took a step backward the second recognition hit him. "Theo?"

The man stumbled into Juliette's apartment. "Caleb?" The man's eyes widened, and his voice rasped like a man who'd been stranded in the desert for ten days.

"It's me. Here, have a seat. We'll get you some water and call an ambulance. But what happened?"

Juliette handed Theo a bottle of water, which he drained in a few big gulps. She introduced Caleb to Alana Flores.

"Alana, where'd you find him?" Juliette whispered.

"Crumpled up by the mailboxes on the side of the road in front of the house," Alana said. "I've already alerted the FBI. I was out back when I heard a car, but by the time I rushed to the street, it was gone. I heard a groan and spotted this guy. I cut the zip ties on his hands and feet and brought him in."

"How are they tracking us?" Juliette voiced Caleb's concern.

A knot tightened in his gut. He needed answers now, because these hackers were keeping one step ahead of them. "Theo, what do these hackers want?"

Theo put the bottle on the table, wincing from the movement. He looked Caleb in the eyes.

"They want you, Caleb. They're coming for you."

NINE

What kind of strange plot twist was this?

The bad guys had dumped their captive off in the road in front of her house. What was their motivation for letting Theo go? To deliver a message to Caleb?

And how were the hackers tracking their every movement? The FBI had the laptop and phone. Juliette was over-the-top diligent in sweeping for bugs and trackers.

Caleb looked from Theo to Juliette and back to the bruised and battered man.

"What do they want with me?" Caleb asked at the exact moment Juliette said, "Do you remember anything about your kidnappers?" Their words tumbled over each other.

Theo held a shaky hand to his forehead. "In answer to your question"—he pointed at Juliette—"I don't know what happened. They kept me drugged for the most part. I'm not even sure where I was."

Another knock at the door, and Juliette let Agent McGregor and Matt Williams into her house, followed by the paramedics.

Juliette sat at the table across from Theo, resisting the urge to pepper the battered man with questions. But Caleb didn't possess the same self-control. "Did they say what they wanted? Why did they take you?"

Theo shifted in the chair and winced as one of the paramedics dabbed something on the cut on his forehead. "Something about wanting a laptop they think you have. It didn't make any sense to me."

And it didn't make sense as to why they'd let Theo go without the laptop. Unless they'd realized the laptop was in police custody. At least they'd let him live.

"Can you identify any of the perpetrators?" Agent McGregor asked, hovering in the corner with his notebook and pen handy.

Theo squinted for a minute as if conjuring up images from his horrible ordeal. "There were two men. Both big and muscular. I'm not sure of a physical description beyond that because they wore all black and kept ski masks on. I didn't see their faces. And with the drugs in my system, my memory is foggy."

Alana brought Theo another bottle of water, and he took it with a thank you. "My wife?" he asked after a sip. "She must be worried sick."

Caleb pulled up his phone and dialed Theo's home number. "Georgia? I have someone who's desperate to talk with you." He passed the phone to Theo, whose eyes lit up for the first time.

"Sweetie? I'm so glad to hear your voice." Tears dripped down the man's face and soaked his blood-stained T-shirt. They all moved a few steps away to give the man some privacy to reconnect with his wife.

"We're taking Theo to the hospital to get checked out," one of the paramedics said.

Theo stood and handed Caleb the phone. "Georgia is going to meet me at the hospital. What do these guys want with the laptop? And why kidnap me for it?"

"It's a long story with what has transpired in the last twenty-four hours. I'll let Agent McGregor fill you in."

"But will you be safe? They're after you. Do you have a place to stay that's off the grid?" Theo started to sway, but one of the paramedics grabbed his arm to steady him.

"We'll be fine," Caleb said. "Juliette and I are going to check out the office damage on our way to a place where we can lie low for a while. But you need to take some time to rest and heal. Don't worry about us. Take care of yourself."

The paramedics ushered Theo out the door. Agent McGregor followed, lobbing questions at the man along the way.

Juliette glanced at Matt, hoping he would keep her informed as much as he could with the investigation. He gave her a curt nod, silently communicating he'd be in touch. Theo had been returned to them basically on her doorstep. And the man didn't seem like he'd observed much in his time of captivity. They hadn't learned much of anything from him. If anything, the drop-off was disconcerting.

"You two need to lie low for a while—somewhere else," Matt said. "I don't like this one bit. These perpetrators know your precise location. You've got to find somewhere off their radar."

"Something—or someone—is tipping off the bad guys," Alana said, looking between Caleb and Juliette. "Do you two have a safe place in mind?"

"Jules and I will be just fine," Caleb responded matter-of-factly. "We're moving to a safe house today."

All eyes shifted to Juliette, and the room fell silent. Alana's eyes went wider than the Grand Canyon. Matt shifted from one foot to the other.

"What?" Caleb asked.

"Um, you just called Juliette"—Alana lowered her voice in a mock whisper and put one hand next to her mouth—"*Jules.*"

"She threatened to kill a man who called her that once. I witnessed the whole thing." Matt shook his head. "She doesn't let anyone call her that. Any man who values his life knows this."

Caleb shrugged, a hint of crimson coloring his cheeks. "I forgot about that. After all these years, you still don't let people call you by a nickname?"

Alana rolled her eyes. Juliette would have some explaining to do for her coworkers' benefit. Because, for some reason, *Jules* just sounded perfect coming from Caleb's lips.

"I'm just going to keep an eye on things outside," Alana said with a quirky smile as she left, Matt trailing right behind her. She'd be teasing Juliette about this later.

Caleb and Juliette were alone again.

"Now for a cup of coffee," Juliette said. She poured them both a mug.

"At least Ivy can sleep through anything," Caleb said, accepting the coffee. "But it's seven thirty, so she should be waking shortly, and we still don't have a plan for the day."

She set the mugs down on the table and sat next to Caleb. Her mind still reeled from his vulnerability last night when he'd shared about his mother. She hadn't known the depth of the pain he'd carried for so long.

I can't lose her. His words about Ivy had pierced her heart. He'd lost everyone else. And Juliette had left him too. The same way his mother had—walked out the door without so much as a goodbye.

How could she have been so careless?

And then he'd lost Tessa. If they didn't get one step ahead of these hackers, Ivy might be next.

She sipped her coffee. "We need to head to the safe house. Get Ivy settled in."

He nodded. "She's not going to like missing school. Her team is in the semifinals for a robot-building competition this weekend. She's worked so hard, but I can't send her. I'm so glad there are three bodyguards now. It's nice to have you, Alana, and Noelle. You three make a pretty formidable team. Especially Alana. I wouldn't want to run into her in some dark alley. She's lethal."

Juliette chuckled. "Alana is the sweetest once you get past her protective armor. They've both been great partners and friends. I trust them with my life. See, we all need someone to watch our backs now and then." She and her colleagues had their differences, but Juliette had learned to appreciate the value of different perspectives on a situation. Her respect for her colleagues ran deep.

His hands circled around the mug of still-steaming coffee. "While I want to get to the safe house as soon as possible, I want to see my office. Find out what's left of it. Maybe there's another clue." He tilted his head. "At least one of the hackers works for Cyberskies. It's the only thing that makes sense. How else did they get that program into the bank's laptop with my security program?" He paused, running a hand through his hair. "It might even be two people—they were leaving each other messages on the hard drive."

"The police have closed the office building. We'd have to see if the fire marshal would even let us in. Plus, I'm sure the FBI has gone through every inch of the place hunting for clues to help their investigation."

"I know. But for some reason, I need to see it for myself. Maybe they missed something."

Juliette moved to the kitchen to clean up the breakfast dishes. "Who would do something like this? Do you have any suspects in mind?"

Caleb blew out a loud breath. "Blake and I employ seventy-five people. A lot of the positions are remote, but there's maybe twenty of us in the corporate office. And before you say it, I can't imagine Blake being behind this. I've known him since college. I trusted him enough to go into business with him."

Since their days in basic training, Caleb had always been an excellent judge of character. His eidetic memory caused him to notice details most people overlooked.

Juliette stood. "What if I make breakfast for us? Then maybe we can send Ivy to the safe house with Noelle or Alana. I'll drive you to the office, and we can check it out before heading out of town, as long as we can get access for us to go in."

He gave a slow nod, his gaze locked on hers. "I like the idea of Ivy getting to the safe house as soon as possible. We'll stop off at the office on our way."

Together.

Just like that, they were a team again, moving as a single unit. He'd saved her life that day on the mountainside.

And she'd lay down her life if it meant protecting Caleb and Ivy.

———

THURSDAY, 10:00 A.M.

God, please keep Ivy safe.

Caleb rode in Juliette's Prius, the steady hum of the engine the only sound as she drove to his office. Noelle had taken Ivy directly to the safe house.

"Not easy letting Ivy out of my sight." Caleb shifted in his seat to face Jules. "But thanks for taking me by the office. I feel like, if these hackers were bold enough to work for me, they may have left more evidence behind. The fire may have been a way to cover their tracks."

"Ivy has the best bodyguards on her protection detail. Let Noelle and Alana stand watch while we figure things out with your office."

His phone buzzed with a text from his neighbor, Abby, asking about the robotics competition this weekend and whether Ivy needed a ride. He responded with the truth.

At this point, I'm not sure. I'll let you know later.

Abby meant well, but sometimes he felt like he had a mother always looking over his shoulder. On the one hand, she'd watched Ivy and had even tutored her after school. He should be grateful to live next door to a former college professor. But when Abby sent a follow up text asking if they'd be home, he ignored it.

"This needs to end," he said as Juliette found a space in the garage across from the office building. "Ivy needs to be in school. She'll be devastated if she misses her competition. She's worked so hard, and her team qualified for the championship round."

"I think as long as you're with her in the safe house, she'll understand about missing out on the competition. She wants you to be as safe as you want her to be."

She might be right about that.

They walked across the street. Juliette had called the fire marshal and received permission to enter the building to retrieve files and whatever else was salvageable.

The office complex was deserted since the fire department had closed the entire building, despite the fire being contained in just Caleb's office. When Juliette opened the door to the lobby, they ran into Blake heading out.

"What are you doing here?" Blake asked, juggling the box in his arms. Papers, computers, and files stuck out the top.

Curious. Why was Blake taking office documents and equipment?

"I'm checking on the damage and wanted to see if there was any evidence left that might point us to the hackers."

Blake nodded. "I'm gathering personnel files per the police's request and heading to the station to give yet another statement. After that, I'm leaving, taking my wife and kids, and going to my in-laws' out of state. We may have to shut our doors, Caleb."

"It's not over yet, Blake. The FBI is involved. They won't get away with—"

"They threatened my family." Blake set the box on the tile floor. "Rushmore sent me pictures of my kids playing on the playground. They gave me an ultimatum to step down as the CEO, or they'll go after my family." He showed Caleb the email on his phone with the photos. "I might just do it. No job is worth the lives of my wife and children."

"Did you send this to Agent McGregor?" Juliette asked.

Blake gave a humorless laugh. "He has all the information. But I'm not waiting around for Rushmore to strike again. They've blown up our office, kidnapped our employee, and robbed our client. I'm no coward, but I will protect my family."

Caleb related all too well. "Ivy and I are going off grid. Someplace with no internet or phones. We've got to figure out how these hackers are one step ahead of us. But I'm not ready to surrender yet."

"Well, stay safe, and we'll keep in touch. Maybe we can salvage what's left of the company once these criminals are behind bars."

Blake picked up the box and left the building.

"Let's hope he's not taking evidence with him," Juliette whispered after Blake was out of earshot.

"You think Blake is working with Rushmore and made up that story about his family?"

"At this point, I'm suspecting everyone. I can ask Matt. He'll tell us if Blake is making a statement today." She texted while they walked through the lobby.

They headed for the stairs, but a security guard stopped them. Even with permission from the police for them to be there, the security guard insisted that Juliette not bring in her service weapon. She huffed and muttered under her breath the whole way back to the car to lock up her gun.

They reentered the building and were waved through. The

elevators weren't working since the building didn't have electricity, so they hiked up six flights of stairs.

Once they hit his floor, the stairwell opened into a generic office building hallway, complete with stark white walls and flat gray carpet. The acrid smell of smoke grew stronger with each step they took toward his office suite. Remnants of water-damaged furniture and office equipment had been pulled into his reception area.

"This place is a mess," Juliette muttered. Once they passed the reception area, the open floor plan showed the true damage.

He stifled a gasp and pointed. "That's my office. Or what's left of it." His charred door had fallen off the hinges from the blast, and water from the sprinklers had streaked soot across the once white walls. Wind whistled from a hole leading outside.

"If I'd been here…"

She put a hand on his arm. "Don't. You weren't here. We need to keep moving forward."

Caleb stood in the middle of the open floor plan and stared at the ruined remains of his dream. The visual reminder that he was the intended target. The smell of burnt wood hung in the air, and every inch of cubical space was covered with a fine layer of ash.

A generator hummed, providing power to a few portable lamps the recovery crew must have installed. Leave it to Juliette to come prepared with a flashlight.

"We're not going to find much in your office," Juliette said. "If the fire didn't destroy everything, the water damage from the firefighters would take care of the rest."

Caleb walked around the cubicles, shaking his head. "These hackers went to a lot of trouble to get to me. But I still suspect it's someone that works here. God, just leave me one decent clue as to who is behind all of"—he waved his hands around his devastated office space—"this."

Juliette walked around while Caleb sank into a chair at one

of the less-damaged cubicles and stared at a half-melted monitor. Usually the whole office was lit up with screens and chatter. Today, everything was still. Until voices made him jump. He stood and noted Juliette grasping for her missing sidearm, but it was just two building engineers surveying the structural damage.

They'd eventually reopen the building, and the fire would be a distant memory. Companies would get back to work and move on as if nothing had happened.

But could Caleb move on? He and Ivy might wind up in hiding indefinitely. Blake may have to run the company without him—assuming the hackers didn't run the company into the ground with their relentless attacks or force Blake to resign. Everything he'd worked for had come crashing down around him in the span of three days.

Caleb stood. "Let me just check the server room. It should be up and running with a generator so that our offsite employees can keep working. For now."

Juliette placed a hand on his shoulder. "We're not going to let these hackers win. They can't destroy your company. It's just not right."

It might not be right, but if the bad guys figured out how to release the ransomware, he'd have a line of clients out the door, calling it quits.

They headed to an office tucked into the corner of an interior wall behind the reception area. Caleb used his keys to unlock the door to the server room. The tight rectangular closet had shelves lining three of the four walls. Fans buzzed, keeping the machines from overheating. A box of laptops sat on one of the shelves. "Agent McGregor's team didn't take these."

He moved to the interior of the room to inspect the laptops, Juliette right behind him.

A click sliced through the air. Juliette froze.

Caleb tried the door.

Locked.

"Someone locked the door," he whispered. "It locks from the outside, not the inside."

A sizzle ripped through the air and plunged the closet into inky blackness. All of the equipment came to an abrupt halt.

"We're not alone," Juliette said. She pulled out her phone to call for help but couldn't get a signal. She turned on the flashlight and positioned it to illuminate the computer rack.

"Our office tends to not get a signal, especially in the center of the building."

Juliette sucked in a breath. "Well, security knows we're here, and we just saw two maintenance workers." Her voice faltered. "Maybe someone will be by soon."

"Just be honest with me. I know we're in trouble." He sniffed, a strange odor tickling his nose. "What is that? Smells like a campfire." Nausea made him clutch his stomach. The scent was familiar—

Kerosene!

"No. No. No. No. No." Juliette pounded on the door. "Help. We're in here."

She shone the flashlight on the door, where smoke filtered under the crack.

"They're getting rid of any evidence. Jules, we've got to get out of here."

If they didn't do something, the computer room would double as their coffin.

TEN

Juliette pounded on the door, mentally thumping herself for walking them right into a trap.

"How do they even know we're here?" Caleb muttered. "It's not like we're broadcasting our every movement."

Unless Blake had told someone he'd seen them there. Juliette couldn't help suspecting Caleb's partner, even if Caleb refused to consider it. "We just need to get out of here. And we faced tighter situations during basic training, right? This shouldn't be too difficult. I mean, it's not a no-win situation." She yelled to be heard over the clang of the fire alarm.

He nodded. "There's always a way out. That's what we've got to believe."

They surveyed the room to see what they had to work with. The metal storage racks lined each wall floor to ceiling, housing servers and spare computer parts.

She pulled on one of the shelves. "I think this can hold our weight." She climbed the first few rows, thankful the whole unit had been bolted to the wall. She hit the fifth shelf and stopped at the ceiling. The ceiling tile gave way with a push, and she stuck her head through the crawl space above. "We should be able to shimmy through the air duct toward the other side of the locked door. Hopefully they just lit a small fire and didn't set the entire place ablaze."

Juliette hoisted herself through the hole in the ceiling. Smoke had reached the three-foot-tall ductwork, but not enough to cause breathing or visibility issues. For now.

Caleb climbed up behind her but hung back with just his head sticking through the vent. He shone the flashlight for her, illuminating the shiny silver metal duct. She crept along, praying the airway would hold her weight. After a few feet of inching through the narrow passageway, she found an air vent that led into the hallway below, on the other side of the door to the server room that doubled as their prison.

She looked back and saw Caleb's head sticking up into the ceiling. "The fire isn't coming through the door, just a lot of smoke."

Juliette pried off the air grate with a pocket knife the security officer hadn't confiscated. She stuck her head out of the ceiling a few inches and saw the source of the fire. A trash can full of paper and cardboard had been set ablaze right outside the door to the server room.

She was about to let Caleb know to follow her when a man walked directly under the air vent. At least he didn't spot her in the ceiling. She inched her head back into the crawl space. The guy wore all black, including a ski mask, and was talking on his cell phone. He probably had fifty pounds on her. She turned the best she could in the tight space and held up a finger to indicate they had company. Caleb nodded and stayed put.

The work lights lit the area below, enough for her to see. She tried to hear the conversation, but it sounded muffled. Escape options were limited—either they take on this guy or stay trapped in a not-so-fireproof room.

The man turned around and stopped directly under her position. A crazy, Hazard Pay Montgomery–style plan formed, but it was risky, knowing there were two men to contend with— the big lug below and whoever was on the other end of that call. But she had to get herself and Caleb out of that locked death trap.

The hole was maybe a foot wide and eight inches deep. Just enough space for her to drop down and startle the creep. She held her breath and waited for the perfect moment.

"I'll meet you out front," the man said to the person on the phone. "They aren't going anywhere. I made sure of that."

Juliette crawled over the hole, rolled, and pointed her feet through the opening. Bracing her hands on either side of the vent, she lined herself up with the man and let go. She dropped onto his back and wrapped her arms over his throat in a choke hold. He couldn't yell for help with the pressure on his windpipe. The guy flailed and smashed her against the wall. She sucked in a breath but doubled down her grip. He wasn't getting away.

The building's sprinkler system kicked on with a hiss. Water saturated them, and her slick arms slipped from around his neck.

The big guy had no issues with his grip, and meaty hands wrapped around Juliette's throat. He shoved her up against the wall until her feet dangled. She kicked and clawed at the man's face, but he pressed down on her neck with a mighty force. Her vision blurred and she gasped for air.

A crack sounded and the pressure on her throat relented. Another thud and the man hit the floor. Her vision returned and landed on Caleb, standing over the man, holding a laptop like a hatchet.

Her throat was raw, but she managed to croak out, "Run. Second man."

"We need to see if this guy has any weapons."

Caleb bent to check the man, but Juliette grabbed his hand. "No time." The sprinklers had doused the trash can fire, but the smoke was sucking the oxygen from the air. Juliette's eyes burned as they raced to the reception area. How had these guys made it past security? She shuddered at the idea that these men may have taken down the security guard at the front of the building.

They were on their own.

Juliette skidded to a halt and put her hand on Caleb's chest as he was about to open the front door. "There's a second guy," Juliette said. "The guy you took down said he was going to meet someone 'out front.' I'm assuming he meant the front of the building, like maybe with a getaway car, but just be careful. We don't want to be ambushed."

Caleb nodded and opened the door a crack. "The hallway is clear other than smoke. Let's proceed to the stairs and keep an eye out for our adversary."

He pushed the door open wide, and they entered the hallway, both swiveling their heads from right to left. Juliette glanced over her shoulder as they moved forward. Her brain wouldn't let go of the premonition that they were walking into a trap.

"He could be hiding in the stairwell," Juliette whispered.

"And I don't trust that the guy we knocked out will stay down for long." They approached the metal door to the stairwell. Caleb pushed the bar to the door, inching it open so as to not announce their presence.

"Clear," he said. Juliette followed behind him, her hand on his back, peering through the gaps in the stair railing to check for any signs of movement.

She put her foot on the first step, but the sound of pounding footsteps from below sent ice through her veins. She froze.

"Don't take another step."

Now she regretted her decision not to stop and frisk the other guy for weapons. Because the second man rounded the corner of the stairwell with a gun in his hand. The guy must have heard them coming.

The masked man stood halfway up the stairs and leveled the weapon at Juliette's head.

"Move and she dies."

———

THURSDAY, 11:00 A.M.

Caleb's pulse jackhammered in his ear at the sight of a gun trained on Juliette by some punk in a ski mask.

He wasn't going down like this, and he'd fight this guy hand to hand if it meant protecting Jules. His thoughts flashed back to their basic training days. Hazard Pay had always managed to get out of tough spots. Maybe if he thought like her...

Her eyes widened, reading his mind as if they shared a brain. He gave her an imperceptible nod. Without allowing himself a chance to second-guess this plan, he pivoted, put his feet on the edge of the top step, and launched himself at the man. Solid muscle broke his fall, and they tumbled down the remainder of the stairs. Caleb landed on the man's chest and ducked a punch. He pinned the man's arms down. This guy wasn't going anywhere.

"Run, Jules. Call for help."

Of course, she wouldn't. She retrieved the guy's gun and turned it on him—at his temple. "Now you don't move."

The man sagged in defeat. Caleb rolled off him to check his pockets for other weapons. He passed Jules some zip ties, and she secured the man's hands to the handrail.

The door above them clanged. Smoke filled the stairwell, and the other gunman emerged.

"Time to go," Juliette said. She whipped the man's ski mask

off, and Caleb got a good look before Juliette grabbed his hand and pulled him to his feet.

He'd never seen that man before. They raced down the stairs. "How many men robbed the bank?"

"Four," Juliette said over her shoulder as she took the stairs two at a time. He'd hoped to identify someone from his office as the culprit, but these two weren't the only criminals.

Crack! Plaster rained down on them. "I guess the big guy is awake," Caleb said. A bullet hole marked the wall right above their heads.

The second they tumbled into the first-floor landing, Juliette had her cell phone out checking for a signal. He heard her calling 911 as they moved through the lobby. Caleb wasn't taking any other chances of another ambush, but he needed to put as much distance as possible between them and the stairwell shooter. He kept his eyes peeled for trouble.

Speaking of trouble, how had these two clowns gotten past security? "Where's the security guard?"

Juliette shrugged and swept the confiscated gun around the lobby as they walked. "We need to get out of the building," she said. "The police are on their way, but those intruders will probably pursue us."

Caleb reached the guard desk and peeked behind. "The guard's been knocked out." He hurdled the desk and helped the uniformed man up off the floor.

The man wobbled a bit but was able to stand on his own and waved them off. "I'm okay. I'm okay." But blood trickled from a wound on his forehead.

"I'll stand guard," Juliette said. "I didn't hear footsteps behind us, so maybe the gunman decided his best option would be to flee."

"He might sneak down the stairs and exit from the back of the lobby."

Juliette nodded. "I'll keep an eye out for him."

Caleb found someone's sweater stashed in the desk and pressed it to the wound on the man's forehead. Sirens outside competed against the blaring fire alarms inside. Within seconds, paramedics, firefighters, and police rushed into the lobby. The cavalry had arrived.

Juliette snaked arms with Caleb. "Time to go. We're too exposed in this open lobby. Agent McGregor texted and will be pulling up in a moment." A paramedic took over to assist the security guard, and Caleb headed out the lobby door with Juliette. Four firefighters in full gear with a thick hose passed them. If the bad guys were smart, they'd be long gone. If the good guys caught a break, the stairwell shooter would leave his friend tied to the railing for the police to find.

The instant their feet hit the sidewalk in front of the office, two black SUVs raced up in front of them.

The passenger side window of one vehicle rolled down, and Agent McGregor stuck out his head. "Get in."

The back door swung open. They slid in next to the agent as several police, fire, and armed FBI agents swarmed the area.

"How did you find us so fast?" Caleb asked.

Agent McGregor turned his head toward the back seat. "I heard the call come in about a second fire in the building and knew you two had decided to tempt fate and return to the scene of the crime. Do either of you need medical attention before we hightail it out of here? We need to get you to a secure location. We'll sit down and take your statements for the police when we know you are safe."

Juliette rubbed her throat. She might be sore, but there didn't seem to be any damage to her vocal cords. "I don't think either of us is injured, and the smoke wasn't that bad because we were able to get out of the area where the fire started," Juliette said.

Caleb nodded, but Juliette had fatigue written all over her face. When had the dark circles appeared? And bruises were forming around her throat from where the guy had tried to choke her. Neither of them had slept much in the last few nights, not to mention his tumble down the stairs, so he assumed he looked equally as rough.

McGregor pulled onto the street, and soon they were heading to the outskirts of Savannah on the back roads. They passed Bonaventure Cemetery, the legendary cemetery he and Ivy had yet to visit. Live oaks dripping with Spanish moss lined the roadway. The serene beauty of Savannah contrasted with their tragic circumstances.

Would he and Ivy find peace? He prayed these terrorists would be caught so they could regain their lives.

Juliette had texted Noelle and confirmed that Ivy had already arrived.

Agent McGregor handed Juliette some bags. "I'm going to need your phones and any electronics. Anything that can be traced. Because we're going old-school at this safe house. No electronics of any kind."

No electronics?

How was Caleb supposed to flush out these hackers and save his business—not to mention the bank—without a computer? But it made sense. If he wasn't online, the hackers couldn't track his movements.

He shook his head and deposited his phone into the bag. "What's Ivy going to do when she finds out there isn't any Wi-Fi at the house?"

Juliette shot him a weary smile. "We'll make Noelle tell her. The least we can do is make it fun for her. Maybe we can finally eat junk food and binge-watch *Star Wars*."

"Which is your favorite *Star Wars* character?"

She stared at him. "I want to say Spock..." He couldn't contain his laughter. Despite his many attempts to get her hooked on his favorite, *Star Trek*, she still hadn't a clue.

"At least you have the fighting skills to make it as a bodyguard. Because you're not cut out for nerd life. I mean, if you can't tell the difference between a Vulcan and a Wookie, I can't help you."

"Fine. I'll give it another try. Maybe Ivy can explain it to me in terms I can understand."

"Probably not." He snickered. She responded by sticking out her tongue.

They drove the remainder of the trip in silence, Juliette staring out the window, no doubt evaluating plans for the security detail at the safe house. Caleb relished the moment of peace in the back seat of the sedan. No one was chasing them, and Ivy was protected. His head pounded a steady beat from the stress of the past few days. He closed his eyes.

The vehicle stopped, jarring him awake. They'd arrived at a house in a residential area.

"Uncle Caleb," Ivy called as she ran out the front door, Alana at her heels. "I'm so glad you are okay." He enveloped her in his arms and led her inside, not trusting either of them would be safe outside.

Ivy gave him a tour of the house like she owned it. Maybe he needed to get her out of the city, at least for a vacation. But this house would make a fabulous getaway place.

"The decor is modern farmhouse." Ivy droned on as if she'd memorized the script of one of those home makeover shows. "And did you see outside? The neighbors at the end of the property have horses." Caleb crossed the living room and peered to the patio, which opened up into green pastureland spotted with some trees. In the distance, two horses hung out by the fence line, munching on some tall grass.

Maybe this *would* be a vacation, since they'd have to entertain themselves with no electronics. If only he could convince Agent McGregor to be the one to tell Ivy. But she'd probably already figured it out.

He finally just bit the bullet. "You understand that there can't be any Wi-Fi here. No connections of any kind."

Ivy rolled her eyes. "I know." But her face indicated her complete displeasure and ruined life.

"I mean it, Ivy. You can't get online, or you'll run the risk of tipping off the bad guys to our location. This house is safe. We have to abide by the rules."

Her bottom lip jutted out. "But if anyone can track down these hackers, it's us. I know you can find them. You're the best hacker alive."

"We just need to let the FBI do their job. They're the professionals."

"You don't ever take any risks, Uncle Caleb. Your skills are way better than these other guys. Why are we hiding in this house when we should be working with the FBI to stop these bad guys?"

The simple answer—he'd never risk Ivy's life for anything. "You know why. It's not safe."

Ivy rolled her eyes and pulled a device out of her bag. "Can I at least have my Kindle? Without Wi-Fi, I won't be able to do much, but at least I'll have my books."

He caught the attention of Agent McGregor, who had turned the formal dining room into a makeshift command center with papers, half-drunk cups of coffee, and blueprints spread across the wooden farmhouse table. The agent shrugged his consent. How much trouble could Ivy get into with a Kindle and no connectivity?

"Yes, you can keep your Kindle," Caleb said.

Ivy hugged the Kindle and raced toward the guest bedroom she'd already claimed as her own. His niece just didn't get it. Men with guns had hunted him and Juliette. This wasn't one of those games he used to play with her where he'd send Morse Code messages through the flashlight app on her cellphone. The stakes were too high.

He walked into the formal dining room and saw Agent McGregor and Juliette, deep in discussion about security plans. The agent motioned for Caleb to join them. Noelle headed off to check on Ivy.

"As I was telling Juliette, we'll have two agents stationed here around the clock. They'll work the perimeter, and the Elite Guardians will take shifts to help with inside security."

Caleb nodded. "What are you doing to find these hackers and put a stop to them before they destroy my company and take down a bank?"

The man leaned back in the wooden chair and steepled his hands in front of his face. "I still think our best shot is Ivy. I think having her meet with the hackers may be our only way to stop them. She can make connections with them in ways we can't. She could reach out to them and convince them that she wants to join their ranks—"

Caleb huffed, silencing the man. "I can do the same thing. Use me, not her."

Agent McGregor sighed. "They already know you're not interested. And they've already established that they're willing to prey on her naivety. They don't know that Ivy told us about the meeting with CyberLane. We have the cell phone. I think Ivy should try to make contact. Set up a meeting."

No. Just…no.

"I want to do it." He hadn't even vocalized his answer.

He turned around and saw Ivy standing in the doorway to the dining room. "Ivy, it's not safe." He pulled out the chair next to her so she could sit with them at the table. The adult table. Why couldn't she just be a kid? This wasn't her burden to bear.

"I don't want to sit around and do nothing. We can get these guys and all be safe, or we can hide out here. I know I can help."

Caleb stood. "Conversation over. I'm not letting you risk your life, Ivy. These men are dangerous."

"But your life is on the line too." Ivy's eyes pooled with

tears, and his heart melted into a puddle. "They blew up your office, thinking you'd be in it. I've lost my mom and dad. I'm not going to let anything happen to you, too."

———

THURSDAY, 3:15 P.M.

Ivy sat on the bed in the guest room of the safe house, feeling anything but safe. These hackers needed to be stopped. They'd gone after her uncle again.

The FBI agent, even Juliette, seemed to understand that Ivy could help. Agent McGregor knew that Rushmore would make contact. And they had.

If her uncle wouldn't let her help, she'd do it on her own.

Tears flowed down her face. Why wouldn't he see that they needed to do something?

Willing herself to calm down, she rummaged through her backpack until her fingers touched the wooden beads. Why had she kept the friendship bracelet that Layna had given her when she knew Layna had lied to her?

Part of her wished for a friend. The logical part of her brain told her that Layna was part of Rushmore. The girl had only been interested in Ivy's skills, not a friendship. But had everything the girl said been a lie?

What if there was some part of Layna that hadn't wanted to betray Ivy? If she could get a signal, she'd send a message. Let Layna explain. Maybe she wasn't all bad and would turn on the other members of Rushmore. They would work together and set up the meeting with Rushmore like the FBI guy wanted.

But this prison of a house had no Wi-Fi, and they'd gone to great lengths to jam all cell phone signals. Not to mention an FBI agent had confiscated all of her electronics.

Except one.

She grabbed her Kindle from the nightstand. It had a built-in web browser, and all she needed was access to her free email account. Uncle Caleb would be furious, but he wasn't doing anything. Why did he always have to avoid taking a risk?

Now was her time to shine. Because if Ivy could discover more about Rushmore, she would have tangible evidence to hand over to the FBI. Uncle Caleb would be safe. They'd go back to their apartment and pretend none of this had happened.

Ivy tossed the Kindle onto the bed. If she did this, she'd have to disable the security alarm and sneak out the back door when the FBI wasn't patrolling. Maybe she could reset the alarm to the factory setting and give it a new code. She'd watched a YouTube video once on how to do it.

On the way into the neighborhood, she'd spotted a playground next to a park a few houses down. She could walk all the way there or even just head near the neighbor's house and use their Wi-Fi. Not everyone on the block was locked up like a prisoner.

But was it worth the risk? She could bargain with the hackers. She had information that would complete their program, and she could exchange this for Uncle Caleb's life. If whoever was behind Rushmore got what he wanted, there'd be no reason to attack Uncle Caleb.

Ivy decided on a nap, especially since she'd be up all night with her escape attempt. Her uncle's life depended on her staying focused and sharp and she wouldn't let him down.

Juliette might be able to protect him, but it was up to Ivy to get information for the police to take these guys down.

ELEVEN

If looks could kill, Ivy would have obliterated the entire room.

Juliette appreciated the girl's fire and tenacity to protect her uncle, because she related. But that drive to help might put Ivy in even more danger. When she'd stormed out of the dining room, she'd scattered sparks of fury in her wake.

Not that Juliette needed the internet to entertain herself, but she needed something to keep herself busy. Being trapped in this house with Caleb brought back a slew of memories she'd rather not deal with right now.

The kitchen was way more stocked than the one at her house. Last night she'd made an embarrassing offer to Caleb and Ivy of canned soup and some saltines. But here…

Someone had gone shopping for them, and there were plenty of ingredients to make tacos. The spacious kitchen had modern appliances, so she made herself at home. She knew next to nothing about kids, but who would turn down tacos?

She was pulling items out to start prepping the food when a voice behind her said, "You'd let her do it, wouldn't you?"

She turned.

Caleb had slid into a seat at the kitchen island. "You'd let her jump in there and try to make contact with these hackers."

Juliette turned to face him, the island separating them. She grabbed a cutting board and started dicing tomatoes. "I wouldn't rule it out so fast. And if you're there right next to her, you'll be able to see everything she does. Right now, I'm afraid she'll do something on her own."

He blew out an exasperated breath. "I just couldn't live with myself if I let anything happen to her."

"I know. But I understand where she's coming from. You're concerned with protecting her, but she's worried about your safety. And she wants to act, do something, to make sure nothing happens to you. She's the risk taker you never were."

She concentrated on cutting more veggies for the tacos to avoid Caleb's gaze. Even though Caleb was back in her life, however temporarily, it wasn't the same. Too much time and awkwardness had built up between them. She saw brief hints of the laid-back friendship they'd once had. While they'd made some strides in the past few days, they had miles to hike before their camaraderie kicked in.

"How do you do it, Jules? You always follow your gut instinct and face any obstacle in your way head-on. How do you let go of the fear that drives most people to make sane—albeit safe—decisions?"

"Are you calling me insane?" She shot him a smile, and she noted the tinge of pink surfacing on his cheeks.

"Sometimes you are. And it generally pays off. But what if it doesn't?"

She chopped harder. The tomatoes would be salsa by the time she was done, but she didn't want to face her past, let alone share it with Caleb.

But she remembered one of those nights in basic training where they'd both drawn the short straw and had guard duty.

They'd talked all night while on patrol. Caleb's insights had always been what'd attracted her to him. He had a way of seeing things she couldn't.

She put down the knife and placed both hands on the counter. "I'd rather die being the hero than live life on the sidelines. If there's a chance I can save a life or protect someone, I'll take it."

"But now? Have things changed since you're not on active duty? You're not in a war zone anymore."

His prying annoyed her, and she had a knife. He'd better watch it. Oh, he was still waiting for an answer. She sighed. "After dealing with breast cancer, I realized that circumstances can spiral out of control in one deep breath. I watched everything I'd worked for go up in smoke—nothing I could do about it. I had to focus all my energy on getting better. Fighting for my own life."

He reached over the island and covered her knife-free hand with his, a gesture she knew meant a lot.

"I know it was a tough ride for you, Jules."

"The toughest part was knowing that I couldn't be a Ranger any longer. I—I felt like such a failure."

Had the word *failure* actually come out of her mouth? But that's what she was. She'd failed Laz and Tank. And her disappearing act had cut Caleb to the core. She pulled her hand away and walked to the fridge. Maybe if she cut some onions, Caleb wouldn't see her choked with emotions. She would blame her watery eyes on the onions.

She dumped the onions onto the cutting board and watched Caleb as he processed her pitiful announcement that at the end of the day, she, the fighter and warrior, had failed.

The rhythmic tapping of the knife on the cutting board matched the pace of her beating heart. Caleb watched her.

"Why?" was his one-word response.

"Why did I fail?" She shrugged. "Because of me, Laz and

Tank had died, and I was sent home to lick my wounds and take care of myself."

"Don't, Jules. You can't shoulder the burden of what happened to Tank and Laz."

"It was my impulsive decision to get out of the car. Maybe we could have gotten them out if we'd worked together. If I hadn't fallen..."

"You're not responsible for their deaths, Jules," he whispered across the island. "And you don't have to be a Ranger to protect people. You're doing just fine as a bodyguard."

She stared at him. "But Joe was a Ranger." Her brother. Her hero. All she wanted to do was protect her family.

Because it was the last thing Joe had asked of her before he'd died on a mission.

Caleb moved to the refrigerator and grabbed the beef and a sauté pan from the cabinet. As he walked past her, she caught a whiff of his familiar aftershave. The smell brought her right back to her basic training days. From day one, all she'd wanted to do was follow in her brother's footsteps. Be a warrior who would make him proud.

Caleb placed the pan on the stove and turned to her. "Is Joe the *why* behind Hazard Pay Montgomery?"

She'd never told anyone why she took risks like she did. Lived like she had a death wish.

"Yes." Her voice snagged and she swallowed. "Right before he died, he'd been stateside and we had a Fourth of July picnic. I was a lot younger—twelve when he died—but for all those years, I idolized my brother. He was always the life of the party, and the whole family was so proud of his service."

She tried to move away from Caleb—to walk away from this conversation—but he covered her hand again. They stood over the chopped food, which resembled the pieces of her life, diced into a thousand fragments after the death of her brother.

"Tell me." His voice was soft, reminding her that he didn't have a judgmental bone in his body.

She left her hand under his. "Joe told me the most noble thing a person could do was protect their family and care for those that can't defend themselves. He made me promise that I'd do that—rescue those I love. Fight for justice. When we lost Joe, there was this big hole in our family, and I've worked hard every day to fill that void."

"Do you think you've let down your family by not being a Ranger?"

She sighed. "In a way, yes. I mean, my parents weren't too keen on me jumping out of airplanes behind enemy lines. But I know they thought of Joe every time they saw what I'd accomplished."

"And beating cancer wasn't an accomplishment?"

Why did Caleb always get to the heart of the matter? "I never really thought of it that way. I was more focused on cancer killing my career."

"But you have a new career. One with good friends like Alana and Noelle. And you're here, at the right time, to protect Ivy. But my issue has always been, who's got your back, Jules?"

"I take care of myself."

"But doesn't that get tiring, always having to be the one who keeps everything from falling apart? What are you going to do when exhaustion hits and you're faced with a situation where your usual tactic of fighting your way out of it won't work?"

She removed her hand from under his and picked up the knife to massacre a green pepper. "I guess here's the part where you tell me to trust in God, not myself."

"Without faith, the situations we can't change will destroy us. Without hope that God's in control, we wear ourselves out fighting battles we're never going to win. Battles we weren't meant to fight in the first place. Sometimes we just need to stand still and let God fight for us."

While she wanted to believe these words, her heart wasn't fully on board. She grabbed a red pepper and kept chopping. She couldn't look at Caleb, so she kept her eyes fixed on the cutting board.

His words resonated in a place deep inside her. A place she'd kept locked and sealed.

The reason she took risks and fought as hard as she did was because she couldn't live with herself if she let others down.

Just like she'd failed Laz and Tank.

It's what Joe had fought and died for—protecting others.

"I fight so others don't have to. Joe died a hero and I refuse to disgrace his legacy. I won't sit on the sidelines and do nothing."

"That's an awfully big burden to carry, Jules. Because we all know that some things are out of our control, no matter what we do."

But was stepping aside and trusting in an unseen God the answer?

THURSDAY, 5:00 P.M.

The freight train had hit him hard, and even with all the warning lights and whistles, Caleb hadn't seen it coming.

Juliette had walked away from him once, and logic dictated that he'd lose her again if he let his guard down. He refused to allow his heart to want something more.

But now the *something more* was standing in front of him, hacking vegetables like she was cutting her way through a jungle with a machete. The rhythmic chop-chop-chop of Juliette's knife never slowed. He headed to the stove to brown the meat while his head swam at her confession. He'd known about Joe and how hard she'd mourned his loss, but he hadn't realized how deep the connection ran.

"Have you decided what you're going to do about Ivy yet?" she asked, jarring his thoughts back to the situation at hand.

He couldn't muster a response, mainly because he just didn't know.

"Look," Juliette said, spinning to face him with the knife in her hand. "You just told me that God is in control. If you believe this, then shouldn't that coverage extend to Ivy?"

His own words slapped him in the face. He used a spatula to stir the meat—anything to avoid eye contact with the knife-wielding Juliette. "God doesn't promise that we'll never deal with loss. And while I trust him, I don't think my heart can take it again. I've lost everyone I've ever loved."

Well, maybe not *everyone*. If he were honest with himself, he'd loved Juliette. But after she left, he'd refused to let that admission see the light of day.

"You just asked me what I would do if a risk I took didn't pay off." Juliette set the knife onto the counter with a clink. "But what would happen to you if a risk *did* pay off? You could be missing out on so much by…sitting on the sidelines—to use my own analogy."

She kept working on the dinner prep, adding the chopped vegetables to a bowl, saying nothing. She flung a fistful of onions into the container. "All I'm saying is that sometimes the rewards are worth the risk."

She blew out a breath of frustration and turned her attention to laying taco shells on a tray. She was the only woman he'd ever let get this close to him, physically or emotionally. Expressing his feelings didn't come easily, because most women didn't want sentimental things dictated to them in the form of an algorithm.

Three years ago, she'd left him. Broken his heart. Could he take a risk now that she was back in his life?

"I—ah—" Sizzling caught his attention. "The meat is burning."

"Way to dodge the tough stuff, Styles."

He busied himself with cooking the meat but wasn't able to shake Juliette's words. His whole life, he'd calculated everything. It gave order to the chaos, and he never took risks where the odds weren't in his favor. But if he trusted God instead of his own logic, he might not be devastated in the end. In fact, he'd possibly gain more than he could even imagine. But without letting go, he'd never find out.

Maybe it was time for him to loosen his grip on Ivy's safety and Juliette's desertion. Rely on a God that was bigger than his circumstances.

Was loving Juliette worth the risk?

Maybe he should start by telling her how he really felt.

Sucking in a deep breath, he spun around to face her, but instead he knocked into her with a tray full of hard taco shells in her hands. The tray flipped through the air, raining corn shells all around the kitchen. She lost her balance, and Caleb grabbed her around the waist to steady her.

"I've got you," he whispered. She threw her arms around his neck, and he wound up dipping her like they were dance partners.

Breathe, Caleb.

He was millimeters from her face. The logical part of his brain was screaming for him to put her down, run away. Flee. But his pounding heartbeat drowned out his thoughts, and he leaned into their embrace. Before logic kicked in, his lips covered hers. Her eyes widened, and then she closed her eyes and sank into the kiss with total abandon, tangling her fingers through his hair.

Time froze. Juliette was in his arms. The taste of her lips was sweeter than he'd ever imagined. This was where he belonged. They were better together.

A voice from behind him shattered the moment.

"What are you two doing?" Ivy asked as she entered the kitchen.

Juliette righted herself out of Caleb's grip and let go of his neck. "We kind of collided over the tacos," she said. A beautiful red hue crept up her neck and colored her cheeks.

Ivy surveyed the taco shell carnage on the floor and sized both of them up. "Do they deliver pizza to FBI safe houses?"

"Not to worry, Ivy," Juliette said. "There's another box of taco shells in the cabinet."

Caleb turned back to the meat, which had turned into charcoal.

Had he just made the biggest mistake of his life, kissing the woman that had walked out on him three years ago?

Safe or not, his heart was there already. He loved Juliette Montgomery.

———

FRIDAY, 2:00 A.M.

Ivy never went to bed. She lay awake, staring at the ceiling.

She'd stayed up all night, watching the two FBI agents on patrol, memorizing the patterns they took in their paths. Noelle and Juliette would take turns staying up and watching inside. But if she got past whoever was on guard duty, and disabled the alarm, she could head back to the bedroom and go out the window.

All she needed to do was get far enough from the house to avoid the signal blockers. She'd watch the signal and trust her gut as far as deciding whether to walk to the playground up the street or stick close to the neighbor's house for Wi-Fi.

She needed to get a message to Layna. If she arranged the meeting, she'd let the FBI know the time and place. She'd calculated the risks. Of course, this had *danger* written all over it. But Uncle Caleb had been in the Army. How could he not want her to use her skills to defend and protect others? Juliette understood.

And what was up with the two of them embracing in the kitchen? It'd seemed like she'd interrupted a kiss. On the one hand, Uncle Caleb needed to find someone to fall in love with. He'd been alone too long, and she liked Juliette.

But it had been her and her uncle for so long. What if he spent more of his time with Juliette? Would she lose him?

She got up from the bed and paced. All she needed was for Layna to give her a time and place to meet, and she'd turn everything she knew in to the FBI. Uncle Caleb would have to let her go undercover to the meeting, to try and get evidence. They needed real names, not just fake screen names.

Uncle Caleb would finally be safe.

She also wanted to warn Layna that her brother was a bad man. Layna seemed nice, not the kind of girl who would do illegal things, which meant she probably still had time to get out of Rushmore.

One of the agents was about to take a fifteen-minute break, and the backyard would be empty for a few minutes until the other agent swept in. Now was her chance.

She cracked the bedroom door and tiptoed down the hallway toward the living room. She didn't see Noelle or Juliette but knew that at least one of them would be up, so she had to act fast. Near the garage door, she located the keypad to the alarm. She recalled how the guy on YouTube had been able to reset the password to the manufacturer's setting and prayed it worked. Otherwise, she'd set it off.

She tapped one button, and it let out a faint beep. In the still of the night, it might as well have been a car horn blaring, but she held her breath and nothing stirred. So she kept going, disabling the device.

No turning back now.

She really needed a code name for her operation. Something cool and edgy. She'd have to think about it when she wasn't stressed about accidentally setting off the alarm and waking up the whole neighborhood. But she managed to do everything the man in the video had, and with three long beeps, the alarm lights turned off.

That was close.

And she'd managed to do it all without running into Juliette or Noelle. Maybe she could take a chance and walk right out the back sliding glass door.

She headed to the door and peered through the blinds to make sure agent number two wasn't early with his routine. With the backyard empty except for some creepy shadows, she pushed the sliding door open just enough to duck out. The cool night air sent a shock through her system. Why hadn't she brought her thick jacket? But there wasn't time to go back. It was now or never.

"Busted."

She stifled a scream as a hand clamped down on her shoulder.

She turned. Juliette and Noelle stood behind her.

"Ivy, what exactly are you doing?"

TWELVE

"Did you really think you could sneak out of this house, knowing there are two professional bodyguards on duty?" She tried to keep the sharp edges out of her tone, but this girl kept pushing the edges of Juliette's patience.

Ivy stared at the ground but said nothing. For being so brilliant, Ivy had a lot of life lessons to learn. Why would the girl put herself in jeopardy like this?

Juliette hadn't anticipated Ivy sneaking out, but she'd been wide awake in bed, replaying the events of the evening on a loop in her mind.

Because there'd been something spicy going on in the kitchen earlier, and it hadn't been the salsa.

She and Caleb had kissed. Her lips tingled at the thought. How was she supposed to do her job when her insides went all school-girl crush when he walked into the room?

Okay, Montgomery, time to get your head in the game.

She was a professional bodyguard, and Caleb, a client. She couldn't run around fawning over a man when she needed to have one hundred percent of her attention focused on his protection. Not to mention that she and Caleb weren't meant to be together.

When she'd heard Ivy's feet padding down the hall, instincts had kicked in and she'd followed her. The girl wasn't going anywhere on Juliette's watch.

"Ivy, what's this about? You understand that your uncle and I are trying to protect you, right?"

Ivy sighed. "I just want some fresh air. Can we at least sit on the patio for a few minutes?"

Juliette looked into Ivy's eyes and saw the stress and sorrow she carried. She turned to Noelle. "Why don't you get some rest, and I'll stay up on watch. I'll radio the FBI and see if they're good with us sitting on the patio for a few minutes."

Noelle nodded and stood guard by the sliding glass door. This situation had more to do with Ivy acting out than anything else. Juliette knew Noelle wouldn't rest but would stay up and guard the door while she and Ivy chatted.

Juliette picked up the analog two-way radio from the end table in the living room and asked the FBI agent on duty if they could sit on the patio. A crackle responded, and then: "We'll sweep the backyard for any signs of trouble, and you two stick close to the house. But it should be okay for a few minutes. We'll be watching."

They headed outside to the patio, which consisted of a screened-in concrete slab with a table and chairs. It would be quaint if it weren't two a.m. and they weren't being hunted by dangerous madmen.

They sat on two metal chairs at the bistro-style table. "Give me the device, Ivy." Instinct told Juliette that the only reason Ivy would be so determined to sneak out was if she were searching for a signal.

The girl's eyes widened. She pulled the Kindle from inside her jacket and handed it to Juliette.

"What are you thinking, Ivy? There's a reason for all the security measures."

The girl scuffed her sneakers on the cement floor. "If I can find out where the hackers are, I can help save Uncle Caleb. Then they'll stop attacking him. I can't lose him, Juliette. Why won't he let me help the FBI?"

Juliette wished Ivy didn't have to deal with such adult things. "You hired me to be his bodyguard. Let me do my job."

Ivy shook her head, a tear streaking down one cheek. "I can't sit around and do nothing. I know I can help."

Juliette's heart melted. The little girl's fierce determination to protect Caleb resonated in the deepest parts of Juliette's soul. "You can't do it alone." The words resonated in her own heart as they came out of her mouth. How many times had she heard the same lecture?

"And you can't do it by sneaking around and lying. I remember your Uncle Caleb once telling me something very important. He told me that God fights for us, but we have to stand still and let him."

Where had that come from? Her relationship with God had been on the rocks for years. But somehow, spending time with Caleb had thawed her heart ever so slightly toward God. She'd even suggested going to church with him. A total one-eighty from her prior convictions.

"I can't lose *him*." Tears welled up in Ivy's eyes. "Where was God when my parents died? I'll do whatever it takes to make sure nothing happens to Uncle Caleb. He's all I have."

Juliette couldn't blame the girl for being mad at God. How many times had she uttered the same thing and rolled her eyes when someone told her that God was on her side? She and Ivy had a lot more in common than she'd first thought.

But right now, Juliette needed to focus on keeping her safe. "Who were you going to call?"

LYNETTE EASON & KELLY UNDERWOOD

Ivy refused to lift her head and make eye contact with Juliette.

"I can't do my job if you're not going to be a hundred and ten percent honest with me."

Ivy snickered. "There's no such thing as a hundred and ten percent. That doesn't make any sense. You can't give more than one hundred percent."

"But I'll take that extra ten percent and use it to keep your uncle safe. You know, by coming clean and telling the full truth, you might actually help save your uncle because the police can find and stop these bad guys."

Ivy continued to stare at the ground and mumbled. Juliette leaned across the table to hear. "I wanted to see if Layna would give me information on Rushmore. Maybe she isn't all bad and she might help us. I know I can get her to join our side."

Juliette bit back the sharp retort. Layna had preyed on Ivy's vulnerability. Of course Ivy longed for friendship.

"Ivy, look at me." The girl met Juliette's eyes, full of conflict. Here was a girl with a determination to grow up, warring to risk her childhood innocence.

"It's not your job to catch the bad guys. It's not mine either. The FBI has trained professionals that will bring this group to justice."

"So what, I just stand still? Because, you know, *God?*"

Trusting God was a good place to start, but Juliette wasn't ready to admit that. "I think we should start with the truth. You can't make plans and go off on your own. You need to be honest with your uncle and with me."

The house burst with a blaze of lights. "We need to go in. I bet your uncle woke up and found us both missing."

"Oh no," Ivy groaned. "He is going to freak."

Juliette grabbed Ivy's hand, and they slid the patio door open. For the first time in a long time, Juliette prayed. Because she was all-in on Caleb and Ivy's protection duty. They'd managed to work their way into her heart in just three short days.

And Juliette needed all the help she could get to keep Ivy from going rogue.

––––––

FRIDAY, 2:15 A.M.

"Where is she?" He saw Juliette emerging from the patio and didn't even try to hide the panic in his words. "What happened?"

Breathe, Caleb. Let her respond.

"Ivy and I just needed some fresh air." Ivy trailed Juliette from outside.

"I found her bed empty. Why would you two risk going outside at two a.m.?"

Juliette walked over to him and touched his arm. "I cleared it with the FBI agents, and they said we could sit right by the house on the screened-in patio. I saw them patrolling the whole time."

Noelle yawned. "If you don't need me, I'm going to get some rest." She headed back to the guest room, leaving the three of them alone.

Ivy threw her arms around Caleb. "It's all my fault. I disabled the alarm and was going to sneak out. I wanted to find a signal and email Layna. I thought I could help. I'm so sorry for being dishonest."

His niece had been adamant about helping the FBI, but he'd underestimated just how far she would take this. He ran a hand through his bedhead hair.

"I—I just wanted to help. You're keeping me on lockdown. I just wanted to talk to a friend. I know Layna's not all bad."

He took several deep breaths, leaned down and hugged Ivy

again. "You can't go after these hackers alone, Ivy. Layna isn't even a student at your school. She was pretending, so you can't trust her."

"But—" Her shoulders slumped.

"I need to keep you out of danger, and you're running headfirst into it. Please promise me you'll be careful." He tipped her chin up and pleaded with his eyes. She needed to see the truth here. See the danger.

Juliette squinted her eyes and gave an almost imperceptible nod to Caleb. Code for *We'll talk later.*

Caleb kissed the top of Ivy's head. "Why don't you try to get some sleep?"

"Why, so I can be bored tomorrow without the internet all day?"

"You're grounded, remember? So it would have been an internet-free day anyway. We'll play board games and watch movies like we did when I was a kid."

Ivy rolled her eyes and headed to the bedroom. A knock at the door startled him, but Juliette let the FBI agent in so he could reset the alarm.

He would never get any rest when it came to Ivy. Caleb handed the Kindle to the agent, who dropped it in an evidence bag. Once the agent reset the alarm, he headed out to patrol the perimeter.

"I have no business being a parent." He sat on the couch. "I can't keep her out of trouble. Maybe I should give Ivy's grandparents custody. They're nice people and can give her a nice life. A safe life."

Juliette sat down next to him. "Don't say that, Caleb. This isn't your fault. On the positive side, at least she didn't get a signal to turn the device on."

Caleb's heart squeezed at Juliette's nearness. "She's twelve, Jules. Sure, she sees herself as some sort of Robin Hood white hacker that wants to use her skills to help people, but she doesn't think things through. I just want her to be a kid again."

"I hope Agent McGregor can track down this Layna," Juliette said. "Ivy thinks the girl is a friend, that she can get Layna to turn on Rushmore."

Caleb shook his head. "Last time I asked, they didn't have any new leads on the girl's real identity. I can't believe I didn't realize she's so desperate for a friend that she can't see Layna is using her."

Juliette covered Caleb's hand with hers. "You're doing the best you can. Being a parent is new for you."

"I love her so much."

Juliette cleared her throat. "You know, Ivy said the exact same thing you've said—that she can't lose you. She's concerned God will take you like he took her parents."

Caleb's throat constricted. He'd had no idea Ivy blamed God for taking her parents. But how could he help her when he battled his own demons of insecurity? "I know how she feels. It's hard to love after so much loss." He looked into Juliette's golden-brown eyes that somehow managed to sparkle in the dim lighting of the living room. Could he risk loving this woman, knowing that she wouldn't hesitate to throw herself in front of a high-speed train if it meant protecting someone else?

Juliette shrugged. "Without the risk, you might miss out on so much more. You have to take the bad with the good sometimes. The good is that much sweeter when it costs something."

She was still talking about Ivy, right? "You know a thing or two about sweet things with your sugar addiction."

She playfully punched his arm, but just having her near him gave him a peace he hadn't experienced in a while.

Silence settled in the room, but he never needed to fill every empty space with words, and she often offered him quiet moments to reflect. His mind worked at unraveling the unsolvable problem staring him in the face.

Should he allow himself to be swept away by the woman in front of him? No.

Did he want to miss out on the potential for something great if he were open to love?

Another no.

And then there was that kiss on a replay loop in his mind. That was wreaking havoc on his emotions. What would happen if she left again?

Time to clarify things with Juliette. They needed to talk about the kiss. "While we're thinking about risk, um...I'm not sure we should have kissed, Jules. It just complicates things. We make a great team, but we both know we're not destined for more."

Juliette leaned closer to him and rested her head on his shoulder. "I'm so sorry I hurt you by leaving. I made the wrong choice. I hope you can forgive me. I'm not leaving again."

"Of course I forgive you, Jules."

Forgiveness was the easy part.

But how could he keep his distance from her when he was caught in her tractor beam and being drawn closer to her with every beat of his heart?

THIRTEEN

FRIDAY, 6:00 A.M.

Juliette stayed up all night on watch duty, paying extra attention to Ivy's room. That girl was a handful but had passed out in the guest room bed without any further incidents.

The coffee pot sputtered. The smell of fresh coffee sent her to her happy place. Juliette watched out the kitchen window. Caleb dozed on the couch, and Ivy still hadn't emerged from her room.

Noelle came out of her room, dressed and ready to take over watch duties. She grabbed a cup of coffee and sat at the table. Alana would be by later with some supplies.

"You two are really good together," Noelle said. "I can see why you held out."

She glanced at Caleb, who was sleeping like a rock.

"I didn't hold out." She joined Noelle at the table. "It just wasn't the right time."

"And is now a better time? Because he makes you smile in ways I've never seen."

Juliette shrugged. "We've both changed over the years.

Maybe it's possible to explore a relationship." Oh, how she wanted that to be true. A second chance with Caleb.

But he'd already said their kiss was a mistake.

Noelle changed the subject. "What I wouldn't give for a run."

"I know. This morning is the perfect weather. Cool, with a mist blanketing the yard. Everything is so still and peaceful."

Then a chill crept up her spine. *Why* was it so still?

"I can't remember the last time I saw the two FBI agents on patrol. They took shifts all night." She moved to the window and peeked out the blinds. The agents had been hanging out in their SUV when not actively patrolling.

The car was there, but with the tinted windows, she couldn't see if the two agents were in the vehicle.

Noelle had put down her coffee and joined Juliette. "I don't like this."

Juliette agreed. Something was off. "You stay here, and I'll go outside and check on the agents. I'll bring them some coffee. I'm sure everything is fine."

She poured two mugs and was grateful they'd given her the alarm code. She tapped in the six-digit number, and the alarm chirped off. Neither Caleb nor Ivy stirred. They needed the rest. She heard the beep as Noelle locked the door and reset the alarm.

She headed out the front door with the mugs in hand and approached the passenger side of the SUV. The car was running, but as she peered through the windshield, it didn't look like the driver was moving. The rest of the tinted windows made it hard to see, but as she got close, she noted the agent in the driver's seat was slumped against the wheel.

The coffee mugs hit the sidewalk and shattered. In a fraction of a second, Juliette's gun was in her hands, and she ducked behind the passenger side door. She opened it to peer inside the car. The driver's lifeless eyes stared back at her, and blood streaked down the side of his face. No need to check his pulse. The man was gone. No passenger.

She surveyed the area and didn't see any movement, so she sprinted through the front yard and bolted to the door. Noelle opened it the second Juliette arrived.

"We've got to go," she said.

Caleb jumped up off the couch, ready for action.

"What's wrong?" he asked. He grabbed his Glock off the end table and crept next to the sliding glass door. Noelle returned to the living room with a sleepy Ivy.

Juliette kept an eye on the front yard and heard Caleb take a sharp breath. "FBI agent, down on the ground. He's not moving. Blood on the concrete walkway outside of the patio could mean a gunshot wound to the head."

"The other is dead in the car. Same wound."

Caleb motioned for Ivy to stand behind him. The girl trembled but complied without saying a word. Juliette watched out the front window for any signs of movement. A car parked across the street three doors down had her concerned.

She held her breath, willing her pounding pulse to steady. "We've got company." The car door opened. A man dressed in all black slipped out and stood in the shadows of the neighbor's shrubbery, creeping closer to the safe house. Sunlight glinted off the gun in his hand.

"The front is not an acceptable escape route," she announced and flanked the other side of the sliding glass door, across from Caleb.

She fixed her eyes on him. "Do you think we should make a run for it?" she asked. Somehow that didn't feel safe, but with the man creeping around the front yard, what options did they have?

Caleb held up one finger. "Listen. What's that noise?"

Juliette swiveled her head, trying to locate the source of the high buzzing sound. She dashed to the front window to keep a visual on the intruder. She didn't see anything in the front yard, but the humming grew louder, like a swarm of bees. Or maybe it was—"It's a drone," Ivy said. Juliette watched as a mechanical box with four propellers dropped into view of the window. She raced back to the sliding glass door and caught Caleb's attention. "We've got to go. The drone has a gun mounted on it."

Noelle darted to the back bedroom and returned with two shotguns. "I thought we might need extra protection, so I packed accordingly." She handed one to Caleb and stood against the wall with Ivy, all of them staying well away from being seen in the window. Caleb gave Juliette a tight nod. "We'll run through the yard to the fence at the back. There are some trees that will offer limited protection, but there is a house about a quarter mile back. Maybe we can get help."

"But that drone is going to target us the second it spots us."

Caleb racked his gun. "You and Ivy run. Noelle and I will take care of the drone."

Shots rang out, and the picture window in the front of the house exploded. They dove for the ground, glass fragments flying everywhere. Juliette met Caleb's eyes. "It's now or never."

At Caleb's nudge, Ivy crawled across the floor next to Juliette. Juliette squatted by the door and cracked it open. She froze. "Do you hear that?" The humming sound intensified.

Caleb stood, sticking to the wall while trying to stay out of view from both the front window and the sliding door. He parted the blind slats to take a peek. "I don't see the drone," Caleb whispered.

"It's drones," Ivy said. "Plural."

No time to argue about a plan that put them all in the direct line of fire, because based on the sound, the hackers had sent a drone army to attack them. Caleb could defend himself. But Ivy? The girl put on a brave face, but this was more than any twelve-year-old should have to deal with. They needed to run across the patio to the yard, but that would take them right past the fallen agent.

"Ivy, we're going to run." Juliette stood and pulled Ivy up. "Look straight ahead. Focus on the rooftop of the house at the end of the pasture. Aim for the small group of trees near the fence."

Juliette nodded to Caleb, and he moved into position behind her, with Noelle guarding the rear. Ivy wrapped her hand around Juliette's arm.

They all stepped onto the patio and froze.

"What's going on?" Juliette's whisper was lost in the steady thrumming noise. They clung to the side of the house, under the awning of the patio. Multiple drones descended across the backyard. There had to be at least twenty of them dropping out of the sky, lining up in a grid-like pattern across the lawn.

"It looks like a chess board," Ivy whispered. "They're quadcopters. Expensive."

The whirring stopped as the black rectangle machines with four propellors settled into the grass, unnerving Juliette more than the incessant noise. They stared down at the drone army parked across the backyard.

"It's like a scene from a science fiction movie. What are they waiting for?" Juliette asked.

Caleb's face paled. "Us."

———

FRIDAY, 6:15 A.M.

Caleb could only rationalize one reason these terrorists would blanket a bunch of sophisticated drones across the backyard of the safe house in three-foot intervals.

"Bombs," Caleb said. "They've strapped these drones with

something. Probably C-4. We're going to be walking through land mines to get out of the yard."

"You've got to be kidding me." Juliette's wide eyes conveyed the danger of this situation, because if Hazard Pay was spooked, Caleb was downright terrified.

He watched Juliette shield Ivy from the fallen agent on the patio with her body.

Armed drones in the front yard. Landmine drones in the back. They were sandwiched in the safe house.

"They're FPV drones," Ivy whispered, staring at the sky. When Juliette's mouth hung open in confusion, Ivy clarified. "FPV stands for First Person View. No radio frequencies or GPS. They're being piloted by remote control. Which means the bad guys are close. And probably more drones are coming."

"But what do they want?" Juliette scanned the sky for more signs of trouble. "Do they want to trap us, flush us out into the open, or kill us?"

"At this point," Caleb said, "it's a toss-up. If they think Ivy knows something, they wouldn't strike this hard. But my gut says they want to chase us out of the house."

Whirring propellors announced the arrival of more gun drones, confirming Ivy's guess. Caleb counted three of them. But more could be waiting on the other side of the house. "They're trying to drive us out of the house and through the yard." He racked the shotgun. "You're going to have to take Ivy and run. The second you step into that yard, the gun drones will go after you. I'll take them down, but you'll have to dodge the land mines. Unless we can stop the drone pilot, our only other option is to get to safety."

Juliette hesitated, then nodded. They both knew this was their only chance.

Caleb prayed. Because if anything happened to either Ivy or Juliette...

With one hand, Caleb counted down. Three...two... On one,

Juliette hoisted Ivy onto her back and moved toward the edge of the stone patio. Caleb and Noelle aimed shotguns at the sky and watched for any signs of movement.

Dear God, please let this work.

Juliette took off at a fast clip, and Caleb watched her weave around the first drone. The buzzing intensified, and Caleb turned his head to watch behind himself. One of the drones gave chase, heading straight for Juliette and Ivy.

Juliette sped up, mindful of where the drones were strategically placed throughout the yard. She wouldn't be able to steer clear of all of them. Caleb aimed and fired at the one stalking Juliette and Ivy, taking off two of its four propellers. The machine lilted to one side and tumbled out of the sky before it could get off a shot.

Caleb's head throbbed from the gunshot explosion. This was their lives, not some video game. He lowered the gun and flexed his fingers, itching to get his hands on the drone pilot. But these cowards hid behind screens.

Juliette weaved through the drones on the ground, and he followed in her trail. She slowed to avoid stepping on a drone. Noelle hung back by the house, patrolling the skies.

"I don't like this," Caleb said. "What if they detonate all at once?"

Juliette grunted and shifted Ivy's weight on her back. "Don't even say that."

Another thump-thump-thump and Caleb's heart stopped. Behind them, two more gunship drones rose over the house.

"Run!" Caleb yelled, and Juliette took off while Caleb spun and faced off with the two warships. A crash sounded as Noelle's shot took down one of the drones.

The drone chased Juliette, and Caleb shot at the descending invader. It exploded in the air. Juliette had made it halfway through the land-mine drone maze, and Caleb needed to help her. He didn't trust that one of these bombs wouldn't detonate, and that might set off a chain reaction. He couldn't watch the sky and the ground.

"Go," Noelle said. "Watch Juliette's back, and I'll defend from here."

He was so thankful for all of the Elite Guardians. "Don't forget about the man prowling about. And we still don't have eyes on the drone operator. Be careful." He took off running after Jules, following the same path. But before he reached her position, he stopped short. One of the drones nearest him on the ground lit up with a red blinking light. He changed direction and ran away from the activated drone.

The earth rumbled, and heat seared his back. The drone exploded in a fireball, taking out the yard around it but not touching the other drones. At least the others hadn't detonated. These guys wanted to play with Caleb and Juliette to drive them out into the open. How had they figured out where the safe house was?

Caleb's skin pricked with goosebumps at the sound of more beeping, and several other red lights appeared.

"Keep moving!" Caleb yelled. Booms rang out from Noelle's shotguns while she took down more drones.

They sprinted for the back fence, weaving in and out of the land-mine drones. Trees dotted the fence line and might give them some semblance of protection from the air attack. Another explosion sent them ducking from falling debris. Gunshots rang out, and Caleb didn't even stop to look. They hit the six-foot picket fence, and Caleb climbed up first. At least the horses had scattered, although they might have made good getaway transportation.

He reached back and grabbed Ivy from Juliette, hoisting her to the top of the fence. Ivy hopped up and over, and he reached a hand to pull Juliette. Bullets pinged off the side of the fence.

Juliette's feet hit the ground with a thud, and while Caleb straddled the top of the fence, he took aim at the last air drone.

Firing twice, he nailed it center mass, sending splinters of plastic material flying. The fragments took a nosedive and crashed onto one of the land-mine drones, creating a yellow and red fireball.

Caleb jumped off the fence and ran. More land mines exploded, sending pebbles and earth pieces high into the air. Despite some tree covering, debris rained down around them. Smoke from the charred plastic burned his nostrils and stung his eyes.

Whirring sounded behind him, and Caleb turned. Two more gun drones patrolled the edge of the property.

Juliette slowed her pace. "I don't think the drones can navigate through the trees."

"That makes sense if they're being piloted by remote control," Ivy said.

Juliette relaxed her shoulders, the tension in her face easing a bit. "If we walk straight back, we should come out at the neighboring house."

Caleb frowned. "But that would also be where they would expect us to exit. And we lose the tree covering."

Juliette put her hands on her hips, not bothering to mask her frustration. "You've got me. This is the first drone attack slash land-mine encounter I've ever tried to outrun. I must have been sick the day the Army had their class on outrunning a robot invasion."

Caleb suppressed a smile. It was good to see Juliette's feisty spirit return. The churning the drone propellers kept humming as they pushed farther through the patch of trees toward the roofline of the neighbor's house. But they soon came to the end of the wooded area that separated the two houses.

"Is there a road on the other side of this property?" Juliette asked. "I'm sure you memorized the map of the entire area."

Before Caleb could respond, Ivy said, "If we walk point seven miles north, we'll come out on Magnolia Ave." Caleb and

Juliette both gaped at Ivy. "What?" she said. "I checked the map before I snuck out. I'm not that dumb."

"Well, that's my girl." Caleb slung his arm around his niece.

Juliette checked her phone. "Finally. A signal. I'll text Alana for backup and let Agent McGregor know we've been attacked." Her phone pinged. "Alana was bringing my car to me this morning. She's already on her way. I'll tell her to meet us at the house on Magnolia."

They took a chance and raced for the patio of the house.

Juliette stood on her tiptoes, cupping her face with her hands to peer through the sliding glass door. "I don't see any signs of life. Maybe this is a summer home for someone. It's as nice as the safe house before drones went all scorched-earth on the place."

Caleb gave the door a heavy knock, but no one responded. "At least we're not putting anyone else in danger, but we still need to find a way out. We can't hide here. It would be too obvious."

"The drones are still patrolling the area," Juliette said. "It's only a matter of time before they discover us here."

Caleb nodded. "Let's move to the front of the house and see if they have a car or some kind of vehicle we can...um... borrow." He didn't want to trespass on someone's private property and then steal, but they needed to leave the area.

Juliette looked like she wanted to argue about the plan but offered no alternatives. Caleb watched the skies, and they smashed themselves against the wall of the house and crept toward the front.

Sirens wailed in the distance, signifying help would soon arrive, but they didn't have time to wait around.

They rounded the corner of the house, and Caleb spotted an older model sedan parked in the driveway. The buzz of drones had died down, but he refused to let his guard down for a second.

Juliette dashed to the car and found the driver's door unlocked. "Yes! It's an old car. Should be easy to hotwire, and won't have GPS for someone to trace. Win-win."

Caleb tossed her a Swiss Army tool he fished out of his pocket, and she caught it over the roof of the car. In no time she had the dashboard removed with the tiny screwdriver, and she connected wires until the engine purred to life. Caleb and Ivy jumped in.

"Let's get out of here," Jules said.

"I'm glad those days in the motor pool taught you a thing or two about hot-wiring a car," Caleb said as Juliette backed out of the long driveway.

"Thank goodness it's not a current model, or we'd still be sitting there."

When she hit the street, she let out a yelp.

Directly in front of their windshield hovered a drone with a gun mounted underneath it, blocking their escape.

FOURTEEN

What else could go wrong? Juliette had already faced off with drones, dodged land mines, and run for her life. And it wasn't even seven a.m.

"Ivy, get on the floor." A gun-strapped drone hovered right in the path of their car.

The girl complied without a word.

Juliette blinked, willing the scene in front of her to change. But that thing blocked their way. She could hit reverse, but the drone would follow. Or worse, shoot the car up. Her pulse hammered in her ears.

Caleb raised the shotgun, but he'd be no match for the machine gun mounted on the front of the drone. Ivy sucked in a breath from the floor in the back seat of the borrowed sedan.

If there was ever a moment she needed God, it was now.

Out of the corner of her eye, movement whooshed from the wooded area across the street.

The drone exploded, raining fire and mechanical parts in front of the car.

170

Alana stepped out from behind a tree and lowered a handheld RPG. She waved them on. "Get out of here! I'll cover all of you."

Juliette hit the gas, and the sedan engine revved. As she followed the road to the turnoff for the subdivision, another fireball shot across the view in her rearview mirror. Behind them, Alana jumped up and down in triumph, fist pumping the air.

These hackers—no, make that *terrorists*—were relentless. Juliette's blood boiled. "We're being followed." Another drone bobbed and weaved behind their racing car. How many drones did these guys have?

Enough to create a terrifying army.

Caleb racked his shotgun and rolled down the passenger window.

Juliette watched the scene unfold through the rearview mirror with one eye while she watched the road with the other. Before Caleb could get off a shot, Alana ran into the middle of the road with the RPG, and the grenade sliced through the machine, sending its parts scattering.

Juliette stomped on the gas pedal and raced to the main road, the stress coursing through her veins faster than the spinning tires of their stolen vehicle. Even if the threat was over, she wouldn't relax until they were out of this car and off the radar of these madmen with attack drones.

"A drone attack in broad daylight?" Caleb said. "Seriously?"

"I've never seen anything like that in my entire life. Whoever is orchestrating this Rushmore group is well funded. They blew up millions of dollars' worth of equipment today."

Caleb stared out the window. "I need to call Blake. He might be a target as well."

"I'm not sure that's a great idea," Juliette said. "We don't know who we can trust at this point. We have two dead FBI agents. It seems like these hackers are monitoring our every move."

"But how?" Caleb turned to Ivy in the back seat. "Ivy, you said you never turned your phone on since we got to the house and you never got a signal."

"I didn't. I was going to, but Juliette found me before I could."

"Did Layna give you anything else other than that phone?"

Ivy hesitated. "She did give me a friendship bracelet." She shook out her sleeve, and a beaded bracelet slid down her wrist. She passed it to Caleb.

He turned it around in his hands. "I've never noticed this before. Why didn't you tell us that Layna gave you this?"

Ivy shrugged. "It didn't seem like a big deal. The phone could be tracked. This is just a stupid bracelet."

Caleb sighed and examined the beads.

"What did you find, Caleb?"

He blew out a breath, betraying his exhaustion level. "One of these beads has a tracker in it. It's different than the others."

Caleb broke the strand of string holding the beads together and rolled them around in his palm. "It's probably emitting a low radio frequency. They've been able to locate us this whole time." He dropped the questionable bead on the floor and smashed it with the heel of his shoe. He tossed the pieces of the bead, along with the rest of them, out the window.

Juliette stared at the open road ahead. "Well, they won't know where we are, but right now, we have no place to go."

"I'm hungry," Ivy said, her voice soft. Juliette's heart broke. The girl had endured a terrible ordeal today—one that might shape her future. This threat needed to end so Ivy could get back to her life.

"There's a diner a few streets over from here," Juliette said. "I've been there before. It shouldn't be too crowded this time of day, and we can make a few calls and use their Wi-Fi. We'll figure things out from there."

Caleb's eyes were fierce. The man was gearing up for a fight. "Can we stop at a place where I can buy a laptop?" he asked. "I feel lost without one. I won't do anything to attract attention to myself. No one will track me. I'd trust a brand-new computer way more than any of my old ones. Someone working for Cyberskies has to be in on this hacker group. It would be the easiest way for someone to bypass security and gain access to the bank."

"Who do you suspect?" She agreed it might be an inside job, but they needed proof. Or at least a lead.

"I can't imagine it would be Blake. He's been a great friend for a long time. I trust him, or I wouldn't have become his business partner."

"But anything is possible."

Caleb shrugged. "He would have the highest level of access and the knowledge to pull this off. But why physically rob banks? Why not just finish the program and send the ransomware? And Blake would know how to complete the program."

Juliette had no answers as she navigated the country roads, her anxiety ratcheting with each passing mile. Within fifteen minutes, she pulled into a big-box computer supply store, having had no revelation as to their next steps. Once Caleb had the supplies he needed, they'd head to the diner for breakfast along with the opportunity to regroup.

The Elite Guardians Agency had two clients in desperate need of protection.

Juliette had developed a soft spot for both of them. Caleb's kiss didn't help squash the desire that took up residence in her heart. She needed to get her head out of the clouds and into her job. Caleb was first and foremost a client.

She refused to let her personal feelings jeopardize his safety.

Because she'd do whatever it took to keep Caleb and Ivy safe. Even if she had to put her own life on the line to do it.

———

FRIDAY, 9:15 A.M.

The back booth of the café resembled a display rack at Best Buy. Caleb had bought two MacBooks and an iPad. All machines ran at the same time. He'd have bought more, but considering he and Ivy were homeless at this point, he decided to make do with just the essentials.

"What can I get you, hon?" the waitress asked Caleb. She pulled a pen from her bun and poised it over her notepad.

"I'll have the shrimp and grits." He couldn't go wrong with a classic Savannah dish, even though the drone chase had stolen his appetite.

The diner thrummed with voices and dishes clinking and smelled of coffee and sugar. Juliette had already ordered an entire pot of coffee plus some cinnamon buns for the table before they'd sat down. Now she added a platter of bacon, eggs, and hash browns just before the waitress scurried off to take an order from another table.

"Where are we going next?" Ivy asked, the normal sparkle in her eyes now dull.

Juliette nursed a cup of coffee with both hands. "I called Agent McGregor. He's on his way over."

Great. The man who couldn't protect them would come up with another brilliant plan. Why didn't he just hand Ivy over to the hackers? That's all McGregor wanted—to use Ivy.

Caleb turned his attention to his laptops strewn about the table. He'd hunted for the least sticky spot before placing them down and was using three menus and twelve napkins as a buffer. He accessed his own system, hunting for any signs of the hackers. A nagging in the back of his mind wouldn't quit. This had to be an inside job. These hackers had manipulated his system and had been passing messages back and forth right in front of him. And he'd employed them. But Cyberskies had seventy-five employees, so he needed to narrow the pool of suspects.

He ran a hand through his hair and then remembered the sticky table situation. "I need a shower."

Juliette smirked. "Yeah, you do."

"Speak for yourself. You've got a nice streak of dirt across your T-shirt." That was putting it mildly. Her white T-shirt showed streaks of dirt like it'd been dragged through the mud a few times.

She frowned at her attire. "I guess that's to be expected when dodging robotic land mines. Sorry you ruined your favorite nerd shirt. But I know you keep backups for your backup shirts. For emergencies like this."

He glanced at his blue *Star Trek* shirt. Pajama shirt, since their flight from the house had been an abrupt one. At least he'd been wearing jeans and not his flannel bottoms with the Spock heads on them. And how did Juliette appear so put together despite outrunning a drone army and having mud on her shirt?

Ivy stared, saying nothing. The food arrived, and the waitress arranged plates in between the laptops and cords.

"I guess I'm right on time for breakfast." Agent McGregor strode in and pulled a chair from an empty table. He sat down at the head of the booth. Caleb kept watch outside and saw a vehicle pull into the parking lot with two occupants. Feds. He relaxed a bit. Even though the safe house had wound up being compromised, any reinforcements were appreciated.

"I'm not sharing." Juliette covered her mountain of food with her hand.

McGregor laughed. "I'll be surprised if you can finish that platter."

Caleb snorted. "Oh, just watch her. I have no idea where she puts it."

The agent asked the waitress for coffee, and she returned with a cup.

Caleb knew the man had news, and he hated small talk more than anything else. "What's the plan now that the hackers destroyed the not-so-safe house, Agent?"

Grief flashed across his features for a fraction of a second, but then it was gone. Caleb winced at his insensitivity. This man had lost two colleagues in their battle. "I'm sorry."

"When we weren't able to get ahold of our agents on the sat phone, we sent backup. A little too late though." The agent sized up the ragtag crew at the table. "But thanks to you folks, we've apprehended two suspects that we think are involved with Rushmore."

Finally, a win for the good guys. The agent continued. "First of all, we found the man you two tied to the stairwell of the office. Guess his partner left him behind. His name is Daniel Archer. Ring any bells?"

Juliette froze with her fork dangling in midair. "I know that name. But I don't have an eidetic memory, so give me a second. I need the coffee to kick in." She finished her bite, took a sip from her mug, and squinted. "Wait. I think he was the security guard at the bank. The one that was robbed."

Agent McGregor's face crinkled like he was holding in laughter at Juliette's antics, but he held his professional demeanor in place. "Well done. He worked as a night security guard for First United."

"That's how they were gaining access to the bank," Caleb said. "They had a man on the inside."

Agent McGregor took a sip of his coffee. "More good news though. We were able to locate one of the drone pilots. He was a few houses down in a parked car. His name is Jeff Kline. He's a highly skilled computer programmer. But it gets better, as the guy has a scar across his cheek—as if someone had whacked him in the face with a 'best in customer service' award."

"So the hackers were the ones robbing the bank," Jules said. "And this is the guy that pushed Caleb in front of the streetcar." She stabbed another bite of eggs.

"We think they hired a couple of ex-military guys for some added support, but it looks like they're doing their own dirty work. Whatever their mission is, it's personal to them. These Savannah Rushmore members have gone rogue. None of the other cities where Rushmore operates have reported bank robberies or drone attacks. But it's a big win for us, because we believe Jeff's code name is the Architect. He may be the creator of their ransomware."

"Does this mean they can't launch the program, since their architect is in jail?" Juliette asked, right before taking a big bite of the cinnamon roll.

"That's why we need to keep Ivy safe," Caleb said with a glance at his very quiet niece. She moved food around on her plate with a fork. "If Ivy can recreate their program and make it work, they don't need their architect." He stirred his coffee with more force than necessary to combine the cream and sugar.

The man cleared his throat. "We'd like to take both you and Ivy into protective custody."

Instant irritation. "But how can you keep us safe?" Caleb never hid his emotions well. "What are you doing to find these hackers and stop them?"

The plastic cushion on the agent's chair squeaked when he shifted. "Ivy's made more inroads with these hackers than we have. And that's tough for me to admit. We'd, uh...we'd like to proceed with having Ivy make contact with them—"

Ivy's eyes pleaded with him.

"Did you not see the drone army they unleashed on us? It doesn't feel safe to put a twelve-year-old out there as bait. There must be another way." Several customers stared at their table, and he lowered his voice. "Use me. I can do the same things Ivy can. I've gone over their program and can fix their bug. I can act like I want to join them. What better way to take down the bank than to have the guy that created the security software on their side?"

Juliette shook her head. "They'll see it as the trap that it is. Rushmore has tried to kill you several times. And they'll still come after Ivy. She's the easier target."

The fine lines around Agent McGregor's eyes deepened. His job carried a world of stress, and maybe Ivy was the man's last resort. But what if something happened to her?

The agent cleared his throat. "We'd still like to have her contact Layna. Let them think that Ivy's not told you anything. We'll think of a reason that the tracker got damaged, like Ivy lost the bracelet. But if she makes contact, we can—"

"No. Find another way." Back at the safe house, he'd told Juliette that he'd consider it. But after drones had chased them out of the supposed *safe* house, he refused to let Ivy be dangled as bait.

His niece rested her hand on his arm. "Uncle Caleb, I want to help. I know I can do this."

"Just because you can do something, doesn't mean you should do it. These are dangerous people. You saw the drones. They're ruthless."

"Just think about it, Caleb," Juliette said, still working on her pile of hash browns. "That's all Agent McGregor is saying."

"You want her to meet in person? Couldn't she meet them online?"

The agent sat back in his chair. "We'd like to arrange a meeting between Ivy and Layna. In person. Someplace public. We need to draw the hackers out into the open."

"And when Ivy gives them what they want? She becomes the very definition of *expendable*."

Caleb ran a hand through his hair. This conversation was going nowhere. He turned to Juliette.

"Your job is to protect Ivy first, remember?" Why couldn't she see the danger? Memories of that day on the mountainside assaulted him. This woman was too quick to take risks, and now she wanted to put his niece in the crosshairs.

Not going to happen.

"You're not taking chances when it comes to her life, Jules."

Fire sparked in her eyes, and she practically slammed the fork to her plate. "Do you really think that little of me? That I'd put her in harm's way? I plan to be right beside her the entire time. I'm not letting her do this alone. But if it helps catch these guys, I think we should at least hear the agent out."

Everything within him wanted to protect them both...

"I need some air." He scooted out of the booth and headed to the parking lot. On the way out, he passed Alana heading into the restaurant. Caleb nodded but kept moving.

A hand on his arm stopped him at the restaurant's exit. "It's not safe to be outside, Caleb." Juliette stood between him and the door. She nodded to a section of the restaurant where there was a private table.

"Fine," he muttered. He followed her to the private section and sank into the vinyl booth. An old-school jukebox brandished a rainbow of flickering colored lights across the back wall.

How had things spun so far out of control? The building blocks of his world consisted of numbers, order, and logic. This situation was chaos, unpredictable. No instruction manual existed. And the thing that bothered him the most?

He was falling for Jules, but at what cost? How could he trust her to protect Ivy when the woman who had his heart refused to play it safe?

From his spot, Caleb could see Ivy talking with Agent McGregor and Alana. His eyes were glued on Ivy until Juliette gave him a soft kick under the table. "Ivy is fine. Alana came in and won't let her out of her sight. For the record, I'm not siding with Agent McGregor. I'm just saying hear the man out. That's all. You know I'd never risk anything happening to Ivy. Or to you."

He nodded, a lump forming in his throat. "I refuse to let go of her. Or you." He stared at Ivy again, who laughed at something Alana said. When was the last time Ivy had giggled like that?

Juliette reached across the table and squeezed his hand, letting her fingers tangle in his. "We will get through this. The three of us. We will make it to the other side, and I'm not resting until we do. But we need to lay out all our options. I would think you, as Mr. Logic, would want to study all possible outcomes."

He shook his head. "Be serious."

"I am. I have my focus a hundred percent on protecting Ivy. No matter what. I'm not going to let anything happen to her."

Caleb sighed. He'd have to trust Jules to do her job and protect Ivy.

Because he was the one who would be hunting these criminals down to protect all of them.

"I know this is a terrible situation all the way around. But just last night, we talked about trusting God with Ivy."

His own words stabbed him like a thousand bee stings. He couldn't argue with his own words.

"I don't know, Jules. I feel so helpless. I close my eyes, and I'm back on that mountainside with Laz crushed in that Humvee, and I can't do anything to pull him out. And I watched Laz and Tank die on an endless loop in my mind some nights in my dreams. It makes me want to play it safe. Especially with Ivy's life."

Juliette hadn't released his hand, but their connection ran deeper than physical touch. She understood him. They'd both had a front row seat at the same horror show. It haunted them both.

His throat constricted. "I trust you, Jules. I know you'll protect Ivy. And I know I have to let go of control here."

"We're a team, Caleb. I've always got your back. Remember how we fought our way out of the unwinnable training exercise? What did you call it?"

"The Kobayashi Maru. You changed the rules of the exercise. How can you forget?"

Her lip quirked up, like she was trying to stifle a smile in a somber moment. "I don't speak Klingon."

"It's not—never mind. But I get your point. We've faced circumstances where the odds were stacked against us, and we found a way out."

She leaned in closer over the table, her fingers still entwined in his. "I'm all-in, Caleb. I'll watch out for Ivy. Even if I have to Kobayashi Maru my way out of the situation. I'm not running away this time. We're in this together. As a team."

Oh, how he wanted to lean over the table and kiss her again. But Juliette defined *dangerous*, and right now, he needed all of her attention on Ivy.

Because he was going to let his niece help the FBI take down a dangerous gang of criminals, while trusting that God had all of their backs.

FIFTEEN

"I'm going to let Ivy work with McGregor on the investigation."

Indecisive Caleb had decided, and the matter was resolved. Juliette watched Caleb rise from the restaurant booth and walk toward Agent McGregor. Despite her being in the protection business, she was doing a terrible job at protecting her heart.

For starters, when had she fallen for her client? One peek in Caleb's dark brown eyes and all common sense vanished. She watched him stroll with confidence across the restaurant and slide into the booth next to Ivy while she mentally inserted herself into their future. Because being with Caleb these past few days had made her long for more chances to spend time with him and Ivy. When they weren't running from drones.

What would it look like to be a family? They were a team. His strength of intelligence and logic balanced out her irrational emotions. He made her feel complete, whole. Plus, she admired his reliance on God. If she were honest with herself, she wanted that kind of faith. Loosening his grip on Ivy took guts.

She shook her head as if that would get her mind back on her job. But Caleb's and Ivy's lives depended on her sharp skills.

Juliette made her way back to the group's table and slid into the booth next to Caleb and Ivy.

"I'm willing to hear you out, Agent McGregor." Caleb stared the man down. "I can see the merits in Ivy working with you. But I need a plan to keep her safe."

They listened to the agent's plan to flush the hackers out from behind their computer screens. "The goal is to have Ivy text Layna and get her to agree to meet in a public place. We'll have undercover agents on standby to take Layna down when she shows up."

"It's not going to work," Juliette announced, louder than she'd intended. "If Layna's with Rushmore, she has inside knowledge of the drone attacks. You don't think they'll see the FBI coming and smell a trap?" If the FBI was going to risk Ivy's life, they needed a rock-solid plan. This mission was deadly, and it relied on the acting skills of a twelve-year-old. Could Ivy sell this?

The wooden chair creaked as McGregor shifted to Ivy. "We'll need to make Layna think that you want to defect to her side, that you're ready to work with Rushmore. I believe if you agree to meet, they'll think that they've won you over. Especially if you're rebelling by ditching your uncle."

Ivy chimed in. "I can text her to meet me after school by the bleachers where I met her last time."

The man shook his head. "I think a public park nearby might work, and I like your thinking. But Layna needs a reason to trust you. She has to be convinced that you want to work with Rushmore."

"I can pull the whole teenage moody thing and tell her I'm fighting with Uncle Caleb. That I'm tired of being under surveillance and am sneaking out to meet her at the park."

Caleb blanched, and Juliette felt the same queasiness over

Ivy calling the shots and creating an elaborate lie to catch a criminal. And she did it with such ease.

McGregor pulled the phone—the one Layna had given Ivy—out of his jacket pocket and set it in front of him. "We made sure there aren't any trackers on the phone and set it up to show a fake location."

He slid the phone toward the center of the table. "I think you need to go bigger. Let them know you want to be a hacker and work for Rushmore. What is something that would prove your loyalty?"

Ivy reached across the table and took the phone. Her fingers flew across the screen. She put the phone down and slid it back to Agent McGregor. "Does that work?"

He retrieved the phone, read her message, and smirked. The agent flipped the screen so Caleb and Juliette could see it.

Meet at the park across from school. Noon. I'm done with my uncle holding me back and want to show the world what I can do. I'm all in. I can disable Cyberskies' security system.

"I'm not really going to do it, Uncle Caleb. I just need her to think I'll betray you to work with Rushmore. I know Layna will believe me. Please let me do this."

Juliette shivered at how easy it was for Ivy to concoct a plausible story, as if lies just rolled off her tongue naturally. The power of a genius mind in the petite twelve-year-old body. If only she didn't have to grow up so fast in a world that played loose with the truth.

There was no way Caleb would allow her to—

"Okay," he said, his voice a whisper. And just like that, Caleb consented. On the outside, it seemed like he'd made peace with the decision. But inside Caleb's genius mind, Juliette knew, grief and anger were churning up a storm.

The agent passed Ivy the phone, and she sent the text to Layna. Within thirty seconds, Ivy had a response.

"She said she'd be there. I'm in." She said it with no

hesitation in her voice. The girl reminded Juliette of herself. Always ready for the call of duty without a second glance at the consequences.

And now she saw why taking risks sometimes shot terror through the hearts of those who had to stand on the sidelines and watch.

God, please be with this girl.

"Is there enough time to get agents in place?" Juliette said, checking her watch.

Agent McGregor stood. "I'm going to make some calls. It's a shorter time frame than I was thinking, but I've had agents on standby working on nothing but this case. I'll get everything set up."

He turned to Caleb. "Will you two bring Ivy to the park and drop her off maybe a block away? We'll have agents trail her as she walks to the meeting."

"What about the car we stole?" Ivy asked.

McGregor chuckled. "I had an agent deliver a new car for you. It's parked right out front. We'll compensate the owner of the car you *borrowed*." He passed a set of keys to Juliette.

They headed out of the restaurant. Alana wanted to get a jump start on security and headed off to let Savannah PD know about the operation. Juliette, Caleb, and Ivy headed to a nondescript four-door sedan and got in.

Juliette followed Agent McGregor's car and watched her FBI tail in the rearview mirror. The plan was that once they got near the school, the agents would fall back a bit, in case someone was watching the area.

Caleb sat in the passenger seat, typing away on his laptop while they drove.

"Uncle Caleb?" Ivy's small voice came from the back seat.

He paused his typing and craned his neck toward the back seat. "What's up?"

Ivy sniffed. "You know I have to do this. If I can help the

agents, then I need to. But I can't do it alone. Remember? I need your help. And God's. You taught me that."

Juliette stiffened, because that was the same lecture he'd preached to her all those years ago.

"Right," Caleb replied. "But I'm not sure putting you in danger is the best way to bring about justice."

"But what if it is?"

He turned in his seat so he could face her. "Maybe you're right. You're smart, Ivy, and if you can help and feel that it's the right thing to do, I'll support you a hundred percent. I've got your back."

Juliette could see Ivy's smile in her rearview mirror.

"And maybe Uncle Caleb should take a piece of his own advice," Juliette said. Caleb swiveled his head toward the front of the car. "I know you're trying to track these hackers on your own, outside of the FBI. Make sure you don't forget that you're part of a team. My team."

Agent McGregor's car ran through a yellow light, but Juliette stopped. They were about two miles from the park. So far, she hadn't spotted any trouble. But now she'd have to catch up to the agent's car. He'd probably pull off and wait for her.

The light seemed to take forever, with cars stopped at all four intersections. Maybe her suspicious mind needed a rest. But after a minute of sitting at the intersection with all cars at a four-way stop, her bodyguard senses kicked into overdrive. "Something's not right," she muttered at Caleb, whose fingers hovered over the keyboard.

He didn't say anything but commenced typing. For a former Army analyst, how could he be so oblivious—

"They hacked the lights," Ivy said. "Didn't they?"

Caleb nodded. "They're in the system and changed those lights to mess with our protection."

Juliette's stomach clenched. She checked her rearview mirror to confirm the agent was still behind her. "We need to get out of here. They're coming for us."

She pulled into the intersection, but it was too late. Two trucks raced toward them. One T-boned the FBI agent that had been following them.

The other headed straight for them.

———

FRIDAY, 11:45 A.M.

Caleb's mind processed the scene as if it were happening in slow motion.

The truck barreled toward the driver's side of the vehicle.

Ivy screamed.

The side of the car crumpled around Juliette. Metal creaked and popped as if all the bolts and nuts holding the car together were stretched beyond their limits.

The impact shoved Juliette toward the crumbling center console, almost into his lap. Her seat belt kept her in place, but the whole driver's door pressed inward. The passenger-side airbag deployed, filling the front seat with a cloud of white powder. The impact knocked the wind out of him, and he gasped.

His mind sped up. The movement stopped, but Caleb's stomach continued to somersault. Juliette groaned. He reached over and touched her cheek.

"I'm alive," she rasped.

"Ivy, are you okay?" No response.

Caleb craned his neck toward the back seat. Ivy stared out the side window.

"No, no, no," Ivy muttered. "They're here."

The car door was flung open. A masked man reached in toward Ivy.

Ivy kicked the guy and scrambled across the back seat, trying to open the opposite door.

Caleb tried to extricate himself from the squished front seat, but the side console kept his seat belt from unlatching. "Ivy!"

The man wrapped his hand around Ivy's ankle. She flailed, but he dragged her from the vehicle.

Juliette fumbled with the crushed center console. "It's jammed, and my gun's in there." She smashed the compartment with her fist. "Come on. Open!"

Caleb wrestled with the seat belt. "Stop!" Caleb's scream was muted by police sirens screeching toward the scene. But they wouldn't arrive in time.

The man wrapped his arms around Ivy with her feet dangling in the air. One last sob escaped her before he injected her in the neck with a needle. She fell limp in his arms. Then they disappeared.

"They're too late." With a grunt, Caleb finally untangled himself from the seat belt. "She's gone. They took her."

Tires squealed. Burnt rubber clung to his nostrils, sending his gag reflex into overdrive. The bad guys, with Ivy, backed up their truck and sped off. But not before he memorized the make and model of the truck along with the license plate number.

Juliette beat the console, and Caleb echoed the sentiment. He wanted to put his fist through the windshield. "What are we going to do?" he whispered.

Tears rimmed Juliette's eyes.

He'd lost Ivy.

"I think I can get out," Caleb said. He rotated in his seat. He tried the door, and though it stuck for a moment, with a shove of his foot, it swung open. When his feet hit the pavement, he turned to help Juliette shimmy under the steering wheel, over the crushed console, and out the passenger side door.

The second her feet hit the ground, Juliette morphed into

soldier mode. "I'm calling Agent McGregor." She pulled out her phone, and Caleb marched toward the nearest police car.

"CXD8302. Silver Dodge Ram 1500 with a quad cab, 2018 or 2019 model. Right front bumper will be smashed in. Dark tinted window."

The officer had just stepped out of his vehicle. "What? Slow down."

Caleb was about to lose it. "I need you to put out an alert for the truck that sped off with my niece."

The officer had Caleb repeat the information as he took notes.

Juliette put a hand on Caleb's arm. "Agent McGregor is on his way."

"I'm going to go call this in and will be back to get your statements," the officer said, and walked away with his radio to his mouth, relaying Caleb's description of the vehicle.

Juliette spotted one of the FBI agents and took off. Caleb passed her and got in the man's face. "What happened?"

"We were hit by a truck. Same as you. I had to crawl through the back window, just as the truck fled the scene." The man's face reddened. "Sorry, but we were trapped. And my partner was injured in the crash." Caleb wanted to pummel him, but it wasn't this guy's fault.

It was his. Why had he agreed to this plan? The hackers had cut them off before they'd even gotten a chance to implement their plan.

Smoke poured out of the engine of the FBI agent's crumpled car, which had fared far worse than their own.

"This was the plan all along," Juliette said. "They wanted to kidnap Ivy." She wretched like she was going to lose her lunch.

"Are you sure you're good?" Caleb asked. Her face was pale, but she didn't have any visible cuts or bruises on her.

But she'd be beating herself up for losing Ivy. They both would.

"I failed. I didn't see it."

"Stop, Jules. Just stop. It's not all on you."

"We have to get her back."

A car raced up to them, and Agent McGregor was out the door before the car slowed to a complete stop. Other police vehicles and an ambulance pulled up to the scene right behind him.

"Are you two hurt?" The man's concern morphed into terror, probably because Ivy wasn't with them. He ran a hand across his mouth. "They took her?"

Juliette nodded. The veins in Agent McGregor's forehead throbbed like they were about to burst. "I stopped on the side of the road to wait for you, and one of the trucks drove by and shot my tire out."

Agent McGregor put his hands on Caleb's shoulders. "We will get Ivy back. I'll have every agent in the department working round the clock to find her. I'm calling everyone—"

The man's words hissed louder in his ears than the sizzle of the agent's crumpled radiator. Caleb shook out of the man's grip. "I don't want to hear all your plans. Just get out there and find her."

But Caleb had no confidence this man would find Ivy. Juliette relayed her version of the attack while Caleb's mind spun an intricate plan that would flush these men out of hiding. He had the skills to track them online. And if he could make himself useful to the hacker group, he would trade himself for Ivy. He'd join them if it meant Ivy could walk away from this. Of course, by *join* he meant he'd exact his vengeance from the inside and take them down.

But he wasn't going to involve the FBI. Or Juliette. He wouldn't ruin Juliette's career or reputation if things went bad. Now to find a laptop. Maybe he could salvage one from Juliette's wrecked car.

Juliette called Alana, and Caleb heard her discuss plans to get them back to the Elite Guardians office.

The second she disconnected the call, he pounced. "I need to go back to my place. I have all the equipment I need to track these hackers. I'll make more progress than these guys." Police taped off the area. Agent McGregor stood off to the side, talking with other agents. Probably planning some other lame attempt to find Ivy.

No, he was Ivy's best shot. "We need to get a car. Can Alana pick us up?"

Juliette hit the mute button on her phone. "We should head to the office to regroup. I'll get you whatever you need to track Ivy, but we've got to get out of the open, and your apartment isn't safe."

A different FBI agent approached, his FBI blazer flapping in the breeze. "We need you to give a statement."

Caleb counted to three, because otherwise he'd punch the man. "We just talked with Agent McGregor. And you should be out there hunting these terrorists and tracking down Ivy, not rehashing every detail we've told the previous agent." He clenched his fists in his pockets to keep his hands busy, because everything within him needed to be at a keyboard, searching for Ivy.

Alana picked them up after what seemed like an eternity and drove them to the Elite Guardians office. Caleb stewed. He didn't relish being social on a good day, and he sat in the back seat, his mind conjuring up worst-case scenarios.

"Once Ivy gives these men what they want, she's expendable," Caleb said. "She could fix their malware, and they could launch it against the bank. I've already sent out messages to the bank alerting them to not open anything suspicious, and Blake is locking their system down. We might need to take all systems offline. But all it would take is for Rushmore to have someone on the inside of the bank to open the ransomware on a bank computer."

"What can we do to help?" Juliette asked.

"I need to call Blake, but I don't want to think about work right now. I just need to get online and see if I can find a clue to where these hackers took Ivy. If they think she can help their cause, they may force her to work on their program. Maybe she'll be online. We have to find her."

At the Elite Guardians office, they offered Caleb an empty office and a computer.

Caleb sat in the swivel chair and stared at the blank screen.

Then he sucked in a deep breath and booted up the laptop. Within a minute, he'd sent a public message to the hackers with an easy code for them to break—and an offer they couldn't resist.

He'd offered himself in exchange for Ivy.

———

FRIDAY, 4 P.M.

Ivy's head pounded. The stale air made her gag.

She pushed the haze from her mind and tried to focus. The last thing she remembered was a man in a ski mask grabbing her from Juliette's car. Whatever had been in that needle had knocked her out—for how long? The drugs must still be in her system a little, because even the slightest move made her want to vomit.

Rough carpet scratched her cheek. She reached to feel the fibers, but her hands were tied behind her.

Where was she? The room was pitch black, and she couldn't see a thing.

Ivy stretched her legs and hit what appeared to be a chair.

She sucked back a sob, but tears leaked down her face, wetting the carpet. How would Uncle Caleb and Juliette find her?

And what was in store for her?

A door opened, and light blinded her.

"Morning, sunshine."

She squinted and tried to focus on any identifying features of the man, but he was covered head to toe in black, including the dumb ski mask.

Wasn't it a good sign that he didn't show his face? On TV, that meant they might let the person go. So maybe this was a good sign. But the light glinted off the knife in the man's hands, and Ivy shuddered.

She had to convince these hackers that she was on their side. Just like the school play she was in during second grade. If they believed that she could help them, they wouldn't kill her. Right?

"What...what do you want?" Her throat burned, and the words came out all gravelly. Her eyes adjusted to the light, and she saw a desk with a computer and several monitors. The room had no windows and only the one door that the man had shut behind him.

He picked her up and dropped her in the chair. He used the knife to slice whatever was around her wrists. She wanted to rub them but was afraid to move.

Her hair hung in her eyes, the strands trembling right along with the rest of her body. The man spun the office chair around and wheeled her into position in front of the three monitors. The wooden desk was bare except for the computer equipment.

The guy bumped the mouse, and the monitors sparked to life. She recognized it instantly—the malware program. Designed to freeze all of the bank accounts and let the hackers take control of the bank.

"We know you can finish the coding." The man's voice was deep, as if he was trying to disguise it. It sounded vaguely familiar, but even with her eidetic memory, voices didn't always stick with her. And she might have never run into this person before.

The man took something out of his pocket. Some sort of remote control. He clicked it and a clock on the wall lit up. 60:00.

"You have one hour and no internet access. Don't try anything. We will know. If you don't finish in the hour, we will kill your uncle and then you."

"I can't finish this in an hour. It will take me days—"

The man turned and left the room. Ivy heard the lock click, and she let out a deep breath. She would rather be alone than with a masked knife-wielding stranger, but how was she supposed to concentrate on coding with Uncle Caleb's and her lives on the line?

Her fingers shook over the keyboard. Bile rose in her throat. If she complied, would it actually keep her uncle safe? These men couldn't be trusted. The clock flickered and changed to 59:00.

She'd better get started. Maybe she could make them think she'd completed the program but keep a flaw in it so they couldn't do any damage with the program. Or better yet, she could sabotage the malware to attack the hackers' system.

Ivy poked around in the computer, well aware of the camera with the blinking red dot above her shoulder. They'd know in a second if she got online. But if she could...

"Ah, man." The bad guys had jammed all signals. There wasn't a thing she could do about getting online. Where were they keeping her?

A beeping sound came from outside her door. It sounded like a truck.

The only source of light came from the monitors and the countdown clock. Ivy turned away from the screen and blinked a few times. Better. Now she could make out the layout of her prison. A bed was shoved up against the back wall, across from the door. Besides the desk, there wasn't any other furniture.

But sounds were definitely coming from outside her prison. She spotted an air vent at the top of the wall, above the bed.

She pulled up the program the men wanted her to work on and started making some keystrokes, in case they were monitoring her activity. But the air vent might be her ticket out of here.

Voices filtered through the room. She strained to listen. The vent must lead to a hallway or another room. She stood and acted like she was stretching. If she got on the bed, she'd be under the camera pointing at the desk. Maybe she could hear something useful that might help her get out.

She stood on the bed, under the vent, and waited.

Two people. A man and a woman were having a conversation on the other side of the wall. How long would it take for them to notice that she wasn't at the desk working?

The man's voice rumbled. "He'll come. He'll do anything to rescue his precious niece."

The woman responded. "We'll draw him out. Set a trap with Ivy as bait."

No. No. No. Uncle Caleb would come to her rescue. She needed to warn him. But without any connection to the outside world, how could she get him a message?

The camera moved, and she sat down on the bed and forced herself to cry. It wasn't too hard. All she had to do was think of Uncle Caleb, devastated by showing up somewhere only to find that Ivy wasn't there.

And then the bad guys would kill him.

She swiped at her face as the camera panned over her. Time to get back to work.

She sat back at the desk and started typing. The door was flung open, and a different masked man returned.

Not a man.

A woman. She was smaller, and Ivy smelled perfume.

She stopped typing. "I need more time. I can't finish in an hour—"

The slap came hard and fast. Ivy grabbed the chair to keep from falling over. Her cheek was on fire, and tears fell from her watery eyes.

"You now have thirty minutes to complete this task. No more stalling."

Ivy held a hand to her cheek and stared at her abductor.

But the woman had made a mistake. Ivy could see out the open door. And she caught a glimpse of where they were keeping her.

She had to send a message to her uncle. He needed to know that Rushmore had set some kind of trap for him. The only way she could get a message to the outside world, someplace her uncle would find it, would be to launch their program. Uncle Caleb had taught her a special code when she was younger. If she could add a hidden message to the program, the bad guys might not understand it. Hadn't they lost their programmer?

It was worth a shot, but it meant the bad guys got what they wanted. But they might kill Uncle Caleb if she didn't finish the program. So either way, she had to work for them.

But how long until Uncle Caleb and Juliette found her?

Because the clock on the wall now showed thirty minutes.

SIXTEEN

Juliette knew in the depths of her soul how Caleb intended to flush out these hackers from their hiding spot.

Because it was exactly what she'd do if given the opportunity to sacrifice herself to bring Ivy home.

She stood outside the office door in the hallway, hearing the click-click-click of Caleb's keyboard. All she wanted to do was ease Caleb's pain, promise him that they'd get Ivy back.

But she'd already failed him. Again.

Her hands throbbed from the tight fists clenched at her sides. How could she face Caleb, knowing her mistakes had cost him everything? Because she should never have agreed to let Ivy work for the FBI. Why hadn't she taken the girl and Caleb and run?

Part of her just wanted this to be over so they could try being…together. He made her feel whole, secure.

Loved.

But even if they had run, Caleb's program would have drawn

him back. This wouldn't be finished until the bad guys were behind bars.

But she was the reason Ivy was missing. Without knocking, she pushed the door open. "I'm not letting you sacrifice yourself to get Ivy back. We're in this together."

His face paled. "What makes you think I'd do that?"

She couldn't stop the eye roll. "I know you. It's the most logical choice. Give the bad guys what they want, which is the ability to take down the bank's systems. And you're the perfect guy for the job. They've tried to get rid of you, their competition. But if they saw you as an asset, they might trade Ivy."

He turned the laptop screen. "I've already sent the message."

Her anger toward herself refocused on a new target. "What's the plan, Caleb? Just waltz in and they'll give up Ivy? They'll use you both. And you've already said, what happens when Ivy becomes expendable? You are not doing this without me."

Her voice growled the last two words. She put her hands on the side of the desk and stared Caleb down. He shifted in his seat, refusing to meet her eyes.

"If anything goes bad, I need you here to be there for Ivy. Make sure she gets to her grandparents if anything happens to me. I have to do this alone." He kept his eyes glued to the desk and fidgeted with his hands.

She crouched across from him, getting into his field of vision. "This is too big of a risk, Caleb. You of all people should know this. Ivy needs you. Alive."

He slapped the desk with his palm. "She needs me to find her."

"Then let me help."

They stared at each other until Caleb nodded. The ding of the computer sent Caleb spinning in his chair, his attention returning to the laptop. Juliette stood and moved to read over his shoulder.

"It's Rushmore," Caleb said. "They want to meet. In one hour."

"I'll let Agent McGregor know." Juliette pulled her phone from her pocket.

"They said no police or they'll kill Ivy." He turned the laptop toward her.

Meet us at this address. Thirty minutes. Tell no one. If we think the police are following, we will kill Ivy. We'll consider a trade. Ivy for you.

A picture followed the message. Ivy's emerald-green eyes stared blankly into what looked like a computer camera, her face streaked with tears. Juliette sucked in a breath.

A countdown clock showed the time ticking down. They now had twenty-nine minutes to get to Ivy.

"We can't go in alone, Caleb. This could be a trap." She headed for the door to find Alana and Noelle. Maybe they could help Caleb see reason.

Caleb grabbed her arm and spun her around. "We've got to go now. The address they sent is a marina about twenty minutes from here. There's no time. Either you're in or out."

Juliette shook out of his grip and faced him with her hands on her hips. "We need to call the FBI—or at least Matt. Let them handle it. They'll be able to be discreet. We can't do this alone."

In a complete role reversal, Juliette was telling him to play it safe. But her heart thumped with every second that ticked by. They couldn't waste time arguing.

He shook his head. "No. We need to surprise them, not swoop in with sirens and a SWAT team. These men will kill her if they get backed into a corner. I'm not taking any chances of spooking them."

"Caleb, some risks aren't worth taking. I know you love Ivy, but think this through. They aren't playing by the rules. They will kill you both."

"You know what?" Caleb grabbed his laptop and stuffed it into a backpack. "I'm going. Can we take Alana's car?" He marched out the door, presumably to find Alana. Juliette's car was still at the crime scene, so they needed a new ride.

"Fine." Juliette huffed her displeasure at their lack of a plan. What had happened to her logical Caleb? "You need to channel your inner Spock and think things through logically. But we can take my grandmother's car. I haven't sold it yet."

He nodded and Juliette led him down the hallway, out the back door, and toward the parking lot behind the house. "For the record, I don't like this idea. It's not like you to go rogue. But as your bodyguard, I go where you go. Let me get Alana and Noelle and let them know what's up."

"You used to run into danger all the time when the situation called for it," Caleb said. "What happened to Hazard Pay Montgomery? I need her to show up and fight hard."

She shot him a glare to send the message that he'd pushed her too far, but he ignored her silent clue and kept on talking. "I'm just saying that now is the time to take risks. I can't wait around for something to happen. We need to get Ivy back."

"Stop." She turned and put her hand on his chest. "I said I'm in, even though I don't agree. At least let me tell Alana and Noelle in case things go south."

"Text them from the car."

She relented and handed him the keys. She fired off a quick text to Alana and Noelle.

If ever she'd needed her teammates, it was now. Because how was she going to rein in her client if he recklessly walked into the bad guys' trap and surrendered?

———

FRIDAY 5 P.M.

Nothing was stopping Caleb from getting to Ivy. He'd risk everything, including his own life, to get to her.

He stopped short at Juliette's car, or rather, her grandmother's ancient Lincoln Town Car. The vehicle looked like it hadn't been driven since 1993, and when he cranked the engine, the car chugged.

"She didn't drive it a lot," Juliette said while she hammered out text messages. He hit the gas, and the car lurched into reverse. Dust blew out of the air-conditioning vents, and he coughed.

He needed to apologize to her. But he wasn't backing down on his decision to leave without backup. These hackers played by their own rules, and he could speak their language.

"Jules, I'm sorry I snapped at you. But you understand my position. I can't do anything that will put Ivy in jeopardy. If they said no cops and we cross that line..."

"Right," she huffed. "You'd rather put yourself in danger instead."

"I'm barely hanging on to my life, Jules. My company might go under. Ivy's grandparents might take her away. She's all I have left."

A voice in the recesses of his mind chided him. Ivy wasn't the only one he loved.

He loved Juliette. He just couldn't say it. Because once those three words were put out into the atmosphere, he couldn't take them back.

Everyone he'd ever loved had left him, whether by death or by choice. And she'd already left him once. Love just wasn't worth the risk.

He took a deep breath and debated running a red light. At the last second, he slowed. No sense in getting into a car accident before they arrived at the marina.

His smartwatch chimed a fifteen-minute warning.

"I texted Matt and Decia the location," Juliette said. "Alana and Noelle are going to head here in their own cars, so they'll blend in and not look like the police. But Matt could help."

Caleb swallowed hard. "They'll kill her if we make one wrong move. I'm not even sure you should be here. They said for me to come alone." He refused to trade Ivy's life for Juliette's. He needed to protect them both.

Like she'd said, he always played it safe. But not now. Not with Ivy's life on the line.

"I need you to hang back, Juliette. Let me go in. You have to watch my back and wait for backup once they release Ivy."

"This is a bad idea. You're assuming they'll release Ivy. They aren't going to give up that easily."

They rode in silence, with Caleb's foot heavy on the gas the whole trip. They approached the entrance to the marina. Caleb pulled onto the side of the road and cut the lights. "I have to do everything within my power to get her back." He stared out the windshield at the docks leading to the parked boats and million-dollar yachts.

Juliette put her hand on his shoulder. "Stop shutting me out. We've always been a team. I'll hang back and look for trouble."

He stared into her eyes, and longing hit him like a freight train. His mind muddled and he needed to get out of the car before he had a chance to do something stupid.

Like kiss her again.

Juliette jumped out of the old Lincoln, breaking the spell between them. She'd go in on foot to remain undetected. Meanwhile, Caleb drove into the marina and parked in the lot in front of the docks.

The place had three docks that had boat slips on the right and left, with probably fifteen boats on each side. He picked the center aisle and started walking. The crisp fall air gave him chills, but the coldness revived his senses. He surveyed the area, committing everything to memory. From every boat name to the number of yachts parked in the marina, he'd remember every detail.

The dock extended out into the Intracoastal Waterway. He checked each boat, searching for signs of life or clues that it might belong to a hacker. People had the strangest names for boats. A forty-five-foot yacht heralded the name *Nacho Boat* across its stern. Another one read *Sea-Sick*. He needed a break, some name to jump out at him as a possible location for Ivy. Or maybe just a big neon arrow falling from the sky, pinpointing Ivy's exact location. Was that too much to ask for?

He glanced behind him and didn't see Juliette, but he could feel her eyes watching his every move. In front of him, boats rocked back and forth in the waves, but none of them had any signs of life. Was Ivy on one of these boats?

Part of his logical brain knew that this whole thing might be nothing more than an elaborate trap. But he had to believe that if he gave the hackers a trade they couldn't refuse, they'd free Ivy. Now he regretted not waiting for backup to arrive. Why had he allowed emotion to win out over sound logic? This wasn't like him.

Had he made things worse for himself by rushing into danger? Even Hazard Pay Montgomery wouldn't take this risk, which should say something about his decision. But if there was one thing Caleb understood, it was the world of hacking. And these men wouldn't pass up an opportunity to have the chief architect of the security software in their clutches.

A bang sounded from one of the boats at the end of the dock. He raced down the wooden planks to the last boat slip and stopped short.

The yacht had *The Rushmore* painted across the stern in thick red spray-painted letters.

This was the place. "I'm here," he called out. "Show yourselves."

The dock rocked under the swell of the waves. He sensed

someone watching him, and not in a good way, like Juliette patrolling the area.

A scream pierced the twilight sky. "Uncle Caleb! Help!"

Ivy! His niece's voice ripped a hole through his heart. The sound had come from below deck on the yacht.

"I'm coming, Ivy!"

He rushed toward a ladder on the side of *The Rushmore*.

Heat and a blinding light knocked him backwards, and he stumbled to right himself. But the force of the blast had thrown him to the other side of the deck. He grabbed the rope guardrail to keep from plunging into the water.

The Rushmore erupted into a giant fireball. The wood deck beneath his feet rumbled, and the fire spread to the neighboring boats. He grasped the rope, but fire began to consume the dock plank by plank until he had no choice but to let go.

A thousand sharp needles of cold water pricked his body at once. His choices were to suffocate above the surface from the smoke and flames, or swim away and pray he didn't drown.

He allowed himself to sink into the water, one thought racing through his mind.

Ivy.

SEVENTEEN

The dock dissolved into the churning water, and Caleb was gone.

And so was Ivy.

Juliette clung to the rail and steadied herself on the rocking remnants of the pier. Alana and Noelle rushed in behind her, flanking her on either side to hold her up. They half dragged, half carried her to the concrete sidewalk, otherwise she might have dived in after Caleb.

They let her go when her feet hit the solid ground, and Juliette paced, searching the waters for any signs of life. "No! I don't see Caleb. And I heard Ivy call out. She was on the boat. She's gone. It's all my fault. I should never have let him come. I knew it was a trap."

Sirens wailed in the distance. Why hadn't she insisted on calling the police sooner? Maybe they would have arrived in time.

Juliette stared at the burning hull of the yacht. There were six other boats between them and the explosion, but Juliette

205

could feel the heat searing her skin. The fire spread, and black smoke poured into the sky.

"He's out there." Juliette grabbed a flashlight from Alana and searched the murky water. "Caleb's an excellent swimmer. We've got to find him."

Alana, Noelle, and Juliette took different sides of the dock, checking the debris in the water in hopes of spotting Caleb. The boat had been obliterated. Pieces of fiberglass and contents from not only *The Rushmore* but the other two parked boats on either side of it were floating through the marina.

Noelle passed Juliette a pair of binoculars so she could scan the area. "Please, Caleb. Be alive."

How could she claim to be a bodyguard? She'd just watched both of her clients blow up in front of her eyes.

"I can't believe I failed so spectacularly," she muttered as she scanned the area. "I've lost them both." Tears pricked her eyes, and she sucked in a breath. Until they pulled Caleb's body from the depths of the ocean, he was alive.

Alana nudged her. "Check that buoy out about a hundred feet. The one to the west." She pointed and Juliette focused the binoculars on the floating orange beacon that marked the edge of the marina.

She saw movement. Just the slightest blur of bright blue.

Juliette exhaled. "It's Caleb. He's on the buoy. I can see his shirt. He just pulled himself to safety."

She watched to make sure he was breathing. Caleb had hoisted himself onto the buoy and collapsed. The device barely held him, and with his added weight, the beacon listed to one side. Juliette watched his chest rise and fall, making sure he wasn't injured. Through the binoculars, he appeared to be in one piece.

But she knew his heart had been ripped to shreds.

"He's okay," she told Alana and Noelle. "He's going to lose his mind over Ivy."

She was thinking about searching the waters with the binoculars for any other signs of life when Noelle put a hand on Juliette's shoulder. "If this was a trap, maybe they had a recording of Ivy so that we'd think she's dead. After all, it looks like they want to keep her alive to complete their program. They've tried to take out Caleb numerous times."

Noelle's words lingered in Juliette's mind, and she chose to have faith that they were true. These men were cowards and most likely ran at the first sign of trouble.

Which meant they still had a fighting chance to save Ivy.

Noelle called the Coast Guard to report Caleb's position and to have them put out a BOLO for Ivy. With revived energy, Juliette now had a mission.

Ivy hadn't been on the boat. This had to be a ruse. They could still save her.

A few minutes later, a US Coast Guard cutter dashed across the horizon, zeroing in on the red beacon. Juliette refused to put down the binoculars until Caleb was safe on board the vessel.

Once Caleb stepped onto the Coast Guard ship, the three headed back to the parking lot to wait. Matt and Decia raced up to Juliette, extreme displeasure carved all over Matt's red face. Agent McGregor was ten seconds behind the officers, and Juliette could almost see steam rising from the man.

"What were you two thinking?" Matt asked, jumping in before McGregor had a chance to yell at her. "Why would you come here without backup? Both of you have military training, and you didn't wait for us? They could have killed you both."

"I know." Juliette closed her eyes and took a deep breath to ground herself. She should have stood up to Caleb, but she'd never seen him so determined. Part of her knew that if she hadn't tried to find Ivy at the marina and something bad had happened, Caleb would have blamed her.

But now her worst nightmare had become a reality. She

heaped more blame on herself. Because what if Ivy *had* been on the boat?

She refused to let her mind go there. She had to be somewhere else.

How was Caleb going to forgive her? He'd told her repeatedly that Ivy came first, and she'd let him down. Let herself down. She always protected those she loved, and she now might lose both Ivy and Caleb.

Because if Ivy were truly dead, Caleb wouldn't open up his heart to anyone ever again.

The Coast Guard vessel docked, and Caleb was met by paramedics. She watched them cater to a listless and soaking-wet Caleb. The man shook from the cold and the sorrow. She wanted to rush to his side, but what was the use?

She'd failed to protect the one person that mattered most to Caleb.

A drop of rain ran down the side of her cheek, mimicking a tear. Storm clouds rumbled over the ocean and matched the war of emotions brewing inside Juliette. She superglued her heart shut and headed toward Caleb.

He sat on the back of the ambulance bay, a tangible heaviness seeping from every inch of his body. His T-shirt clung to his frame, his hair dark and spiky from the water. But his eyes told Juliette that he'd checked out mentally and withdrawn into himself, a place she wasn't welcome.

He caught her staring at him. She walked over and sat next to him. She covered his icy hand with hers and he didn't move.

"I'm so sorry, Caleb."

"Don't" was all he said, and he moved his hand away from hers. He sucked in a breath. "I can't. You were supposed to protect Ivy. And now she's gone."

"We don't know that she was on that boat, Caleb."

He turned and stared at her with glassy eyes. "I know. And I'm holding out hope that she wasn't. Maybe it's all some elaborate trick. But it sounded real. This is why it won't work between us, Jules. Love hurts. What if I lose you too? I can't lose everyone I love."

He loved her.

And she'd let him down. Just like she had the last time she'd walked away.

Yet here she was, standing and walking away again when he needed her most. Because this time, it wasn't rain streaking her cheeks.

The tears were real.

———

FRIDAY, 10:15 P.M.

Oh, Jules.

He watched her walk away. Why had he said those hateful words? Logic dictated that it wasn't her fault, but the pain scorching his heart scrambled his mind, and he was finding it hard to pull his thoughts together.

His brain had created multiple rational reasons why he and Juliette weren't meant to be together, but he never should have lashed out like that. She'd come to her senses and realize that they were destined to be friends. Nothing else.

Her pale face and the dark circles under her eyes showed that grief had wrapped its clutches around her, too.

More fire engines rushed to the scene, and fluorescent lights were set up around the area so the police could comb for evidence. He sat on the back of the ambulance bay, wrapped in towels. Even though temperatures weren't freezing, his plunge into the water had chilled him to the bone. At least his toes and fingers were tingling, a good sign that he didn't have frostbite.

Alana walked up to the ambulance and slid down next to him on the edge of the bay. Several firefighters raced by with hoses. The shell of *The Rushmore* still smoldered, sending black smoke into the air.

"The FBI wants to question you, but I told them I wanted to take a stab first."

"I just lost my niece in a fireball. Can you grill me later?"

"No."

Okay then.

Alana continued. "I don't think Ivy was on that boat. You think you're in these hackers' heads, but they're in yours. You walked right into their trap. They see the value in Ivy. Have hope that she's still alive."

Her words softened the calloused edges of his heart. "Thanks, Alana."

"Don't thank me yet. I've watched you and Juliette dance around each other, pretending not to be madly in love with each other like a couple of middle-school kids. *You* need to think with your heart, not your head. And *she* needs to stop letting her emotions get the best of her. You two are made for each other, but you're both stubborn. And you have to take a chance on love. It's worth a thousand risks if you're with the right person."

Caleb gaped at Alana. The woman was a formidable force, but somehow her words made sense in the midst of the chaos all around. Between sirens blaring, officers yelling orders, and the media crews scrambling for the best vantage point, Alana spoke directly to his heart.

He loved Juliette. She was worth the risk.

He gave Alana a sad laugh. "Anything else?"

Alana sprang to her feet as a man in an FBI blazer approached, then she tossed Caleb a wink over her shoulder. "Yeah. Don't hurt my friend, or I'll kill you and make it look like an accident."

He had no doubt Alana meant that.

Caleb answered all of the FBI's questions. His fingers itched, wanting to be at a keyboard, searching for clues to Ivy's whereabouts.

Because until he saw Ivy's body, he would not give up hope. She could be out there. And he was wasting time at the marina when he could be online tracking these hackers and flushing them out into the light of day. He would bring them to justice.

Once the interrogation ended, Caleb found Juliette sitting in her grandmother's car. He slid in the passenger's seat, unable to face her. If he did, he'd melt into a puddle of shame over the way he'd treated her.

"Please don't shut me out," she whispered as she started the car. "That's all I'm asking. I'm all-in on your hunt to bring these men down, and then we can go our separate ways. I can't let these men win. And I believe Ivy's alive."

He sank back in the seat. "I'm not in my right mind. I can't process things correctly right now."

"I understand that. But just know this isn't a no-win situation. There's always a way out." She put the car in gear and drove out of the lot.

He stared out the window as the world whipped by and wished the wind would carry away his grief. He wanted to apologize to Juliette, tell her that he loved her and that everything was going to be okay between them. But silence remained his only response.

At the Elite Guardians office, he sealed himself back in the room he'd been in, searching online for any sign of the hackers. These guys wouldn't give up. They'd be desperate for ways to launch their malware against his security system at the bank.

If they were successful, they could access the bank's systems. Consumers would panic, and the bank could potentially go under. If people couldn't access their accounts, it would be pandemonium. Sure, the FBI was monitoring the situation and would work to prevent any kind of cyberattack.

But this was personal. He'd never been a fan of vigilante justice—until they'd destroyed his life. Now all bets were off.

A new idea worked its way through his mind. What if the way to beat these guys wasn't to think like a hacker but to think like a hacker's enemy? These guys had factions all over the United States. There had to be some people out there that wouldn't mind spilling the dirt on Rushmore.

He got to work, checking the dark web for any evidence these hackers had left behind. If he got lucky, he might find someone with a vengeance against Rushmore that would testify against them. He left a trail of breadcrumbs everywhere he went with a message that he wanted to talk.

Why, God, why?

Why would God allow him to lose Ivy, too? After losing his father and sister. Not to mention his mother abandoning him.

Alana's words echoed across his soul. *"Love is worth a thousand risks if you're with the right person."*

Juliette was his person. She'd always been his soulmate. They were complete opposites that made each other whole.

A ding rang from his laptop. He'd been running a program through his work server to make sure his security software was doing its job. He clicked a few windows open and blinked.

His security program had flagged some suspicious activity in the bank's system.

A knock at the door sent him jumping a foot off his chair.

"Can we talk?" Juliette said as she entered the office.

Caleb shook his head. "I'm working on something. Can we chat later?"

She shot him a look that said she wasn't going to leave. "You still don't get to do this alone. If you've found the hackers, I want in. This time we call the authorities; we do things right. But whatever it is, I'm right by your side, whether you like it or not. Once we find Ivy, if you want to leave, I won't stop you. But know that this time, I'm not walking away from you."

Hands on hips, fire blazed in Juliette's eyes. He matched her stare, and her lips quirked up in a smile at his tenacity. He loved that fire. "I shouldn't have lashed out at you. You've done everything you can to protect both of us. How about neither of us walk away? We'll find her, Jules. Together."

She blinked, taken aback by his confession. But he didn't give her a second to respond as his computer dinged again and he broke eye contact with Juliette. Good thing, because her eyes drew him, and he needed to get his head in the game.

"What in the world…" He gasped. "They're trying to launch the ransomware. The hackers are in the bank's system. Blake is shutting down the system."

Juliette moved to stand behind him and peered over his shoulder. "Ivy finished the program?"

"Someone did. And managed to get it on one of the bank computers before the bank shut their servers down."

He needed proof. Something tangible that pointed to his niece being alive. He poked around in the program and froze. There were some strange strings of text and numbers in the comments of the code.

One of Ivy's breadcrumbs? Had the hackers been in such a hurry to launch the program that they'd missed this? If so, they were getting desperate and sloppy.

He closed his eyes and studied the code, rearranging each of the numbers to unravel the sequence.

He jumped up and threw his arms around Juliette. "She's alive. Ivy is alive."

"How? What?"

He let her go and showed her the screen.

"In the comments, she left a code. I thought back to some of the ciphers she and I used when she was younger and pieced together the words *trap, alive,* and *warehouse.*"

His adrenaline flowed to the point he was dizzy. "You were right all along, Jules. The explosion was a hoax. Now we just need another miracle to bring her back home. Because Ivy is still alive."

EIGHTEEN

Ivy was alive.

Juliette's first instinct was to throw her arms around Caleb's neck and kiss him until sunrise.

Then reality set in. Caleb's lips weren't hers to claim. Back at the marina, he'd made it clear. Despite his confession of being all-in, Caleb's heart would be walled off to her. Forever.

"Do you know where she is?" Juliette asked.

He stared at her with a blank expression, but she could see his thoughts reeling in a thousand directions. He finally nodded but said nothing. Of course he didn't want Juliette to get involved, because in his mind, she was a target. And he wouldn't risk her life.

But when would he learn that sometimes risks paid off? That with great risks came even greater rewards.

Like love.

His words of rejection had stung like a thousand bee stings, but for the sake of Ivy, she wouldn't let Caleb do this alone.

"I'm going with you. And we're doing it my way and involving the police this time," she said, hands on hips.

He nodded. "We'll do it your way." He sat back at the desk and pulled up a map. "Ivy didn't have an exact location, but check this place out. She mentioned hearing trucks and saw a sign about loading docks."

Juliette read over his shoulder. "This place is a warehouse facility that ships goods all over the southeast. We can go stake out the place and see if she's there while we wait for the police."

Caleb stood. "We've got to go. I'll drive. You drive like a grandmother. No wonder you kept the Lincoln Town Car." He snatched the keys from the desk, and before she could protest, he headed out the door.

"I don't drive like a grandmother," she muttered, then chased after him. Had Caleb just made a joke? No, he really must think she drove like an old lady.

She texted Alana and Noelle for backup. They'd both left to get some rest.

He hopped in the driver's seat. "Just so you know," Caleb said as he slid behind the steering wheel and moved the seat back from Juliette's short-person position, "I sent the data to the FBI so their cybersecurity analysts could get to work stopping the program. They have the same information we do."

At least they'd be on the up-and-up this time. She used the speaker on her phone to apprise Matt of the situation so the police could set up a perimeter to catch these guys.

"I'm at the scene of a car accident," Matt said over the phone. "I'll be there as soon as I can. I need to get a warrant, and I'm not sure the judge will approve it without more evidence. But do not approach. Wait for the police." He hung up before they could get a word in.

"They must have convinced Ivy to finish their program," Caleb said. "Her code tried to warn me that the marina was a trap. She probably had no choice but to comply in order to get that message out to me. I just hope we get there in time to stop them from...from..."

"Yeah," Juliette whispered. "I know."

Caleb navigated the Savannah backroads like he'd lived there his whole life. If only he'd talk to her, open up and let her in. But they drove in silence.

When this ordeal ended and Ivy was safe at home, would she and Caleb at least go back to being friends? Or had that ship sunk like an exploded yacht?

He turned onto a road that headed to the warehouse district. A massive building complex spread out over the property with rows of garage doors stretched out for what seemed like a mile. Caleb cut the lights and pulled the car into the wooded area on the side of the street before the entrance to the warehouse. They'd have to stake out the place from here. He pulled off the road as close to the trees as he could for concealment, while still allowing them to watch the activity below the hill leading to the facility.

"We really should wait for the FBI and the police," Juliette said as she texted Matt.

Matt texted back, the three little dots indicating that he was writing a novel.

Getting a search warrant approved. SWAT team is assembling but Decia and I are stuck at the scene of a five car pile-up. Waiting for backup and we'll head your way. ETA fifteen minutes. FBI is also on the way, but it takes time to mobilize. Do not do anything stupid. This means you, Montgomery.

Caleb shook his head. "The hackers are going to kill her. Ivy's only bargaining chip was the program. Now that they've launched it—verified it's doing what they want—they won't need her and will assume that she can identify most if not all of the hackers."

"I know," Juliette repeated. Ivy was expendable. Her phone buzzed with an incoming text.

"Alana and Noelle are a few minutes behind us. Let's at least wait for them." She'd learned her lesson about teamwork. They needed all the manpower they could get.

Caleb unbuckled his seat belt and shifted to face her. "I meant what I said earlier. I'm not leaving you, Jules. Not now or in the future. I can't imagine my life without you in it. I'm so sorry I hurt you with my words. The truth is, I love you. I think I always have. You're worth all of the risks in the world, whether we're together on this planet for an hour or the rest of our lives."

"I love you too, Caleb. I just didn't realize it all those years ago. But we can make up for lost time, right?"

"How about right now?"

The fake leather seat squeaked as he leaned over the center console of the aging Town Car. She mirrored his movements. Her hand entwined with his. His eyes burned with an intensity she'd never seen. The car smelled like her grandmother's perfume mixed with ten years of dust. Their view out the windshield overlooked a warehouse dumpster.

But this moment was as perfect as it could get.

Their lips met over the cracked plastic divider, and her surroundings faded into a blur. Years of longing were satisfied through the taste of his lips. He ran his hand through her hair, drawing her closer to him. She melted against him as he deepened the kiss. Electricity shot from her toes to the tips of her hair.

She didn't have an eidetic memory, but every detail of this moment would remain etched in her memory forever. From the contours of his face to the way his stubble tickled her neck when he kissed it.

She wanted to live in this moment forever. Until a knock on her window nearly sent her through the roof.

Noelle and Alana stood outside the car. She hit the unlock button, and the two jumped into the back seat.

"To be continued," Caleb whispered, still holding her hand.

"Sorry for the bad timing." Alana racked her nine-millimeter Ruger. "But we've got some bad guys to take down."

"Caleb and I were just talking about how we don't have time to wait for backup."

"Yes, we could see you were talking," Noelle chimed in while Alana racked a second gun.

Time to get her head out of the clouds and focus on the mission ahead of them.

"We know they will kill Ivy now that they have what they want." Juliette glanced in the back seat, glad to have friends and coworkers like these two. Always ready to cover her no matter what.

Caleb scrolled on his phone. "I have a map of the interior of the warehouse. This place is a massive online store. Almost seven hundred thousand square feet of space. It'll take us forever to search."

"What if two of us take the front and two of us take the back and start searching?" Juliette eyed her crew. "That way when the police come, we can hopefully have a place to send them. Then we're not sitting around waiting."

They all agreed. Caleb and Alana would search the back, and Juliette and Noelle would head to the front.

Juliette and Noelle crept toward the loading docks. Some of the two-story garage doors had trucks sticking out of them, and others were closed tight. She counted thirty trucks before darkness obstructed her vision, despite the blinding white security lights strategically placed every fifty feet.

Every fifth or sixth loading bay, they'd spot a solid door granting access to the warehouse. Of course, each door had a keypad with a glowing red light.

Noelle nodded at one of the doors—it had a window at the top. She cupped her hands together to boost Juliette up. Too bad Juliette hadn't been a cheerleader in high school, because she wobbled a bit and clutched the minuscule ledge of the window for stability.

She wanted to scream at her disappointment. All she saw were boxes and crates ready to ship. Nothing they could use. Just as she was about to hop down, a light flickered inside.

Juliette watched. Another flicker, but this time someone walked by a door, dead-center inside the warehouse.

Noelle's arms started to shake, so Juliette jumped down. "I see movement inside."

Click. "Should have spotted the movement outside." A man emerged from the shadow of the building with a gun pointed at Noelle's head.

Juliette couldn't make out the man's face in the darkness, but the voice sounded familiar.

The man kept to the shadows, but the gun never wavered. "Well, it's your lucky day. The General thinks you might be useful to us alive. Hostages might make good bargaining chips for our final escape."

The General? Who was this guy taking orders from? Juliette heard footsteps approaching from behind her, but by the time she could turn around, someone had jabbed a needle in her neck. Ten seconds later, her legs gave out and she crumpled to the ground.

———

SATURDAY, 2:30 A.M.

This had *bad idea* written all over it.

Caleb and Alana crept around the back of the property. The giant warehouse complex stretched out as far as they could see. Rows of garages lined the back wall of the building where trucks pulled in to load or unload.

"The police will be here soon," Caleb whispered to Alana. "Maybe we split up to cover more ground."

Alana nodded her consent and rattled off her phone number. Caleb quickly added her to his contacts. "Text me if you find anything," she said. "Don't go in alone. I know you're an Army man, but you wait for me." She stared him down until he nodded.

"I agree we wait for the police before going in." He wanted to be able to give the police *something* useful to get to these hackers before they killed Ivy.

He pushed out all the worst-case scenarios from his head. Ivy was alive. Every fiber in his body believed this.

After a minute, he lost sight of Alana, who had sprinted to the opposite side of the complex. He checked doors and windows and found nothing. But as he headed up the ramp to one of the closed garage doors, he heard something.

Voices.

Caleb froze. Where were the police? Why was it taking them so long to get the SWAT team in place? He scanned the area. A field with a retention pond lay at the back of the warehouses. Could the police be lining up behind the fence on the other side of the pond?

There were no windows on this side of the warehouse except for at the top of the building. He spotted some small rectangular windows overlooking the interior. If he climbed onto the roof of the parked eighteen-wheeler, he could pull himself up to the window ledge.

Worth a shot. He texted Alana that he'd heard signs of life coming from warehouse number twenty's loading dock. Without waiting for a response, he hopped over the railing of the ramp and climbed to the top of the truck. Light flickered from the window above, and Caleb's adrenaline pulsed. He reached up and grabbed the ledge. If he made it out of this alive, he vowed to hit the gym more often, because hoisting himself up to the ledge was basically the equivalent of a pull-up. And he hadn't done pull-ups since basic training.

He sucked in a breath and planted his feet on the wall, hoping for some leverage to propel him up. His arms shook, but once his forearms crossed the threshold, he grasped the wrought-iron bars covering the panes of glass. He swung his leg up and over the ledge. His breath came in gasps. The ledge was probably a foot deep and three feet wide, giving him just enough room to stand and take in the expansive warehouse floor below. The place was filled with rows of metal storage racks that held a variety of packaged goods ready to be shipped out. Caleb's perch provided a view over the tops of the shelves.

Where was Alana? He checked his phone and realized the message hadn't gone through. Evidence that he was in the right place, since the hackers liked to jam all signals in or out so they could control communication. This had to be where they were keeping Ivy hostage.

In the middle of the warehouse, there was a walled-off section that looked like offices. A man opened a door at the far left end, and Caleb caught sight of the room filled with monitors and computer equipment.

Jackpot. This was Rushmore's lair. In the middle of a bustling warehouse, they had carved out space to run their operations.

Hiding in plain sight.

Toward the right side of the office area, a different man carried a person over his shoulder. He knocked on a door. It swung open, and Caleb nearly fell off his ledge.

Ivy was strapped to a chair. She turned at the man's entrance and gaped when the person dropped the bundle he was carrying.

Juliette's limp body hit the floor.

Where were the police? Noelle and Alana had called for backup before they'd arrived, so the message should have gotten out.

A second man carried something into the room. Or make

that a woman, but from his distance it was hard to tell. Whoever it was, the person struggled with the weight of the load.

He saw a flash of long blonde hair. "Oh no, no, no."

Noelle!

Movement outside his position caught his attention. Alana popped out from behind the truck.

He jumped down from the ledge and onto the roof of the truck, which made more of a crashing sound than he'd have liked. He scampered down and found Alana.

"What did you find?" Alana whispered.

"They've got Ivy, Juliette, and Noelle in a room with no windows in the middle of the warehouse."

Caleb jumped off the dumpster to the lot below. "I think Juliette and Noelle were knocked out—they were both carried in."

Alana growled and motioned for him to follow. They hiked back to the cars.

"I can't call or text," Alana said. "Detective Williams said he'd send backup as soon as he could, but there was that bad accident taking up their time. I wish I had stressed the urgency of the situation."

Caleb blew out a breath, the cool air sending vapors swirling around his face. Every step toward the cars felt like another minute lost.

"How are we going to get them out?" Caleb asked. "Without knowing whether or not backup is on the way, one of us has to go for help."

Alana shook her head. "I'm not letting you run in there all Jack Bauer–like, trying to single-handedly save the day. But the clock is ticking, and we need to do something."

A knock on the window had him airborne in his seat.

Williams and Slaton hopped in the back.

"Wha-da-we-got?" Matthew asked in one word.

Alana turned to the officers. "Ivy, Juliette, and Noelle are being held in an interior room—Juliette and Noelle are unconscious we think, right?"

Caleb nodded. "Looked like it."

"And we can't get a signal to call for backup. Phones worked earlier but not now. I think they jammed the signals in or out of this area. Did you call the cavalry in yet?"

Officer Slaton hissed. "We were at the accident scene and left to check things out here. We got a judge to sign a search warrant, and when I last communicated with SWAT, they were gearing up. That accident has everyone scrambling."

Caleb took charge. "One of you needs to drive until you find a signal to call the FBI and SWAT and get them here now. The rest of us need to go in. I don't think they have much time. The hackers have what they want, and they know we're here. It's clean-up time for them."

NINETEEN

Voices filtered through her brain, but Juliette couldn't focus.

"What are we going to do? I didn't sign up for murder." The voice was female.

Another voice, male, grumbled. "She's not going to want witnesses. These three are a liability. They know too much."

Three?

They must have Noelle. And Ivy? Juliette opened her eyes a slit and was hit by a wave of dizziness. What had they injected into her?

The female voice sounded familiar, and Juliette struggled to place it. She worked hard to adjust her eyes and found herself in a dark, square room. Across from her, Noelle lay crumpled on the floor. But Juliette saw her move her hand to signal she was alert but playing unconscious.

She tilted her head a fraction of an inch and saw the wooden legs of a chair. Attached to the chair, pink Converse.

Ivy.

225

Juliette took a deep breath to keep the nausea at bay. She could still hear voices, but they were distant, not in the room.

"What's the plan? We've patrolled the area and found two cars just outside the perimeter, but no signs of anyone. But with two cars, there have to be more."

When would the SWAT team arrive? The cars were her grandmother's and Alana's. But where were Caleb and Alana? She sent up a prayer that they'd found help. Two against three unfriendlies wasn't good. Based on voices, they were up against two men and one woman. The door creaked. Juliette didn't lift her head. Maybe they'd think she was still unconscious. Three sets of boots marched through the door. No shoes a woman would wear. So three men and one woman? Where was the woman?

"Time to move them," one of the men said. "We'll load them in a truck and take off."

Ivy struggled against her bonds. The chair scraped the floor. "Leave me alone," she cried.

"Police. You're surrounded. Come out with your hands up." A megaphoned voice echoed through the room.

"You morons!" One of the three men shouted commands. He must be the one in charge. Was he the General?

He continued ranting. "You patrolled but didn't spot the police? Get out there and assess the situation. Now!"

Footsteps retreated from the room. A distinct locking sound sealed them in. After a few moments of silence, Juliette dared to sit up and saw Noelle doing the same. But Juliette had to sink back down until the nausea wore off. She checked out Ivy from her spot on the floor.

The girl's left eye was swollen, but otherwise she looked like a survivor. The fierceness in Ivy's eyes fled when Juliette made eye contact and Ivy realized who it was.

"Juliette!" Tears ran down Ivy's cheek. "Where is Uncle Caleb?"

Noelle started working on Ivy's bindings.

"He's here, and probably trying to save us," Juliette said, attempting to stand again. This time, she was successful, the nausea easing and adrenaline kicking in.

A noise froze them all in place. Someone was unlocking the door.

Juliette and Noelle sprang into action and flanked either side of the door. Whoever was unlocking it took a while, fumbling with the mechanism. Someone who maybe didn't have a key?

She shot Noelle a look and mouthed, *Caleb.*

Noelle shrugged.

The door was flung open, but no one entered. "It's me," Caleb whispered, slipping through the entrance and propping the door open. "Don't take me out."

Juliette held back the urge to fling herself into his arms. Mainly because Ivy beat her to it. The reunion made Juliette tear up, but she sucked back her emotions. Now wasn't the time to get sappy.

"We've got to get out of here," Caleb said with Ivy still wrapped around him. "Our distraction worked, but they'll be back. We only have Alana and Detective Williams as backup. They're creating a distraction by making the hackers think they're surrounded, while Officer Slaton has driven off to get a signal to find out where the SWAT team is."

Juliette took Ivy's hand and pulled her away from Caleb so he could pass a gun to Noelle. Her eyes connected with his, and she remembered their kiss. Things weren't over between them.

This was just the beginning.

Caleb had started to toss a weapon to Juliette when the door crashed open. "Weapons down."

They all froze.

The man's identity registered.

"Theo?" Caleb's eyes widened. Juliette's shock mirrored Caleb's. They'd all been fooled. His employee stood in the doorway with the two armed guards flanking either side of him.

Theo shrugged. "I assumed you'd figured it out already. Since you're uber-smart and all."

"How—how could you?" Caleb stared the man down, his eyes flickering with the fiercest look she'd ever seen on his face. "I trusted you. You staged your own kidnapping? How could you do that to me, not to mention your wife and son?"

He shrugged. "It was the best way to throw off suspicions. Hopefully you suspected Blake. Because who would suspect me faking my own kidnapping?" He laughed.

Noelle made the slightest movement, and one of the armed men approached her to relieve her of her weapon. The other security guard patted Caleb down and then moved and did the same to Juliette.

"What's your end game, Theo?" Caleb's face betrayed his anger. "What are your wife and child going to do when you rot in prison? Did you really think you could rob banks and get away with it?"

Theo cocked his nine millimeter and pointed it in Caleb's face. "Well, thanks to Ivy, we'll get our money—the money the bank president owes my family for ruining my business. They owe my son college tuition and a future. The bank stopped lending us money, and my family has suffered long enough because of their greed." With every sentence, Theo raised his voice more. This was not good.

Rushmore had formed as a vendetta against the bank and their lending policies. Juliette decided to keep the man talking. "So, what is Rushmore going to do with the money if the bank pays your ransom demand?"

Theo shifted his gun from Caleb to Juliette. "You, stop talking. You and your bodyguard friend are nothing but trouble."

Caleb shifted closer to Ivy, who sat on the wooden chair. He stared Theo down and took another step sideways until he was in front of Ivy. "Did you go to work for me with the intention of selling out Cyberskies? You thought you could use my company to further your personal agenda?"

"Blake should have made me his partner. He was going to until you came along. Cyberskies should have been mine."

So it was more personal than the money. Theo thought Caleb had robbed him of a position.

Theo glared at Caleb, whose eyes never left Theo's trigger finger. If they didn't do something soon, this man might snap. Jules instinctively knew exactly what Caleb was planning. She shot him a quick wink of acknowledgement. He'd hit Theo, and Juliette would dive for Ivy and get her out of the crossfire. Noelle blinked twice, agreeing to their wordless plan. She'd be Caleb's backup.

But before they could attack, Theo changed the playing field. "This ends now." Theo nodded and the two security guards moved next to Juliette and Ivy.

"I'll let you decide, Caleb. I'll let you save one of your loves. The other one dies. Who will it be? Ivy or your pretty bodyguard? You can only save one."

————

SATURDAY, 3:00 A.M.

Theo Payne was one sick man.

Caleb willed his body to stop trembling, but adrenaline pulsed through him at a supersonic pace. One of the security guards pressed a gun against Juliette's temple. The other trained his gun on Ivy. And Theo blocked the exit, pointing his gun at Caleb.

Ivy. Juliette.

These two were his entire world. How could he choose? He loved them both.

Flashbacks filled his mind. Laz. Juliette. The mountain.

He fisted his hands to keep them from trembling. Juliette gave an imperceptible nod, as if to say, *I'll save Ivy*. Tears streaked his niece's cheeks and dripped onto her shirt. Noelle hovered in the corner, trying to remain invisible, but her clenched fists were ready for action.

"Please, don't do this." Ivy pleaded with Theo.

Was this an unwinnable situation?

Think, Caleb, think. There had to be a way out of this. Theo couldn't get away with his reign of terror. Noelle inched closer to Theo, trying to stay out of his field of vision.

"Stop with the games, Theo. You're not letting any of us walk away. We all know too much." Caleb turned slightly to catch Juliette's attention. She stood frozen, her eyes darting between the three bad guys with guns. He stood ramrod straight in front of Ivy, making himself look as intimidating as possible, despite his hammering heart playing his rib cage like a xylophone.

Refusing to flinch or back down in the slightest, Caleb stared hard. The Army had prepared him for combat. After assessing his opponent, he knew the man didn't have any combat skills—he wasn't holding the gun correctly—but with Theo's finger hovering over the trigger, if anything set the man off, it would spell disaster.

Theo's nostrils flared, but he said nothing. The man was in his late twenties, maybe approaching thirty. He had his whole life ahead of him. And while his Robin Hood vigilante-style justice was hailed by some, his list of crimes would land him in jail for the rest of his life. Assuming they could get him there.

"How much more are you willing to lose, Theo? Your family, your son? Because murder is a much bigger deal than a bank robbery."

"You don't call the shots. I do." Theo's hands trembled, and his eyes twitched. Was the man on something? "You've been the boss long enough. I've stood in your shadow long enough. It's time to take down two Goliaths with one stone—you and the bank."

This man had targeted Cyberskies to carry out his crimes. Theo was smart, but he hadn't operated alone.

"Theo, the police are surrounding the building as we speak. You need to run if you want to have any chance of escaping."

Caleb flicked his eyes to Noelle on his left and Juliette on his right, neither of whom were moving. Where were Alana and Agent Williams? Agent Slaton should have gotten through to help by now. Hopefully Theo wouldn't call his bluff.

"Choose!" Theo's agitation was just this side of unhinged.

As if Caleb could choose. The reason he'd refused to give his heart to anyone was this very situation. It always ended with someone getting hurt. Or worse—death.

"Police. We have the building surrounded." The sound of the police megaphone was music to Caleb's ears, but he needed to talk this madman off a ledge before he hurt the people Caleb loved.

There was only one answer in Caleb's mind. Juliette's wide eyes meant she could read his thoughts. He took two steps forward, straight into the path of Theo's gun.

"Take me. Let Ivy, Juliette, and Noelle go. It's obvious the issues you have are with me."

"That's not how it works. You do as I say. I'll kill them both—" Theo was cut off by a crackle over his radio. They must have set their communications up to get around the signal jammer. A fact he wished he'd known earlier—he would have tried to steal one of their radios.

A voice came through the speaker. "Rough Rider. Get out of there. Police have entered the building." Sirens wailed in the distance. But what struck Caleb was the distinctly female voice. It resonated with Caleb, like it was someone he knew.

Was the voice on the other end of the radio CyberLane? Could she be the mastermind of this whole operation?

"You know what?" Theo waved the gun around Caleb's face. "On second thought, I will take you. I'm getting out of here. You two." He nodded to the hired guns. "Get rid of the rest of them and then run. Caleb's my bargaining chip out of here."

TWENTY

Why did this man always have to sacrifice himself? Juliette started forward, but the gun pressed against her temple halted her.

Think, think, think!

Caleb stared at Juliette as Theo shuffled him out the door. His eyes communicated love and the promise of a future.

Why did love always look a lot like sacrifice? Last time, she'd left him rather than have her problems bring him down. But now?

This man truly loved her. He was risking his life for her. The logical, risk-averse Caleb had willingly put his life on the line to save her. To rescue her.

God, please let us have more time together.

She wanted the rest of her life to be spent with the man now held at gunpoint.

Theo positioned himself behind Caleb and jabbed his gun in his back before slamming the door shut. "Let's go," was the last thing Juliette heard.

Hopefully Theo would keep Caleb alive as a hostage, but his instruction to the two hired gunmen signaled the end for Juliette, Noelle, and Ivy.

The bad guys were cleaning house and running.

Juliette and Noelle exchanged glances. Neither of them would go down without a fight. But before they could act, an explosion rocked the room. Juliette grabbed the back of Ivy's chair to keep herself on her feet. The ground shook, and thick smoke filled the room.

Someone kicked the door down, and through stinging eyes, Juliette watched Alana burst into the room with a high-powered rifle.

"Freeze," Matt shouted over the commotion. "Guns on the ground. Now!" Three police officers followed him into the room.

The men tossed their weapons down. Officers secured the two men, and Juliette relieved one of the security guards of his radio and clipped it to her belt.

Something pulled on her sweatshirt, and small arms encircled her waist. Juliette enveloped Ivy in a hug.

"Juliette, please find Uncle Caleb. You have to rescue him." The girl now looked all of her twelve years of age. Tears trailed through the dirt covering her smoke-stained cheeks.

"That's the plan, Ivy. I'll get him back. Stay with Noelle and Alana."

She nodded at Noelle, who nodded back. Noelle would guard Ivy until this was over. Juliette needed to find Caleb. Now.

"Matt, Theo Payne took Caleb at gunpoint."

"Go, we've got this," Matt said. "This warehouse is a maze, and I have officers searching every corner of this place. Join the search."

She dashed out the door and stood in the middle of the warehouse. The offices where they were held lined the center of the facility. All around her, rows of metal shelving created long aisles, with a main passageway running through the length of the building.

"This place *is* a maze." Alana walked up behind Juliette and pressed a gun into her hand. "I'll watch over things here."

"Thanks, Alana. I have to find Caleb."

While the police had breached the front of the facility, Juliette headed to the back. Theo would be plotting a way to escape.

She headed down one of the rows that almost looked like a road running down the center of the warehouse. The concrete floor showed wear and tear from forklifts moving packages to be shipped. To the left were rows of merchandise. To the right were the loading docks, some with trucks and some empty. The commotion grew softer the deeper she moved into the warehouse. Maybe she could commandeer a forklift, but where was she going?

How was she going to find Caleb in this labyrinth? There was no way she could check each truck or aisle. In the distance, flashlights flickered up and down from officers on search duty. But time was running out. She swung her gun out in front of her whenever she hit a new aisle.

Nothing.

Theo would need to find some way to get as far away from this place as he could.

She raced down an aisle and stared at the maze of shelving units, boxes, and the occasional parked forklift. They could be anywhere.

The situation was out of her control. She clenched her teeth. "It can't end this way," she whispered. "I love him too much."

Caleb's words rushed back to her. *Sometimes we just need to stand still and let God fight for us.* Instead of ignoring his advice, she embraced it and decided to do the one thing that seemed completely unnatural and illogical to her.

She stood still.

In the middle of a dusty aisle in a mile-long warehouse, she stopped running and set her emotions aside. "Okay, God. I'm standing still. I can't do this on my own. I have to find Caleb. Please protect him and lead me to him."

The radio she'd clipped to her belt crackled. An idea struck like lightning.

Theo had a partner, a woman, who had a radio. She'd heard the voice. Maybe she could trick Theo into revealing his location if Juliette pretended to be his partner.

It was worth a shot. She ducked behind a row of pallets shrink-wrapped to hold multiple boxes. She spotted a box cutter and stuck it in her pocket for future use. It might come in handy.

What was Theo's radio name? If only she had an eidetic memory like Caleb and Ivy. Rough something.

Rough Rider?

It was worth a shot. She crinkled some of the shrink wrap, hoping it sounded like static.

"Rough Rider. What's your twenty?"

Silence.

She waited, hoping the other woman didn't respond and bust her.

But a crackle zipped through the air. "In a truck, loading dock thirty-two. Hurry. We have to get out of here."

Thank you, God.

She bolted for that location, praying that the police had already confiscated the radios and had heard the same message she'd just received. Juliette needed to get there before Theo's partner did, because she'd probably heard Juliette's bad impersonation.

The slots were numbered, and she'd passed twenty-five before she'd ducked down this aisle. She raced down the center pathway.

Thirty. Thirty-one. She spotted loading bay thirty-two and

hid next to a stack of furniture boxes to scope out the situation. She didn't see any movement.

A voice from behind made Juliette's heart stop. "Don't move." A woman stepped out of the shadows, but Juliette didn't need to see her to know exactly who the voice belonged to. If only she had put the pieces together sooner.

Because another person close to Caleb had betrayed him.

SATURDAY, 3:41 A.M.

Caleb prayed that Juliette, Noelle, and Ivy were rescued.

Theo had dragged Caleb through the warehouse to the loading bays. He shoved Caleb up against the wall of the eighteen-wheeler truck bed, where Caleb lost his balance and slid to the ground. It didn't help that his hands were zip-tied behind his back. Hiding in the shadows of the empty truck bed, Theo paced. Without his hands, Caleb stood no chance of overpowering this maniac.

He didn't try to get up. Maybe he could kick Theo's legs out from under him if the man got close enough.

"Where is she?" Theo muttered. "We've got to get out of here." The guy was losing it. He'd always respected the man's work, but now his heart broke for Theo's family. His son was barely two.

A scuffle sounded from outside the truck bed. A figure appeared in the door opening. Caleb's heart skipped a beat.

Juliette.

Did this mean they'd escaped?

Juliette stood in the opening, not moving. "Ivy is safe. But we've got company."

Another figure emerged from the shadows. A woman.

Was that—

No.

Before him, with a gun trained on Juliette, stood Abby Prewett. The woman Caleb had trusted to watch Ivy after school.

The woman he'd lived next door to for the past several years, who had been like a grandmother to Ivy, was a part of Rushmore. The neighborhood busybody was working with the bad guys?

All he could say was "Why?"

Abby shrugged. "You know my husband died a slow, painful death. If First United Bank had lent us the money, he could have gotten an experimental treatment that might have saved his life. But my John wasn't given a chance. They just revoked our line of credit. I want them to pay. Rushmore gives back what the bank stole."

No wonder the hacker group knew so much about Ivy's abilities. Abby had spent countless hours with his niece. Another family ruined by vengeance.

Caleb had a knack for reading people, but how had he gone so wrong with Abby? "I can't believe you used me like that."

Abby looked contrite, but Caleb didn't buy it for a second. "I lucked out. You moved in next to me, remember? Once I figured out who you were and what Ivy could do, I joined forces with the other members of Rushmore and formed the perfect plan. Well, until you and the blonde bodyguard ruined it."

Theo huffed. He took out a pair of zip ties and cuffed Juliette's hands behind her back. "Enough chitchat. We're getting out of here. I'll drive the truck."

He nodded toward Abby. "You ride back here and figure out how to deal with these two."

No. No. No. They had to get out of this vehicle before Theo drove five states away and dumped their bodies who knew where.

"You, sit on the floor next to your boyfriend." Abby shoved

Juliette to the ground. Juliette rolled and slid toward Caleb and then sat back-to-back with him. His fingers wove into hers, but both of them were now cuffed.

Abby grabbed a safety strap attached to the wall of the truck, the gun never wavering in her hand. How could the sweet grandmother from next door turn out to be the vigilante holding them at gunpoint?

Theo hopped out the back of the truck and slammed the doors shut. Interior lighting on the sides of the aluminum walls gave them enough light to see. A few seconds later, the semi's bed rumbled from the engine roaring to life.

At least now it was two against one, except they still didn't have the use of their hands. And Abby had a gun that never wavered.

He felt a tug on his binds. Did Juliette have a pocketknife? The zip ties fell off, and he flexed his fingers but kept his hands behind his back.

The truck made several turns, and they swayed with the movement. He prayed the police had set up some checkpoints. They needed to get out before Theo hit the highway. He grabbed Juliette's hand and tapped out a Morse code message on her wrist.

Rush Abby. Get gun. Together.

She tapped back on his wrist, *I'm in.*

His mind drifted back to their basic training days. To their no-win training exercise. Juliette fought her way out of an unwinnable situation. Could they do the same? Because they did need to Kobayashi Maru their way out of this one.

They needed to change the rules, with a lot of divine intervention.

Sure, it was two against one in the back of the trailer, but it didn't seem like Theo had a lot of practice driving a big rig. The cargo bay swayed back and forth. If they moved to take Abby down and the truck made a turn, they'd lose their balance.

It was now or never. He counted down on her wrist.

Three. They moved into a crouching position.

Two. Caleb prayed this would work. That God would get them out of this. And keep Ivy and Juliette safe.

One.

Caleb and Juliette sprang up and threw all of their weight into colliding with Abby. Juliette pinned her down, and Caleb wrestled the gun out of her hand and tossed it out of her reach.

The cargo bay pitched left. The bounce caused Juliette and Abby to lose their footing and the door to unlatch and swing open. Wind blasted through the open space.

Caleb dove for Juliette's hand while grabbing a rope wrapped around a metal tiedown. His hand connected with her ankle, and he held her foot with all the strength he could muster.

"Hang on, Jules." His fingers dug in through her shoe, and he prayed it didn't come off. If he let go, she could slide out the door.

The truck bucked, and Caleb held on tight to the rope and Juliette. Both arms shook, but he refused to let go. A pop sounded, and he sucked in a breath at the blinding pain racing down the arm holding Juliette.

He couldn't hang on for much longer.

Abby tried to stand, but another sharp turn sent her flying out the back of the truck. She managed to catch a metal bar attached to the back of one of the double doors. It pulled her out of the opening, and she clung to the door as it flapped in the wind.

"Help!" she cried.

Juliette inched closer to the wall of the truck, but she still wasn't secure. One more bump in the road could send them both flying out the back. Outside, all Caleb could see was paved asphalt with white dotted lines flying by on the highway. The truck picked up speed.

But Caleb was in no position to rescue Abby. He refused to

let go of Juliette until she wasn't in danger of sliding out of a moving truck bed.

Juliette wiggled her way to the side and grabbed a rope attached to the wall. "I'm good," she yelled over the wind and the rumbling truck. Caleb let her go and clung to the rope, his shoulder throbbing. He fought the urge to pass out from the pain.

The truck slowed and the inside lit up with red and blue lights. Caleb spotted a police cruiser whiz by them.

Theo must have hit a checkpoint. If he were smart, he'd stop and not try to outrun a police barricade. Another car approached the back. Someone hung out the window.

It was Alana, in Juliette's grandmother's Lincoln Town Car, with Noelle in the driver's seat. Several more police cars raced by, and a few seconds later, the truck came to a grinding halt, complete with metal scraping sounds and a dust plume. Noelle got close enough for Alana to grab Abby around the waist and pull her onto the hood of the car. An officer pulled in behind the car and cuffed Abby.

Caleb slumped against the wall and let go of his lifeline. Juliette crawled to him. He wrapped his good arm around her, and she collapsed in his lap.

"It's over," he whispered. "And this time, I'm never letting you go."

TWENTY-ONE

SATURDAY, 5:30 A.M.

Please, God, let Caleb come through surgery.

Juliette paced the hospital waiting room. No way would she rest until she saw Caleb. He had to pull through. He'd torn several tendons in his shoulder while keeping her from being flung out of the back of a semi. She was here, alive, because of him.

And this time, she wasn't leaving. She'd be right here when he woke up.

Ivy sat in the vinyl chair like a statue, staring out the window, with Alana and Noelle flanking her on either side. Matt Williams walked over to Juliette and handed her a cup of coffee. She'd already had three. It didn't matter. She wouldn't sleep until Caleb came out of surgery.

Her heart pounded in time to the ticking second hand of the analog clock on the wall. Waiting was not one of Juliette's strong suits.

"He's going to pull through, Juliette," Matt said, as if reading her thoughts. Not that her emotions weren't written all over her face.

"I don't want to lose him." Her breath caught in her throat.

All she wanted was more time. She and Caleb had years of lost time to recover.

Agent McGregor arrived at the already crowded waiting room and walked over to them. "I thought you might like an update, since you, Caleb, and Ivy were instrumental in stopping this hacker group from attempting to take down the bank."

Juliette wanted to celebrate that the hacker group had been dismantled, but not until she saw Caleb.

"Did you capture all of the Savannah members of Rushmore?" She looked between Matt and Agent McGregor. "We still don't know who CyberLane is. Ivy would have recognized her neighbor in a heartbeat."

The FBI agent shook his head. "Not yet. Based on the coded communications we've uncovered between the members of the group, Theo was Rough Rider, Jeff was the Architect, and Abby was the Liberator. We still don't know the whereabouts of the General, the one that seemed to be calling the shots."

"It's the presidents." Juliette hadn't heard Ivy walk up next to her. "Their hacker names are all the faces of Mount Rushmore."

Agent McGregor let out a low chuckle. "Ivy, you need to apply for the FBI. I can't wait for you to work with us. With all our analysts, no one picked up on that fact."

She shrugged and wrapped her arms around Juliette's waist. Ivy had claimed such a special place in her heart.

But now that they'd started talking about the case, she wanted to know more. "Has the FBI cleared Blake Abernathy?" She scanned the waiting room and spotted Blake, sitting with his wife, waiting for news of Caleb's recovery.

McGregor shrugged. "So far, nothing indicates Caleb's

partner was involved. I have a feeling someone else is still out there, though."

A chill raced through Juliette. "Exactly. What do we know about CyberLane?"

"Theo said they'd hired a young girl to pose as CyberLane. She apparently wasn't part of their group, just an actor from the local community college that they paid a couple of bucks to pretend. We're still searching for her, but assume she probably skipped town."

"And you believe him? He faked his own kidnapping. I think he'd do anything at this point to save himself."

Agent McGregor raised his palms face up and shrugged. "We have nothing to go on to find CyberLane. We did successfully stop their ransomware from taking over the bank accounts. Theo said that if the bank had paid, they would have released all accounts but the ones that the top executives owned. They intended to bleed them dry and take every penny these men and women possessed and deposit the money into other people's accounts, of course keeping a chunk of change for themselves."

"Hardly noble." Juliette shook her head. At least they wouldn't get away with it and justice would be served. "And again, I'm not sure I believe anything he says."

McGregor folded his arms. "These hackers went out of their way to deceive people. They thought they were justified in what they were doing. Jeff Kline had his house repossessed by the bank. Theo claims he lost his business when the bank stopped loaning him money. And Abby's case is sad, but it doesn't justify her actions as part of this group. They *redistributed* thousands of dollars in cash that we might never recover."

A doctor in scrubs entered the room and took off his mask. "Are you Caleb Styles's family?"

"Yes, we are." Juliette rushed to the doctor's side, Ivy right behind her. She wrapped her arm around Ivy and held tight.

"Caleb is going to be fine," the doctor said. "He's resting

comfortably, and he'll be up for visitors once the anesthesia wears off. We repaired three torn tendons, and while he'll need some physical therapy, Caleb is a fighter and should bounce back with no problems."

Juliette felt the tension release from her hand as Ivy relaxed her grip with the good news.

Matt brought some sandwiches from the hospital café, and they ate while waiting for Caleb to wake up.

An hour later, the nurse announced that Caleb was ready for visitors. Juliette and Ivy jumped up from their chairs and followed her down the hall to Caleb's room.

Various monitors buzzed and blipped. Caleb's eyes were closed, and Juliette wanted to reach out and brush the wisps of brown hair away from his forehead. Her heart constricted at the sight of his pale face.

Oh, Caleb.

His eyes fluttered and opened. Ivy tenderly curled up next to him on the bed, on his good side. A sling graced his right arm. Juliette should have stopped her, but the peace that filled Caleb's face made it clear he was fine. He placed his hand on Ivy's head and stroked her hair. Ivy's tears wet Caleb's hospital gown, and Juliette fought her own desire to weep at the scene.

He looked at Juliette, and her face filled with warmth. She sat on the edge of his bed, opposite Ivy, the steady thrumming of the hospital equipment reminding her of what she could have lost.

After a few minutes, Ivy dozed off.

"Jules," Caleb whispered. She tried to tell him not to talk, but he shook his head, intent on speaking. "I thought I was going to lose you. When that trailer door opened, I—"

She leaned across the bed and silenced him with her lips. A tender, slow kiss. One that communicated that this was just the beginning of many more kisses.

"I love you, Caleb. I always have."

He sighed, peace washing over his face. "I'd rather spend fifteen minutes with you, if that's all the time we have, than spend the rest of my life without you. You're worth the risk."

"I love you and Ivy. The three of us are a team." Juliette grabbed Caleb's hand. "I'm never letting go."

———

SUNDAY, 2:00 P.M.

Everything was right in his world. On Caleb's left, Ivy slept curled up by his side on the couch in the apartment.

On his right, the woman he loved had her hand wrapped around his.

No one was chasing them. The ransomware had been destroyed.

He let out a sigh of contentment. After being released from the hospital, Juliette and Ivy had enforced a twenty-four-hour vigil. Aside from Juliette going home to change, she and Ivy hadn't left him alone for a second. Ivy was supposed to compete in the second part of a two-day robotics competition that afternoon, but she refused to go. They'd quit trying to convince her she should.

"Are you sure you want to meet with Theo's wife today?" Juliette asked. "You just got out of the hospital. I'm sure she'd understand and maybe meet Blake at the office later in the week to pick up Theo's last paycheck." The office had closed for renovations. Caleb figured having Georgia stop by would be the quickest way to get the money to her.

Caleb shook his head and winced. His shoulder throbbed, but despite their ordeal, he felt like he'd gotten lucky with just a few torn tendons.

"I can't believe Theo betrayed Georgia and his son like he did. They deserve to have more than a last paycheck. I'm thinking about setting up a scholarship. Something just to make sure his son is taken care of in the future."

Juliette got up from the couch to get Caleb a drink. She monitored the times he needed to take his pain meds, and it was time. She grabbed a bottle of water, and he downed the pills. After Georgia stopped by, he'd take a long nap.

"Sadly, the hacker called the General is in the wind. And I wish they'd find the girl that posed as CyberLane," Juliette said. "I'd sleep a little better knowing that all the bad guys are behind bars."

Caleb nodded. "If she really was just a local college kid, I doubt the threat will continue. It sounds like it was just a ploy to gain Ivy's trust."

Ivy stirred under his arm at the mention of her name. She looked at Caleb and stretched. "I think I'm going to shower and change clothes." She hopped off the couch with all the energy of a twelve-year-old and headed to her bedroom.

Would she have permanent scars from this ordeal? Maybe not ones he could see, but the inside was his main concern. The girl was resilient, and he wanted her to have the best childhood possible. Between her intellect and losing her parents at such a young age, Ivy had been forced to grow up way too fast.

Juliette sat back down on the couch. "What are you going to do about her grandparents?"

He ran his good hand through his hair. "My attorney doesn't think their lawsuit has merit. But I'm going to take a trip to visit them with Ivy. Over Christmas. If we meet face-to-face, maybe they'll change their position. I'm not trying to keep them from her, but she belongs with me."

"I'm sure they'd love that."

"Maybe you'd like to join us?"

She snuggled under his good shoulder. "There's no place I'd rather be for the holidays. Or right now."

A knock at the door ruined the moment. Juliette dashed to open it. She ushered Georgia into the living room.

This woman would be raising her son on her own while her husband served time behind bars. And she just looked so young. Why would Theo put her in that situation?

"Thanks for letting me pick up the check here." Georgia sat on a chair opposite the couch. "I'd rather get it now than wait until the office reopens. Blake is a hard man to track down."

Juliette busied herself cleaning up the kitchen. Caleb stood and handed Georgia the envelope. Blake and Caleb had agreed to give her a substantial severance—even though her husband had tried to ruin the company—and Caleb had insisted that she have the money right away. It was the right thing to do, take care of a family in need. Theo had left Georgia and his son in financial ruin. After his business had gone under, he'd spent all of their money on his plan for retribution.

Georgia took the envelope. "Thank you for this. I know what Theo did was terrible, but this money will help with childcare, because...I've got to find a job."

Ivy headed out into the living room and froze. Her eyes widened and her face paled. He noticed a tremor in her arms.

He watched Georgia, who had her back toward Ivy. He glanced into the kitchen to see if he could get Juliette's attention, but she had already keyed in to Ivy's reaction.

Something was off.

Georgia stood. "I'd better be going. I left my son with my sister." She turned and saw Ivy.

"Ivy, what are you doing here? I thought you were at the robotics competition."

How would Georgia know anything about that?

Ivy's expression turned from fear to anger in a flash. "You. You tried to kill my uncle. You said your name was Layna."

Before Caleb or Juliette could act, Georgia pulled a gun from her pocket and aimed it at Ivy.

"All I needed was this check and I'd have been in the clear. Theo made sure no one could point a finger at me."

Caleb caught Juliette's eye, and she responded with a nod. Who needed words when they were so in sync?

They sprang into action. Juliette inched toward the left, allowing her room to take Georgia down from the side. Ivy dove behind the couch. Juliette's swift kick sent the gun flying from Georgia's hand while Caleb launched himself forward. He knocked Georgia back with his good shoulder. Juliette caught the woman and had Georgia's hands zip-tied behind her back before the woman could blink.

Georgia. The General. Layna. The mastermind behind Rushmore sat on the floor of Caleb's living room, face beet red.

"You ruined everything." Georgia squirmed and fell onto her side, wrestling with the cuffs.

Caleb gave Juliette an exaggerated high five and she smiled. "Teamwork."

Georgia groaned.

"You just happened to have zip ties in your pocket?" he asked as he helped Ivy up off the floor.

"What? I'm still a bodyguard, even if you don't need me to protect you."

"I always need you, Jules."

Heat crept up her cheeks like a beautiful sunrise.

Officer Matt Williams was at Caleb's doorstep in record time, thanks in part to living in the building and always keeping his police radio handy. Caleb opened the door. Matt and another officer carted Georgia away. Now Georgia's son would be raised by her sister because of their greed.

Ivy raced to Caleb's side once Georgia was escorted from the apartment. He wrapped his good arm around Ivy and Juliette in an embrace.

"Now it's seriously over," he whispered to both of his girls. "No one's going to hurt us again."

Ivy wriggled out from under his arm and rolled her eyes at him. "Just kiss her already. What are you waiting for?"

Caleb laughed and caught Juliette blushing. "I'm not waiting anymore." He pulled Juliette close and dipped her with his uninjured arm like they were in a movie scene. She twined her arms around his neck, and his lips met hers. A fire ignited between them like an exothermic chemical reaction. If someone lit a match, the place would explode.

"I take it back," Ivy chimed in. "I'd rather not see that." She grinned and ran off to her room. Caleb pulled Juliette to her feet but didn't let her go.

"I think we should gross her out like that more often," Caleb whispered in her ear.

Juliette smiled. "And to think, this is just the beginning." She pulled him in for another spine-tingling kiss.

"I'm not letting you out of my sight, Hazard Pay. Not even for a second."

TWENTY-TWO

SIX MONTHS LATER

"Are you ready, Jules?" Caleb asked.

Juliette checked her reflection in the bathroom mirror and applied more lipstick.

The things she did for love.

"Almost."

"We're going to be late." Ivy's voice carried through the bathroom door.

What was the rush? The convention didn't start for two hours. How had she agreed to attend her first *Star Trek* convention? But worse, what had possessed her to dress up in a blue Star Fleet uniform complete with Spock ears?

Easy answer. Ivy was the reason.

The girl had begged her to attend, and Juliette couldn't say no. After binge-watching the movies, she'd decided to surprise Caleb and Ivy with her ensemble.

"Well, here goes nothing." She opened the bathroom door and headed to the living room. Ivy and Caleb gaped, their reactions everything she could have wanted.

"What? I thought I'd look the part."

Ivy giggled at Juliette's outfit.

"It's not what I was expecting when you agreed to go to the convention," Caleb said. "But you look great, as always." He twirled her around and wrapped his arms around her.

She was beyond blessed with Caleb and Ivy in her life. The three of them had been inseparable these past few months. When she didn't have an assignment from work, she'd pick up Ivy from school and spend the afternoon with her.

Ivy bounced around the apartment with an unusual level of excitement, more than her typical twelve-year-old girl antics.

"You really are excited for this convention," Juliette said with a laugh. "But why aren't you and your uncle dressed up? If I'm wearing a costume, you two should be in costume."

"Right," Ivy said, winking at her uncle. "I guess we need costumes, too."

What were they up to? The girl's giggle filled the hallway while she raced to change. Ivy had a closet full of choices. Caleb shrugged and headed to his room too, emerging a few minutes later with his own Star Fleet uniform.

Ivy returned, decked out in her matching uniform. "I can't wait. Let's go." She grabbed Juliette's hand and pulled her toward the door.

"I guess we're leaving now." Juliette followed Ivy down the hall and to the car.

Caleb drove and Ivy prattled on about *Star Trek*, giving a detailed play-by-play about an episode featuring the Borg. And for the first time in her life, Juliette could follow the conversation.

She watched out the window, not recognizing the road they were on. "Where is the event? I didn't even ask."

"Uh, it's at a hotel down on the riverfront," Caleb replied without making eye contact with her.

Internal alarms rang.

Caleb couldn't lie. He was up to something. The last thing she needed was a surprise at a *Star Trek* convention. The surprise was her agreeing to go in costume. That was enough excitement for one night.

"We're here," Ivy squealed. Caleb pulled the car around the horseshoe driveway and stopped in front of the lobby doors to one of the swankiest hotels Juliette had ever seen.

"These *Star Trek* fans must make a lot of money to stay at a place like this," she said.

Caleb gave his keys to the valet—who failed to hide a laugh when sizing up their attire—and Ivy raced inside. Juliette followed, but Caleb grabbed her hand. "Ivy will be fine. She's going to get us—um...registered? At the table with the...you know...registration."

Okay. Since when did Caleb let Ivy out of his sight? And why was he so nervous?

Wait...was Caleb going to propose to her? At a *Star Trek* convention? While she was dressed like this?

They walked along the boardwalk to the back of the hotel, which had a stunning view of the river. Tiki torches with flames lit the pathway and created a moment of pure magic.

"This place is beautiful, Caleb. But why are there no people? I expected to see alien costumes and Spock lookalikes. This is so—"

He put his finger over her lips. "There isn't a convention. I— I made it up."

"You? That can't be. You must have had help."

"I wanted to create the perfect moment. Of course I had help. I want to give you the world, Juliette. You deserve every moment to be special." He got down on one knee with a ring, and Juliette forced herself not to squeal in excitement.

"Yes!" she exclaimed.

"I didn't say anything yet."

"Right. Sorry!"

"Juliette, will you marry me? Ivy and I love you so much. We want to be a family."

"Yes! Of course I'll marry you."

He placed the ring on her finger and stood, and she practically tackled him with a hug. She kissed him, relishing the thought that this was just their beginning. She'd get to kiss him this way for the rest of their lives. Because man, Caleb could kiss. Why hadn't she figured that out sooner?

She put her hands on his chest and moved half an inch back. "But this proposal doesn't count."

"Oh please. You mean you want me to do it again?" Caleb's perplexed face caused Juliette to burst out in laughter.

"It doesn't count because we're in costumes, and that's not how I want to remember this perfect moment. I can't tell Alana and Noelle that you proposed to me while I was wearing a Star Fleet uniform with Spock ears."

"Yeah, about that." He grabbed her hand and led her back toward the hotel. "Like I said, I did have some help planning this little ruse."

Bright lights burst on by the resort-style pool. A cheer erupted as they approached. Caleb leaned in and whispered, "Sorry, I guess you'll have to celebrate as Spock. I never in a million years would have guessed that you'd dress up."

Juliette spun around and saw all of her Elite Guardians friends hanging out around the pool. A buffet was set up under a tent with all kinds of island fare. Tropical music played in the background. Even though the temperature was a bit chilly, heaters made it feel like a Caribbean paradise.

Ivy raced down the path and wrapped herself around Juliette's waist. "You said yes! I almost blew the secret. It was so hard to stay quiet. I can't believe you dressed up!"

"And I can't believe you didn't tell me to change."

Juliette walked with Ivy still attached to her. "Is that funnel cake I smell?"

Caleb laughed. "Yes, I requested something made from pure sugar be added to the menu."

They entered the gate around the enclosed patio next to the pool, and Juliette found herself sandwiched between Noelle and Alana in a group hug. Alana whispered in her ear, "Girl, I am not letting you live down this outfit. But if anyone can pull off a skin-tight space uniform, it's you. You look hot." Juliette greeted Jonah and Cash, Noelle's and Alana's significant others.

"I can't believe you all came." Juliette made a beeline for Olivia Savage and her husband Wade. "This is such a surprise." Olivia had started the Elite Guardians Agency and had recruited Juliette.

"I wouldn't miss this for the world," Olivia said.

Quinn and Maddie Holcomb rushed over, a toddler in tow.

"You two came a long way for this party," Juliette said, hugging them both.

"Well, when Preston Whittaker rents out an entire luxury hotel, I'm not missing out," Quinn said.

"I couldn't stop him," Caleb said. "Things really got out of hand fast."

They greeted more old friends until she spotted Laila and Preston. "I can't believe you did all of this for me. You two are the best."

"What's money for if you can't spend it?" Laila said and laughed. The most unpretentious person on the planet had married a businessman worth billions. But Preston had turned his family's company into one of the biggest philanthropic organizations in the world.

"Not to mention that you did save our lives after we crashed on the side of a mountain. We'd do anything for you, *Jules*." Preston stuck his tongue out at Juliette, and she gave him a mock glare.

She wrapped her arms around her fiancé. "Watch yourself, *Whit*. Caleb's the only one that gets to call me that."

Preston grabbed his wife's hand. "We should get this party started with some dancing." He whisked Laila away, and the deejay started playing eighties classics. Others joined them on the dance floor.

Juliette greeted Christina and Grey along with Lizzie and Charlie. It wasn't so long ago that they'd all worked together in Columbia, SC.

The party carried on until after midnight. Many guests had reserved rooms in the hotel, courtesy of Preston. Juliette made her way to the edge of the pool area, overlooking the river. To the spot where Caleb had proposed.

Ivy and Caleb joined her. She put her arm around Ivy, and Caleb put his head on hers. "I can only think of one thing that would have made this night perfect," he said.

"Really, what's that?" With all her friends, the lights, music, food, and laughter, she couldn't think of anything missing from this evening. Other than her wardrobe malfunction.

"This night should never have existed," Caleb whispered. "Because I should have proposed to you the day I met you."

ELITE GUARDIANS: SAVANNAH

Safety. Secrets. Sacrifice.
What will it cost these Elite Guardians to protect the innocent?

HAVE YOU MET OUR OTHER ELITE GUARDIANS?

Brains. Beauty. Boldness.
The Elite Guardians will keep you safe.

GET READY ... THINGS ARE ABOUT TO GET HOT!

SECRETS. BETRAYAL. SACRIFICE.
THIS TIME, THEY'RE NOT JUST FIGHTING FIRE.

With heart-pounding excitement, gripping suspense, and sizzling (but clean!) romance, the CHASING FIRE: MONTANA series, brought to you by the incredible authors of Sunrise Publishing, including the dynamic duo of bestselling authors Susan May Warren and Lisa Phillips, is your epic summer binge read.

Immerse yourself in a world of short, captivating novels that are designed to be devoured in one sitting. Each book is a standalone masterpiece, (no story cliffhangers!) although you'll be craving the next one in the series!

Follow the Montana Hotshots and Smokejumpers as they chase a wildfire through northwest Montana. The pages ignite with clean romance and high-stakes danger—these heroes (and heroines!) will capture your heart. The biggest question is . . . who will be your summer book boyfriend?

This exciting series is available in ebook, print, and audiobook. What are you waiting for? Read the complete series now!

Keep reading for a sneak peek at *Flashpoint* by Susan May Warren, the first book in the thrilling Chasing Fire: Montana series.

FLASHPOINT

CHASING FIRE: MONTANA || BOOK ONE

CHAPTER 1

Clearly, his last hope at a comeback was about to crash and burn.

Maybe he was being a little melodramatic, but Spenser Storm knew a good story.

Knew how to cater to an audience, knew when a script was a disaster.

And this one had flames all over it.

Yes, the screenplay had all the right ingredients—a winning western retelling of a widow and her son who leaned on the help of two strangers to save her land. And they were shooting on location in Montana at a real abandoned western town rebuilt and redressed for the movie, complete with a jail and a church.

They'd even hired an up-and-coming country music star to write original music.

The problem was, the producer, Lincoln Cash, picked the wrong man to die.

Not that Spenser Storm had a say in it—he'd been given all

of sixteen lines in the one-hundred-twenty-page script. But he wanted to ask, while waving flags and holding a megaphone— *Who killed off the hero at the end of a movie?* Had no one paid any attention to the audience during the screening of *Sommersby?*

He didn't care how many academy-acclaimed actors were attached to this movie. Because everyone—even he—would hate the fact that their favorite action hero ended up fading into eternity. And he wasn't talking about himself, but the invincible Winchester Marshall.

Perfect. Spenser should probably quit now and go back to herding cattle.

"Back to ones!" Indigo, the first Assistant Director, with her long black hair tied back, earphones around her neck, raised her hand.

Spenser nudged his mare, Goldie, back to the position right outside town. Sweat trickled down his spine, and he leaned low so a makeup assistant could wipe his brow.

Yeah, something in his gut said trouble. It didn't help that all of Montana had become a broiler, even this early in the summer—the grass yellow, the temperature index soaring, turning even the wind from the pine-saturated mountains into the breath of hades.

But saving the movie wasn't Spenser's job. No, his job was to sit pretty atop his horse and smile for the camera, those gray-blue eyes smoldery, his body tanned and a little dusty, his golden-brown hair perfectly curled out of his black Stetson, his body buff and muscled under his blue cotton shirt and a leather vest.

He wore jeans, black boots, and could have walked off the set of *Yellowstone*. No, *swaggered* off the set. Because he wasn't a fool.

They'd cast him as eye candy. With sixteen lines and the guy who got the girl at the end. Spenser was the sizzle for the audience who was too young for Winchester Marshall, the lead of the movie, although Spenser was just a couple years younger.

But, like Lincoln Cash said when he signed him, Spenser had a special kind of appeal.

The kind that packed the convention floor at comic cons around the world.

Wow, he hated comic cons. And adults who dressed up as Iwonians and spoke a language only created in fanfic world. If he never heard the name Quillen Cleveland again, he'd die a happy man.

He hated to mention to Lincoln that the fans who loved *Trek of the Osprey* might not enjoy a western called *The Drifters*, but a guy with no screen credits to his name for five years should probably keep his mouth shut when accepting a role.

At least according to his agent, Greg Alexander.

Keep his mouth shut, deliver his lines, and maybe, hopefully, he'd be back in the game.

"We need a little more business from the extras." Director Cosmos Ferguson wore a *Drifters* T-shirt, jeans and boots, and his own cowboy hat. "Feel free to cause more havoc on the set."

Behind him, Swen, from SFX stepped out of the house, checking on the fire cannons for the next shot. The set crew had trailered in an old cabin for today's shoot—a real structure with a porch and a stone chimney that rose from the tattered wooden roof—and plunked it down in a valley just two hundred yards from the town, with a corral for the locally sourced horses. It was a postcard of bygone days.

Was it only Spenser, or did anyone else think it might be a bad idea to light a fire inside a rickety wooden house that looked already primed for tinder?

"Quiet on the set!"

Around him, the world stopped. The gaffers, the grips, the second team, the stuntmen, even, it seemed, the ripple of wind through the dusty one-horse ghost town-slash-movie set.

Not even Goldie moved.

"Picture's up!" Indigo said.

At least Spenser could enjoy the view. The sky stretched forever on both sides of the horizon, the glorious Kootenai mountains rising jagged and bold to the north, purple and green wildflowers cascading down the foothills into the grasslands of the valley.

"Roll sound!"

A hint of summer night hung in the air. Perhaps he'd grab a burger at the Hotline Bar and Grill in Ember, just down the street from Motel Bates, where the cast was staying. Okay, the lodging wasn't that bad, but—

"Action."

The extras, aka cowboys, burst to life, shooting prop guns into the air just before Winchester Marshall, aka Deacon Cooper, rode in, chasing them away with his own six-shooter. They raced out of town, then Deacon got off his horse, dropped the reins, and checked the pulse of the fallen extra. "Hawk, C'mere. I think this is one of the cowboys from the Irish spread."

Spenser's cue to ride on screen, dismount and confirm, then stand up and stare into the horizon, as if searching for bad guys.

Seemed like a great way for a guy to get shot. But again, he wasn't in charge of the script.

So, he galloped onto the set, swung his leg over Goldie's head, jumped out of the saddle, and sauntered up. He gave the scene a once over, met Winchester-slash-Deacon's eyes with a grim look, and nodded. Then he turned and looked at the horizon, his hands on his hips, while the camera zoomed in, trouble in his expression.

"Cut!" Cosmos said as he walked over to them. "I love the interaction between you two." He turned away, motioning to Swen.

What interaction? Spenser wanted to ask, but Winchester— "Win" to the crew—rose and clamped a hand on Spenser's shoulder. "One would think you grew up on a horse the way you rode up."

"I did," Spenser said, but Win had already turned away, headed to craft services, probably for a cold soda.

"Moving on. Scene seventeen," Indigo said. "Let's get ready for the house fire."

Spenser jogged over to Goldie and grabbed her reins, but a male stunt assistant came up and took hold of the mare's halter. "I've got her, sir."

Spenser let the animal go and headed over to the craft table set up under a tented area, back from the set, near the two long connected trailers brought in for the actors. The Kalispell Sound and Light truck was parked next to an array of rental cars, along with the massive Production trailer, where the wardrobe department kept their set supplies, including a locked container for the weapons.

"That was a great scene." This from the caterer, a woman named Juliet, whose family owned the Hot Cakes Bakery in Ember. She wore her brown hair back in a singular braid and handed him a sandwich, nodding to drinks in a cooler. Not a fancy setup, but this far out in the sticks, they were beggars. Cosmos had also ordered a hot breakfast from the Ember Hotline every morning.

"Thanks." Spenser unwrapped the plastic on his sandwich. "This bread looks homemade."

"It is. The smoked chicken is from the Hotline, though." She winked, but it wasn't flirty, and continued to set out snacks— cookies and donuts.

The sandwich reminded him a little of the kind of food that Kermit, the cook for the Flying S Ranch, served during roundup, eaten with a cold soda, and a crispy pickle.

Sheesh, what was he doing here, back on a movie set? He should be home, on his family's ranch...

Or not. Frankly, he didn't know where he belonged.

He turned, eating the sandwich, and watched as lead actress Kathryn Canary, seated on a high director's chair, dressed in a long grimy prairie dress, her blonde hair mussed, ignored a makeup assistant applying blood to her face and hands. She held her script in one hand, rehearsing her lines as Blossom Winthrop, the heroine with Trace Wilder, playing the role of her husband, Shane Winthrop.

Who was about to die.

He hadn't seen Trace since his last movie, but the man seemed not to remember their short stint on *Say You Love Me*.

Spenser would like to forget it too, frankly. Another reason why he'd run back to the family ranch in central Montana.

It all felt surreal, a marriage of Spenser's worlds—the set, busy with gaffers setting up lighting, and the sound department fixing boom mics near the house, the set dresser putting together the scene. And then, nearby, saddles lined up along the rail of a corral where horses on loan from a nearby ranch nickered, restless with the heat.

Cowboys, aka extras, sat in holding with their hats pushed back, drinking coffee, wearing chaps and boots. All they were missing were the cattle grazing in the distance. Maybe the smell of burgers sizzling on Kermit's flat grill.

Bandit, the ranch dog, begging for scraps.

They did, however, have a cat, and out of the corner of his eye, Spenser spotted Bucky Turnquist, age eight, who played Dusty Winthrop, chase the tabby around the set. His mother, Gemma, had already hinted that, as a single mom, she might be interested in getting to know Spenser better.

Now, she talked with one of the villain cowboys, laughing as he got on his horse.

"You guys about ready?" Cosmos had come back from where the cameramen were setting up, the grip team working to shade the light for the shot, on his way to Kathryn and Trace, who were rising from their chairs.

One of the SFX guys raised a hand from where they set up the cannons that would 'fire' the house. Not a real fire, not with the burn index so high in this part of crispy, dry Montana. But enough that it would generate heat and look real.

And enough that they'd asked the local wildland fire team on set to keep an eye on anything that might get out of hand. He'd caught sight of the handful of firefighters dressed in their canvas pants, steel-toed boots, yellow Nomex shirts, and Pulaskis hanging out near the fire. They'd brought up a fire truck, too, with a hose ready to deploy water.

"Get a hose over here, Emily!" A man wearing a vest, the word Command on the back, directed a woman, her blonde hair in a tight ponytail, to pull up a hose nearer the building, and hand it over to another firefighter. Then she ran back to the truck, ready to deploy.

According to the script, the cowboys would fire at the house, and then a stuntman would run out, on fire, and collapse to the ground. Cue Kathryn, as Blossom, to run in with a shirt she'd pulled from the hanging laundry to snuff it out while the cowboys attempted to kidnap her.

She'd panic then, and scream for Dusty, and only then would the kid run from the barn. They'd be surrounded, swept up by the villains and taken away while poor Shane died.

At which point the guy would go down to the Hotline for a nice cool craft beer and a burger, then tomorrow, catch a ride to Kalispell and head back to his air-conditioned apartment in LA.

"Ready on Special Effects?" Indigo shouted. She'd reminded him that this wasn't *Trek of The Osprey* and that he wasn't the star here when he'd headed to the wrong trailer on day one.

Whatever. Easy mistake.

"Ready!" This from Swen, who stood away from the house. The cowboys were already in place and Blossom stood at the clothesline in the yard, away from the house.

"Quiet on set!" Indigo shouted. She glanced at Cosmos, who nodded. "Roll Camera. Roll Sound."

A beat. "Action!"

And that's when he spotted little Bucky, still chasing the cat, scooting under the house on his hands and knees.

At the front of the house, a window burst and flames licked out of it.

"Wait!"

The next window burst. More fire.

"Bucky's in there!" Where was his mother? It didn't matter. He took off for the back of the house.

The cowboys in the front yard whooped, shots fired, and of course, the stuntman stumbled out in his firesuit and flopped onto the front yard.

Blossom screamed and ran to put out the fire just as Spenser reached the back of the house.

The fire seemed real enough, with the roof now catching. "Bucky?"

With everyone's gaze on the action, no one had seen him wriggle under the porch. Spenser hit his knees. "Bucky?"

There. Under the middle of the house, curled into a ball, his hands over his ears. "Bucky, C'mere!"

He was crying now, and Spenser saw why—the entire front porch had caught fire.

Sparks dropped around him. The grass sizzled.

Aw—Spenser dropped to his belly and army crawled into the center of the house, coughing, his eyes watering. He grabbed Bucky's foot, yanked.

Bucky kicked at him, split his lip. Blood spurted.

"C'mon kid!"

He grabbed Bucky's arms and jerked him close, wrapping him up, holding him. "It's okay. C'mon, let's get out of here." Smoke billowed in from where the porch fell, a line of fire blocking their escape. But out the back—

Then, suddenly, a terrible crack rent the building, and with a thunderous crash, the old chimney tumbled down. Dust and rock crashed through the cabin, tore out the flooring, and obliterated the porch.

Blocked their exit.

Spenser grabbed Bucky and pulled him close, holding his breath, then expelling the dust, his body wracking with coughs. And Bucky in his arms, screaming.

When he opened his eyes, fire burned around them, a cauldron of very real, very lethal flames.

———

"Stop! Stop the film! There's someone inside there!"

Or at least Emily thought so. She still wasn't quite sure if that was a person or an animal she'd seen dive under the burning house.

In truth, she'd been stationed by her fire truck, watching the house burn, trying not to let her gaze drift back to the beautiful and amazing Spenser Storm, standing near craft services.

The Spenser Storm.

From *Trek of the Osprey*. Quillen Cleveland in the flesh, all grown up and ruggedly handsome, dressed in western getup: leather vest, chaps, black boots, and a Stetson over his burnished golden-brown hair, those gray-blue eyes that a girl could get lost in. He even wore that rakish, heart-thumping smile. The man who saved the galaxy, one world at a time, there he was...

Eating a sandwich.

She'd spotted him almost right off this morning when she'd arrived with fellow hotshot Houston James and her fire boss, Conner Young. The Special Effects department had called in the local Jude County Hotshots as a precaution.

Not a terrible idea given the current fire index.

The SFX supervisor, Swen, had briefed the hotshots before the event—squibs of dust on a lead that would explode to imitate bullets hitting the building. They'd walked through the system that would create the explosion, a tank filled with propane, rigged to burst the window and release a fireball.

She'd expected the bomb, but when the squibs detonated, Emily nearly hit the dirt.

Nearly. But *didn't*. So, take that, panic attack. No more PTSD for her, thank you ten years of therapy.

Except, the explosion hadn't gone quite like they'd hoped. Sure, the gas dissipated into the air, but somehow cinder had fallen onto the porch.

The entire old wooden porch burst into flames.

Black smoke cluttered the sky, and if she were a spotter, via a fire tower or a plane, she'd be calling in sparks to the local Ember fire department. Which would then deploy either the Jude County Hotshots or, if the fire started further in, the Jude County Smokejumpers. The first and last line of defense against fire in this northwest corner of Montana.

About as far away as she could get from her failures, thank you.

Not anymore. This was a new season, a new start, and this time...*this time* the shrapnel of the past wasn't going to eviscerate her future.

So, she'd stood by the truck, waiting for the signal from Conner. Tall, brown hair, calm, he'd been brought in to command the team for the summer while Jed Ransom, their former boss, now crewed the Missoula team.

And that's when, in her periphery, she'd spotted—was that a *person* diving under the back of the house? Black boots disappeared under the footing of the cabin.

Were they out of their *mind*?

Maybe it was an animal—cats sometimes ran toward a fire instead of away.

"*Boss!*" —She had nearly shouted, but that would carry, and with the house on fire, the director only had one take. Instead, she'd headed to the house—

The chimney simply collapsed. A crack, then thunder as the entire handmade stone chimney crumbled. She dropped to her knees, her hands over her head, as dust, rock, and debris exploded out from the house.

From the front came shouts and shooting, the cameras still rolling. She lifted her head, blinking as the dust settled. The inferno now engulfed the front of the house, moving fast toward the back, the roof half-collapsed. "Boss!"

And then a thought clicked in—*black boots*. "It's Spenser! Spenser Storm is under the building!"

No one heard her over the roar of the fire, the shouts from the street.

No one died today. Not on her watch.

C'mon, Emily, think!

She ran over to the truck, grabbed her Pulaski, and then opened the cab door and hit the siren. It screamed over the set as she scrambled toward the house.

Flames kicked out the side windows now, the heat burning her face. She pulled up her handkerchief and dug at the rubble.

The siren kept whining, sweat burning down her back, but in a second, she'd created a hole. She dropped to her knees. "Hello? Hello?"

"In here!"

Smoke cluttered the area, but she made out—yes, Spenser Storm, and a kid.

Oh no, the little Turnquist kid, the son of one of the locals in town.

Emily's eyes watered, but she crawled inside the space, pushing the Pulaski out in front of her. "Grab hold!"

Hands gripped her ankles. "Emily! Get out of there!"

Conner's voice.

"Grab the ax!" she shouted.

Spenser's hand gripped the ax, his other around the kid.

"Pull me out!" this, to Conner.

It was everything she could do to hold onto the Pulaski as they dragged them out from the crawl space. She cleared the building, then launched to her feet even as Conner tried to push her away.

Spenser Storm appeared, like a hero crawling from the depths of hell. The child clung to him, his face blackened, his wardrobe filthy and sooty, his eyes reddened, coughing as he kicked himself free.

"Bucky!" His mother ran toward him, but someone grabbed her back.

Instead, superstar Winchester Marshall, aka Jack Powers, aka whatever hunk he was playing in this western, was right there, pulling the kid from Spenser's arms.

Cosmos pushed through to grab Spenser, helped him to his feet. Spenser bent over, coughing.

"Water! Make a hole!" Cosmos yelled, leading Spenser away.

The movie star didn't even look at Emily as he stumbled to safety.

"C'mon—we need to put out this fire." Conner took off for the hose.

She ran to the truck, still coughing, turned off the siren, then, seeing Houston's signal, she hit the water.

The hose filled, and in a moment, water doused the house, spray saturating the air.

She leaned over, caught her knees, breathing hard. Watched as the fire died. Listened to the roaring on set, and in her heart, subside.

Felt the knot unravel.

No, no one died today. Especially not Spenser Storm.

She stood up, still hauling in breaths. She'd *saved* Spenser Storm. Holy Cannoli.

No, no she wouldn't make a fool of herself and ask for an autograph. And certainly not tell him, ever, that she'd had at least two *Tiger Beat* centerfold posters of him in his Osprey uniform—a pair of black pants, boots and white shirt, leather vest, holding a Vortex Hand Cannon. Never mind mentioning that she'd once attended a Comic-Con just to stand in line for a photo op. He wouldn't remember her, right? Or her status as a Stormie—a member of his official fan club?

"Hey!"

She looked up. Froze.

Spenser Storm was headed her direction, holding a water bottle, his eyes watering, looking like he'd just, well, been pulled from a fire. "You okay?"

She nodded, her eyes widening. C'mon words—

"I just wanted to say thanks." He held out his hand. "You saved my life back there. And Bucky's."

She nodded again. *C'mon words!*

"Maybe I can buy you a drink down at the Hotline sometime?"

"Mmmhmm." *That didn't count!*

Then he smiled, a thousand watts of pure charisma, sunshine and star power, winked, and walked away.

And right then, right there, she nearly died.

CONNECT WITH SUNRISE

Thank you again for reading *Guarding Truth*. We hope you enjoyed the story. If you did, would you be willing to do us a favor and leave a review? It doesn't have to be long—just a few words to help other readers know what they're getting. (But no spoilers! We don't want to wreck the fun!) Thank you again for reading!

We'd love to hear from you—not only about this st   but about any characters or stories you'd like to read in the   ire. Contact us at www.sunrisepublishing.com/contact.

We also have a monthly update that contains sneak ʝeeks, reviews, upcoming releases, and fun stuff for our reader iends. Sign up at www.sunrisepublishing.com or scan our QR co le.

ACKNOWLEDGMENTS

I'm so thankful to everyone who has loved and supported me while writing this book. I have such a wonderful support system of friends and family who have cheered me on the entire way!

Thank you to Susan May Warren and Lindsey Harrel for starting Sunrise Publishing and giving writers like me a chance to shine. Thank you to Lynette Eason for all of your mentorship and time invested in helping me become a better writer.

Thank you to my writing crew that lets me brainstorm, talk, share frustrations, laugh, send memes, and maybe cry a little bit: Kate Angelo, Sami A. Abrams, Lisa Phillips, and Jenn Pierce. I love the friendships and community we have even if none of you are in my time zone. Thanks to Carrie K. for sparking the idea to write a story about a child genius—Ivy was such a fun character to write.

Special thanks: To the Writers' Police Academy – what a fabulous conference and the information I learned is invaluable. Thank you to Appleton Police Officer Matthew Fillebrown for the drone demonstration and spending time talking with me at WPA. It inspired my drone attack scene. I hope I got it right! Thanks to Chad K. for helping me understand bank systems and security, even if I'm still confused.

ABOUT LYNETTE EASON

Lynette Eason is the bestselling, award-winning author of over sixty books. Her books have appeared on the USA TODAY, Publisher's Weekly, CBA, ECPA, and Parable bestseller lists. She has won numerous awares including the Carol, the Selah, the Golden Scroll and more. Her novel, *Her Stolen Past* was made into a movie for the Lifetime Movie Network. Lynette can be found online at www.lynetteeason.com

    facebook.com/lynette.eason
    instagram.com/lynetteeason
    x.com/lynetteeason
    bookbub.com/authors/lynette-eason
    amazon.com/stores/Lynette-Eason/author/B001TPZ320

ABOUT KELLY UNDERWOOD

Kelly Underwood's favorite things are reading, writing, and drinking coffee. She was born in New Hampshire, but don't ask her about snow, because she's been a Florida girl since she was twelve. She writes book reviews for her blog bestinsuspense.com and is an active member of the Central Florida chapter of the American Christian Fiction Writers. She's a sucker for a good suspense novel, the kind you have to read cover-to-cover until the mystery is solved and the bad guys are in handcuffs. If you're looking for her, she's probably on her back patio with a Kindle in one hand and a cup of coffee in the other. Visit Kelly at kellyunderwoodauthor.com

facebook.com/Bestinsuspense

instagram.com/bestinsuspense

x.com/bestinsuspense

bookbub.com/authors/kelly-underwood

goodreads.com/bestinsuspense

amazon.com/stores/Kelly-Underwood/author/B09WGZ13JW

MORE ELITE GUARDIANS

Elite Guardians: Savannah

Vanishing Legacy

Hunting Justice

Guarding Truth

Elite Guardians Collection

Driving Force

Impending Strike

Defending Honor

Christmas in the Crosshairs

Elite Guardians

Always Watching

Without Warning

Moving Target

Chasing Secrets

Made in the USA
Coppell, TX
15 October 2024

38688606R00171